Other Novels by Julian Gloag

Lost and Found

by Julian Gloag

THE LINDEN PRESS
Simon & Schuster NEW YORK, 1981

Copyright © 1981 by Julian Gloag
All rights reserved
including the right of reproduction
in whole or in part in any form
Published by The Linden Press/Simon & Schuster
A Simon & Schuster Division of Gulf & Western Corporation
Simon & Schuster Building
Rockefeller Center
1230 Avenue of the Americas
New York, New York 10020
THE LINDEN PRESS/SIMON & SCHUSTER and colophon are trademarks of
Simon & Schuster
Designed by Irving Perkins
Manufactured in the United States of America
Printed and Bound by Fairfield Graphics, Inc.
1   2   3   4   5   6   7   8   9   10

Library of Congress Cataloging in Publication Data

Gloag, Julian.
Lost and found.

I. Title.
PR6057.L6L6   1981   823'.914   81-934
AACR2

ISBN 0-671-42828-4

Lost
and
Found

H e dreaded the summer. There was nothing to do then. He never went away because it was always possible—remotely possible—that Hélène would come then, during the vacation. In the eleven years since she had left home she had appeared only three times—once for a weekend; once, for almost two weeks; once, with a German guitarist, for a single night—never announced by letter or telegram, but always in the summer. So he waited: in the garden, picking and pruning; in the kitchen, cooking and bottling and making jam; at his table in the attic, looking away across the meadows and the woods and the little river Saye in the bottom of the valley to the mounting series of hills beyond; in the evening, dutifully eating his supper in the parlour; on the terrace on the hot nights, slowly getting through the second litre. When he went out—to a meeting of the communal council or, after a couple of days of good rain, to pick mushrooms in the woods—he punctiliously left a note on the parlour table: *Hélène, I shall be back for lunch—Papa* or *My dear daughter, I shall return not later than five o'clock.*

He never locked up.

But she hadn't come for four years now. Nor written. Nor phoned.

As he climbed the stairs to the attic he clung tightly to the banister, for he'd drunk a litre and a half at lunch, followed by a *marc*. In term time he never allowed himself more than a glass at midday, not because the children might smell the wine on his breath and run off and tell their parents (the entire village probably knew precisely what he ate and drank), but perhaps out of some curious professional pride—a foolish pride, because he was not a very good teacher and might have taught better on a bottle or two of his father-in-law's thinnish red wine.

He reached the head of the stairs and took down his stick from its peg—he had an upstairs stick and a downstairs stick because once, when he'd only had the one, it had caught between his legs and he'd fallen heavily, badly wrenching a shoulder and lying unconscious for several hours.

As he entered the attic, he smiled to himself. His wife's family always invited him to their immense meals at the festivals of the Church—Easter, Whitsun, the Assumption, All Saints, Christmas (but never on secular occasions, such as the harvest or winemaking or even the Fourteenth of July, a distinction which he suspected was his mother-in-law, Thérèse's, method of punishing him for his "anticlericalism," so-called). He invariably went to these repasts, stoically submitting himself to the inevitable round of hypocritical inquiries.

"And how is our dear Hélène?" Thérèse would ask.

"She is very well," he would reply. "I had a letter from her only the other day. She is in . . ." Rome, Athens, New York, naming any town that took his fancy. They all knew it was a lie, because the postman would have informed them at once if Hélène had written.

"She is a clever girl," his father-in-law, Charles, would remark—meaning, what good were all those degrees and diplomas if she doesn't make money?

"She is highly intelligent," he would answer.

"Ah, but my dear Paul, intelligence isn't everything. . . ." And Thérèse would sigh with regret for her granddaughter's wayward refusal to marry a man of position and settle down. Paul realized their reticence required an enormous effort of tact, for which he was grateful.

But four years ago, after Hélène's last and briefest visit, he'd had a telephone installed—using his position as schoolteacher and, therefore, *ex officio* secretary to the local council, to back up his request. So now he would say, "Ah, she phoned me just last week," and they had no way of being certain that it was a lie.

He had in this respect changed the rules of the game. But not in others. He still never inquired about his wife—and he'd not heard from Arlette since the day she left twenty-seven years ago—although he had an idea that Thérèse knew where she was and what she was doing. And they still went through their formal fencing about his other daughter.

"And our dear Agnès?" Thérèse would say with a soulful smile.

"You mean Marguerite," he'd reply, with perverse pedantry insisting on her religious name.

"Of course. You never hear from her?"

"Of course not." And that at least would be the truth; although he had written to Agnès once, the year after she had been received into her enclosed order, and sent her a box of clementines for her birthday. There had been a brief reply—written, she said, with special permission—of gentle rebuke for his gift and with the gracious assurance that every day she prayed for his immortal soul. He had respected that final silence. He had never answered.

He sat down at the attic table with a clumsy movement, almost toppling the bottle of ink. He was tired from the stairs, from the wine perhaps—from letting his thoughts run round in this particular cycle, to this particular end. He had no immortal soul.

Anything immortal that had ever been his he had lost long ago.

He looked down at what he had written yesterday.

The writer's life is one of passion.

It was crossed out, and then:

9

The life of the writer is of an intensity without parallel.

He took up the pen, dipped it in the ink, and crossed that line out too.

Long ago, when he had really been writing, he had thought nothing of it. "The writer's dilemma," "creative adversity"— all such ideas—touched neither his mind nor his heart. Then, he was filled simply with the joy of writing.

He began on May 7, 1945, the day of the German surrender at Rheims. He and his grandfather had listened to the news on the old Bakelite radio in the parlour. Despite Augustin's disapproval, Paul tuned in to the BBC, as he had every day throughout the war.

"Why the BBC?" the old man asked irritably.

"It's not dangerous now, Grandfather. Besides, it was an English general who took the military surrender—it is more their victory than ours."

Augustin said nothing, just lifted his head slightly and touched the waxed tip of his moustache. He'd fought at Verdun in the First War and had survived without a scratch while all his friends were killed. He worshiped Pétain, accepted Vichy with enthusiasm, detested the English, and could never believe even now that anything the old Marshal had done could have been in any way in error. So, as he stood at attention listening to the news of final victory, the May sun flooding the little room with light, he was torn between pride and anguish. He —who believed passionately in Patriotism, Authority, the Family, who had denounced his own son for joining de Gaulle ("imbecile, traitor, Communist"), who had been delighted that the weakness in his grandson's leg from polio had made him unfit to fight—could only take this victory with the bitterness of defeat. Yet, perhaps even more bitterly, he had to struggle with pride—pride in his son, Bernard, parachuted into France again and again, hero of the Resistance, a full colonel with a chestful of medals who had marched only one rank behind de Gaulle at the Liberation of Paris.

"Father will come home now," Paul said.

"Yes." And the old man's shoulders momentarily drooped. On the day after the Americans had swept the Germans out of Croze, the small town on the other side of the hills, a party of the Resistance had come to take Monique, their maid, who had more than freely consorted with the enemy soldiery. But they had not touched Augustin, although his sympathies were common knowledge, because they also knew—and Paul had made sure they didn't forget—that he was the father of Colonel Bernard Molphey. Augustin had lived under that protection, Paul too, during the whole of the Occupation. And so, while Monique was taken off to have her head shaved in the square at Croze, the old man was let alone. He had not accepted the cruelty of that humiliation, just as now he could take no joy in the clear, silvery sound of the church bells in the village below ringing out victory, but turned away with a shrug.

Time had stopped for Augustin Molphey five years before —in 1940. On the wall above the radio was a calendar for that year and, pinned next to it on a piece of red cloth, was a newspaper clipping of the state of the battle in May, with the thick arrows of the German divisions slashing around Paris and stabbing up towards Calais and the Channel. That defeat the old man had counted as a victory. So no later calendar had been posted. Time had stopped in the house too—so that it was just the same now, except for the attic, as when Paul had walked up the lane five years before with his cardboard suitcase in his hand and a raging thirst in his throat.

Paul turned off the radio.

"A drink, Grandfather?"

Augustin shrugged again; he had his back to the room and was looking up hill behind the house. And Paul thought of a different day, three years before, when one summer's morning over the crest had come Bernard, in civilian clothes but

11

with a soldier's stride, whistling serenely a popular English tune—"Roll Out the Barrel," he'd told Paul later. A father to be proud of.

Paul went down to the cellar and brought up a bottle of the precious prewar Volnay and uncorked it with care and filled two of the thick old café glasses three-quarters full.

"Grandfather?"

Augustin turned and stepped slowly to the table. He picked up his glass. "What are we drinking to?" he asked with an effort at his old sarcasm.

Paul hesitated. The wine gleamed like heart's blood in the sunlight. "To the fact that all three male Molpheys are alive, Beau Papa."

The old man's clear blue eyes stared hard at him, then his lips moved in the faintest of smiles and he gave a little bow. "Très bien, mon petit."

So they drank to the slender truth on which they could agree, quite unaware of the falseness of the toast.

After two glasses, Paul started toward the stairs to his attic.

"To work? I am glad to see your euphoria has not diminished your perseverance."

Paul smiled. "Yes." He nodded. Scholarship was the only pleasure the old man had now, and Paul his only scholar. Augustin had retired as professor of literature in 1939, come back to the hamlet of La Roche for a short holiday, then, when the local man had been called to military service, he had accepted the post of schoolmaster at Ste Colombe-sur-Saye. But that had been a duty, not a pleasure, though a duty made more palatable when he could pin up the portrait of the Marshal in the schoolroom. Although he admired intelligence, he disliked children.

"You must concentrate on your Molière—your Molière is seriously deficient."

It was an indulgent understatement. Even after almost five years of his grandfather's lucid tutoring, Paul's interest in Molière remained unkindled. He had done well in the *baccalauréat* before leaving Paris, but he doubted whether he would ever be able to pass the next great academic examination for which Augustin was so carefully preparing him.

And there on the attic table were the books, open and closed, the piles of notes, the labour of nights and winter days. He passed them by and threw open the windows that gave onto the countryside, the meadows rich now with golds and whites and purples, the cows still clean with spring, the air pure, the sky without a cloud, the acacia in the garden below fluffy with pink delicacy. The far hills were etched exact and sharp; they said on a clear day in *le grand matin*—the early morning just after dawn—that one could see the white shimmering shape of Mont Blanc in the distance. But he'd not seen it yet. He looked down at the buildings before him—at Madame Thibault's rose-stone pigeon tower rising to three stories, at her vegetable garden where stood one of the two Lombards, the club-footed one, statuesque, still as the tower itself. Lombard—stranger, said Augustin, who knew the brothers' real name was Martellini. And then the man turned slowly—a movement as surprising as if a scarecrow had moved—and raised his face, swarthy and unshaven, his dark eyes shadowed by his black hat.

"Bonjour, monsieur," called Paul and smiled and raised his hand.

The Lombard stared, then slowly turned away.

And Paul laughed. Leaving the windows wide, he went back to the table. With deliberation he cleared away the books, the papers, the notes.

He sat down and took a fresh sheet of the crosshatched paper he had used so sparingly. He thought for a moment, biting the end of the pen, then wrote in large letters at the head of the page: SIGNALS OF A NEW WORLD.

Today in my village the bells rang out for peace over a dreamless people. But dreams there are . . .

13

Now, today, even at that long distance in time—nearly thirty years—he could remember the first line, the first line and a half. But nothing else.

It was six days later, the first Sunday after the war's end, that the news came. Punctiliously at ten o'clock, as he always did, Augustin had started off for mass. From the attic, where he had been working since breakfast, Paul watched the small, erect figure in an old raincoat and beret march with brisk steps out of the gate, and turn right along the narrow lane until hidden behind the dilapidated old barn that was fast becoming a ruin.

Paul went back to the table and started to write again, slowly but easily—the words falling into his consciousness as gently as the mild spring rain that cloaked the country with softness and silence. After a while the bell began to toll for mass—it was a good twenty minutes walk from La Roche to the village. And then again, silence. Except for the scratching of the pen across the page.

But there was a noise, faint, faraway, to which at first he paid no attention. But it came nearer, impinging on his mind, so that eventually he laid down his pen and listened. There was no doubt about it—it was a car, a sound so rare that he had to think before he placed it. He heard the shifting down of the gear, then down again as it mounted the steep slope that gave into the hamlet from the left. The lane, unpaved, of packed-down rose-coloured gravel, led only from the main road, then down again to join the main road at Ste Colombe—from nowhere to nowhere. The last motor vehicle to come this way had come to fetch Monique, and, before that, years ago, the truck that had rounded up thirty-two of the commune's able-bodied men, including M. Thibault, and carted them off to forced labour in Germany.

But this was no truck—this was a car. Paul rose and went over to the window. He could see it now—a beige-coloured Citroën. A military vehicle, moving very slowly. It stopped directly below him, the window was rolled down, and a capped head looked out. Paul felt a weakness in his left leg; it troubled him in damp weather. Why here? Because of course, he told himself, this was the only respectable house around. Once a farmhouse like all the rest, in the early thirties Augustin had pulled it down and on the old foundations built a sort of stuccoed villa—*une maison bourgeoise*—a "respectable" house. The obvious place to ask directions.

He leaned out of the window. "Can I help you?"

The head jerked left and right, then glanced up.

"Oh! Yes—would you have the kindness to direct me to Monsieur Molphey's house? If this is La Roche?"

"This is La Roche. This is his house. I will come down."

"Thank you. I . . ."

Paul turned away and hobbled rapidly across the attic—it wasn't the rain, but fright that made him limp, he knew. In later years, the doctor had said, in middle age, it might become a serious handicap. He took the stairs cautiously and got to the front door just as the soldier ran up the stone steps and onto the little vine-clad terrace that surrounded the house.

"Monsieur Molphey?" He was a splendid figure with his leather gloves and crossbelt and high boots, his kepi with gold leaf on the peak, ribbons on his chest, and the flaring cavalry trousers which Paul remembered seeing so often in the Phoney War strutting about the Champ de Mars.

"Yes?"

"Dubellay, Captain." He saluted, but he frowned slightly. "M. Molphey, Augustin?"

"That's my grandfather. I'm Paul. He's at mass, but he will be back shortly. Won't you come in?"

The saluting hand came down smartly. "Thank you. If you don't mind . . ." He shrugged. "This rain."

As he turned to lead the way into the parlour, Paul noticed that the glossy boots were already spattered with pink mud from the lane.

"You have come a long way?"

"From Paris."

"You must have started early."

"Before dawn. It's the devil of a place to find!" He smiled, embarrassed at this sudden vehemence.

They stared at each other awkwardly across the table.

"May I offer you something then—a glass?"

"You are most kind, but thank you, no."

"Won't you at least sit down?"

"If you don't mind, I would prefer to stand."

So Paul would have to stand too, though his leg was trembling now, twitching. Because he knew what was coming, he knew what had happened.

"I—"

"You—"

"I'm sorry. You were going to say?"

"No, please. You first."

Dubellay looked down and slowly began to peel off his gloves. He glanced up. "I take it then that you are the colonel's —Colonel Molphey's son?"

"Yes. He is dead." A statement—a knowledge.

The captain nodded. "Yes. I am afraid so." His gloves were off now; he removed his kepi and laid them on the table together. He was ill at ease because, Paul knew instinctively, this was not what he had expected, was not the way he had been prepared to break the news. "I—I am sorry. Your father was a—"

"Will you excuse me for a moment?"

"But of course."

He went out of the front door, down the stone steps, into the cellar. He took a bottle of Volnay out of the rack and stood holding it in the dimness, the slight dankness of the surrounding stone, his head bowed under the low beams. He had an urge to hurl the bottle against the wall, but instead, he turned and went round the back way to the kitchen. He drew the cork softly and put the bottle on a tray with three of the best glasses. Later it would be needed. Wine—Blood of the Lamb—the sacrificial celebration. He shook his head—no, that was Augustin's religion, not his father's, who had none; not even his mother's proud remnant of Protestantism, whose only relic was a poetic fondness for the Song of Songs: "the bridegroom cometh . . ."

As he entered the parlour, Augustin came in by the front door. The soldier, seated, was caught unawares and leaped to his feet.

"Grandfather, this is Captain Dubellay—he has some news for us. Captain—my grandfather."

"Molphey." The old man gave a curt bow.

"Enchanté."

Augustin took off his beret and slipped out of his raincoat and laid them carefully on a chair. He stood erect, spruce in his Sunday best, the Legion of Honour in his buttonhole, the Croix de Guerre sewn on the lapel.

"Sir, I infinitely regret that it is my unhappy duty to inform you that your son, Colonel Bernard André Philibert Molphey, was killed in action ten days ago. He—"

"Ten days?"

"Sir, the delay is inexcusable. But he was on special liaison with the British forces on the Rhine and it was not until late last night that we learned of this unhappy event. The General himself dispatched me at once to inform you—and it is in his name that I offer you the most sincere condolences on this tragic happening. You, sir, as a soldier yourself, will know that . . ."

They listened in silence to the captain's eulogy. Perhaps he had awoken early and had prepared it as he drove through the Burgundy countryside—or perhaps he had written it out before he departed. But he did it well—glory, patriotism, an example to all, the supreme sacrifice, heroism, the field of battle, La France—and not too swelled with his own eloquence.

And when he had finished there was a stillness.

"Did you know my son personally, Captain?"

"No, sir, I never had that honour. But of course we all knew him by reputation, by his deeds. I have a letter from the General which I am—"

"The General?" Dry, dry-eyed Augustin.

"General de Gaulle." Frowning, Dubellay unbuttoned his tunic and pulled an envelope from the inside pocket.

It was a thick white envelope with a red seal on the back and Augustin held it, turning it over in his hands before opening it. He read the letter almost cursorily and handed it without a word to Paul.

Again the same phrases, but better here—steadfast, companion, grief, the future. But not gaiety, none of them mentioned that—the robust gaiety with which he had come marching down the hill that morning, this hill up here, curtained with rain now, and the hard swing of his arm and the laughter and . . .

"Paul!"

"Monsieur—Grandfather. I'm sorry."

"Some refreshment for the captain."

"No, please, I—"

"I insist."

Paul brought the tray from the kitchen and poured. Each held his glass close to the body, as though to protect it from some mortal enemy. There was no sun now to light the wine.

Augustin raised his glass. "Un brave homme," he said expressionlessly—a good chap.

"Un homme de courage," the soldier amended, then ringingly, "un héros!"

"Mon père."

"Mon fils." And a single tear rolled out of the old man's eye and down the side of his nose and trembled on the wax of his moustache. He brushed it aside with a quick gesture.

The glasses touched, and they drank.

The attic, with its uninsulated roof, was still stiflingly hot even in the cooler air of the summer evening. He had dozed off in memory, awakened—to memory. Time lost in time past. Like his grandfather, he had stopped time—lost it, lost the General's *futur*. Yet he persisted in waiting. The specialist's prophecy had been fulfilled—he was desperately lame now, in middle age. But he walked—always walked back and forth to the school, as he had when the twins were little, one hand in each of his. Later, abandoning Augustin's ancient Citroën, he had bought a new car to fetch and carry them from the *lycée* at Croze when they became weekday boarders. And then they were gone. Agnès to—to God knows where, God *knew* where, if anyone did—some imaginary realm of sanctity. And Hélène to Paris and then—then perhaps, he hoped, to some kingdom of true liberty.

The last time she had come—with her German (Paul had never caught his name)—it had been just such an evening as this. He had been shocked by—well, not by her faint air of grubbiness and untidiness, for she had never been the neat one —but by the look about her cheeks and about her dark eyes which dominated, and yet seemed to have a separate life from, her face. They had been hungry, and he had fed them and given them wine—a newer Volnay, but still Volnay—and they had eaten enormously. Afterwards, they sat in the garden and the guitarist played. And then suddenly Hélène had begun to sing. He had supposed the girls sang, although they never did about the house and he had never accompanied them to mass, but he was utterly astonished by that strong, clean soprano. It was a song of the revolution, in Spanish, and he caught only a few of the words—of freedom and love of country and the sweetness of brotherhood—but the melody was one of indescribable yearning. The air was warm, the crescent moon high in the never quite dark summer sky, and as his daughter stood leaning against the apple tree and sang, Paul had been transported, without breath—as though what he had been waiting for had come at last. Often, since then, he had tried to whistle that tune, but without success:

In the morning, a kiss upon the lips, and she was gone. He

had been vaguely surprised to notice the beds had not been slept in.

His daughters—the last of his losses.

No, not quite true. He mustn't forget Fley, the parish priest, his long enemy for years. At Fley's sudden, stupid death, he'd wept—up here in the attic—tears not spent for mother, father, wife or children, tears not even shed for the greatest loss of them all, the missing *Signals of a New World*.

And he thought of that other day of summer, that other tune of joy Bernard had whistled as he swung down the hill.

Paul had run out to greet his father and they met at the garden gate, like young lovers. They embraced and hugged and swung each other around in a kind of dance and he remembered the smell of his father—of tweed and pipe tobacco—and they laughed. Yet he was a stranger too—the immaculately shaven cheek was bristly, the hair awry, the perfectly pressed suit rumpled and stuck with burrs and bits of hay.

"You've grown, my boy. What muscles!" pinching Paul's biceps. "Father's a slave driver, I thought you'd be white and sickly with learning."

"Oh I do that too. But I work in the fields now—all the young men are gone and they're glad to have me." And he thrust out his hands, the palms thick and calloused from pitchfork and spade.

And they stared at each other for a few moments, gravely absorbing the changes.

Then Bernard nodded. "It's as beautiful as ever. We should have sent you here years ago—instead of to England."

"I adored England—despite the consequences." The doctors thought it was during his month in Sussex when he was fifteen that he'd picked up polio.

"There is good even in bad consequences. At least they won't take *you* away." And suddenly Paul saw how lined the face was under the tan, how tired the eyes were—or perhaps sad.

"I could fight," he said.

"No, my boy. You're all we have now. Fighting—there are plenty of others to do that here." And he gestured toward the wide valley beyond the house; it was early and a deep mist lay heavy down below, so that the tops of the trees poked up from a great floating lake of white—like secret soldiers in a dawn attack.

"They wouldn't let me anyway—because of grandfather."

"Pauvre Papa! How is the old bird?"

"The same as ever."

And he'd laughed. "Well, let's see."

And arm in arm they walked down the garden and into the parlour to find Augustin standing in his shirtsleeves at the table. He hadn't moved since Paul ran out—and he still held the big round loaf of bread in one hand, with the bread knife poised.

"Why have you come?"

"Bonjour, mon père." And Bernard grinned. "To blow you all up, why else?"

"Quiet—Monique is in the kitchen."

"Put down your knife, old man—and let's have some fresh coffee. Monique won't betray me."

"Coffee?" said Augustin belligerently bitter, but laying down the knife all the same. "We haven't seen coffee for years."

"Well, here's something to gladden your heart, then." And Bernard opened his jacket, reached inside and pulled out a packet that glittered with green and gold foil as he banged it down on the table—*Fortnum & Mason: Finest Coffee*.

"Coffee! Mon Dieu!" And the old man slowly sat down, as though the shock was too much for him.

"Monique!" Bernard called in ringing tones, and she appeared at once from the kitchen.

"Bonjour, Mr. Bernard." She made a half curtsy—and wore a fresh blouse and a clean apron.

"Monique, you wouldn't give me away, would you?"

"Never!" She shook her head indignantly, then gave her kind

21

of sly, leering smile. She was not pretty, but buxom and healthy, with a head of marvelous chestnut hair.

"Then make us some coffee." And he tossed the packet, which made a little chink of coffee beans as she caught it deftly.

"Oh, Mr. Bernard!" Her small brown eyes gleamed and perhaps at that moment coffee excited her more than the finest pair of creased breeches or polished boots.

And yet, during the next two days, Bernard had not talked in her hearing of what he was doing. Nor had he answered Augustin's question to his face—the old man's disapproval and dread of his activities were clear from his oddly muted manner, his more than usual stiffness. He asked no further questions, not even inquiring about his daughter-in-law, Emily, Paul's mother.

After the coffee, his father had gone directly to bed. "I'm a night traveller these days, Paul—I sleep by day, when I can. Wake me at dusk."

And that evening, after the soup and a special dish of fried eggs in honour of his coming, they went up to the attic and, by the light of a candle, he looked at Paul's books and examined his notes. Paul used Augustin's old service revolver as a paperweight and his father had picked it up and said, "You shouldn't keep this out. Do you have any bullets?"

Paul showed him the box in the table drawer.

"Do you know how to use it?"

"I suppose you just pull the trigger."

His father smiled and pocketed the revolver. "Come on, let's go for a walk, it's dark enough now."

But it wasn't really dark—there was a full moon that shone like polished silver. And as they cut across the lane and down into the meadows, Bernard nodded at it. "That's one of the reasons I'm here—one can't get far in moonlight. Too risky."

They took the long way around to the woods and he didn't speak again until they were darkly shielded by the trees on either side of the little trail.

"I think your mother's dead, Paul."

"M-mother . . ." He halted abruptly, the tremour shaking his leg.

"I heard they arrested her two months ago."

"Arrested her—in Paris?"

"Yes, at the apartment."

"But why?"

In the stillness he thought he could hear a myriad birds stirring restlessly, moles burrowing, a fox stealthily shifting a leaf as he stalked.

"Why?" There was a sudden rasp of a match and, as he lit his pipe, Bernard's face was illuminated from below—mask-like, the eyes sunken, the lines hard, the cheeks fallen in as he sucked. "Why?" He blew out the match. "Because her mother was Jewish—or her mother's mother was."

"I—I'd forgotten." After the flare of fire, the dark of the woods was darker yet.

"Well somebody didn't forget. She never made any particular secret of it, of course."

And he remembered her, small and gay, perfumed for a party, delicate, coming to tuck him in, perhaps reading a few verses from the Song of Songs, then kissing him good-night. "Sweet dreams, my little David." Paul David he had been christened, but only she ever called him by his second name— and somewhere secretly he had always felt there was an inner David-self within him, as beautiful and free as she.

"She should have come with me—to Ste Colombe. She would have been safe here."

"Perhaps. She and Augustin hated each other, you know. And she despised the countryside—she would have died a different sort of death. Paris was the only place in the world for her—she never thought she could be in danger."

"But Maman—she never did anyone any harm."

"Not intentionally, no." The voice was dry—it might almost have been Augustin speaking. Suddenly the pipe glowed redly. "Come—I want to get up to the Mont de Mars—if you can manage it."

"I can manage it." And, strangely enough, as they continued, his leg seemed to grow stronger. It was a long way to the mountain—made longer because they skirted the villages and farmhouses, though now and again a sharp-eared dog would break into a wild flurry of barking as they passed. Otherwise, the moonlight made the silence deeper. They spoke hardly at all, yet Paul felt a great comfort in his father's presence, the smell of his pipe smoke, the lithe step, the way he had of slightly turning his head this way and that, as if noting every detail of the landscape, alert for all unusual movement.

The top of the mountain was heathlike, thick with wild box, crowned with an enormous statue of the Madonna, sickly white by the moon. Bernard took out the revolver and showed Paul how to stand and aim and shoot, how to load and what to expect in the way of a kick.

"Practice, practice—till the movements are quite natural. You won't have much time—just enough to draw and aim and shoot, if you're lucky. Don't hesitate, don't think—just do it."

And Paul stood there, clicking the empty revolver at the great pale Lady, until the sweat ran into his eyes.

"You keep it now," his father said at last, and Paul slid it into his jacket pocket where it hung heavy, a warning and a promise.

The Mont de Mars was not part of a range, but stood alone, with valleys running away, lower hills in the distance, here and there forests or woods sewn like black patches to the fabric of the landscape, the gleaming silver of a river. Not a single light in all the space about them. An owl hooted and then from far away came the sound of a steam engine.

"It's an odd thing, Paul," his father said slowly, his pipe out now, his hands thrust deep in his pockets, "I've been all over the world advising about dams and water projects, surveying for railways, building roads and bridges—always on the move, helping to open, construct, develop. And now I come back here, home to my own country, secretly in the dark—to destroy those very things. I teach them about explosives, blow up bridges, how and where best to derail a train. I am the avenger in the night . . . And you know, Paul, I am getting to like it." And he turned and laughed with a white gleam of teeth.

"But they're the enemy."

"Oh yes, they're the enemy. It's simple. But it's a dangerous thing. To have enemies all around you. Who reported Maman to the police? Who, in the unknown houses where I spend a night or half a day, will betray me? Who is my enemy—it becomes obsessive. It does not fit us for peace. It does not help us to forgive—and yet unless we can forgive, we will have no peace."

"But, Father, when it is all over—"

"It will never be all over. We become what we do. Can we change back—do we want to? Look at your grandfather, for all his religion, unrelenting in his hatred for half his fellow countrymen."

"Then what?"

"I don't know, I don't know." And he sighed. "All I can think is that whatever cause one has for hate and vengeance— in order to survive one must keep some secret part untouched and still and listening, not listening for death in the dark, but for good news in the daylight. Like our countryside here— these meadows and valleys and forests—waiting in patience."

"Waiting for what?"

"Ah—I am an engineer, not a philosopher." And he laughed again and took Paul's arm. "Come on, we must get back before dawn."

The way home seemed easier, and they talked more freely —more freely than they had ever talked before. He had known his father mainly as a taciturn figure hurrying in late to dinner, often absent for long periods, never discussing his work. But now he told Paul about England and the English, what people thought of the war, about London and air raids, the politics of the Resistance.

The moon had set, but there was a predawn lightness in the sky as they traversed the woods, so the trees had vague shapes as they bent over the pair, as though they too were listening.

"Have you found any mushrooms yet?"

"It's a bit too early—and there's been no rain for weeks."

"Too early—yes. I was forgetting." And he stopped to light his pipe again. When it was going, he said, "Your mother."

"Yes?"

"She wasn't an especially good woman, I expect you know that. Nor particularly sensible. But I loved her."

Paul nodded, suddenly too moved, too weary to speak. Had *he* loved her?

"She neglected you. And so did I. But it was the way people brought up their children. After the war it will be different. No more nannies and housemaids. It will be different for your children—better."

"My children?"

"What are you going to do, Paul? Teach?"

"No! I m-mean, I . . ." He was confused, surprised by his own vehemence.

"I know. If you haven't done anything, you've got nothing to teach. And if you have done something—well, you want to go on doing it." He laughed softly; they turned and began to stroll, at a slower pace now that they were close to home. "You like it here, don't you—very much?"

"Yes. It seems—it seems like a dream come true."

"Despite Augustin?"

"Despite Augustin."

"Don't fall too much in love with it. Anything you fall too much in love with betrays you in the end."

As they emerged from the woods, Paul laughed—and as if in answer, a cock crowed; a dog barked, and all the country seemed to stir.

They went up to the house where the bats, warned of the coming day, were weaving backward and forward trying to find perches under the eaves, sometimes hitting the gutter or the wall and falling back to try again. Paul and his father stood in the little sweet-smelling garden and watched until all the bats were stowed away and secure.

"I shall be gone at nightfall, Paul, unless I hear to the contrary."

"Yes, Father." And suddenly his eyes stung and his leg trembled and the weight of the gun in his pocket was a terrible responsibility.

And then, as if by magic, it *was* evening and they were walking together up to the back gate of the garden.

"Take care of the old man, Paul."

"Yes, Father."

"He will have a bad time of it in the next few years—however long it takes us to win—as we get stronger. And we will get stronger."

"Yes, Father."

And at the gate they embraced. Bernard put his hands on Paul's shoulder and looked at him, then suddenly, strangely, leaned forward and kissed his son on the lips. "Adieu, mon brave."

And he was striding away up the hill, at the crest outlined for a moment—a tiny black figure against the summer sky.

Then he was gone.

Perhaps Bernard's departure had touched Paul with premonition, for that summer three years before the war's end it was as if he had done his mourning for his father—working it out, secretly, in advance, as he forked the hay on top of the cart or in the great haylofts of the farmers, streaming with sweat, pricked and bitten, half-choking with the dust, drinking litres of fresh white wine that ran through his body like weeping or shivers of love; in the autumn in the vineyards, bending and cutting the soft, tender bunches of black grapes, white grapes, dewy and delicate . . .

Because when Captain Dubellay left, and Paul and his grandfather stood looking at each other, the General's letter between them on the table, neither one able to offer the slightest comfort, and when Paul had climbed up to the attic and sat down to his work, he could not shed a tear. Perhaps the words were a weeping—for they seemed to gush like clear water from his heart.

From time to time during the next few days, he would lay down his pen and try to force himself to remember. The whole of his childhood and the greater part of his youth—until he was almost seventeen—had been spent in Paris, yet he could catch no more than fragments of it: an enormous apartment, with rose-coloured carpeting in the sitting room and red plush chairs and gilt and marble; the formal visits of strangers generally described as cousins or aunts and uncles; exquisitely wrapped presents on his birthday, not one of which he could recall; once, stealing a *marron glacé* from a silver dish at Christmas (why did he have to steal it?); walking with his parents in the Champ de Mars, little white gloves on his hands—again, was that possible? He must have been very small. More clearly he remembered lying sick with polio in his primrose-coloured bedroom as autumn wore into winter, and doctors and nurses came and went, and he was allowed to get up for Christmas and sit in his dressing gown in front of the sitting room fire while a maid brought him his presents from under the Christmas tree and his mother cooed and clapped her hands as he opened each gift, although she must have known beforehand what most of them would be.

More clearly still he recollected the previous summer he had spent in Sussex with an English family. After a desultory week of trying to entertain him, they had presented him with a bicycle and a map and left him alone. And then and there—in a foreign place—he had, with springing delight, discovered the country. A cosy countryside of sleek villages and fat brick mansions, then further afield to the bleaker magnificence of the Downs, and once to Beachy Head and the great chalk cliffs and the sea spotted with minute vessels far below. Mountainous breakfasts at little inns, huge teas at tea shops, pints of beer in pubs if they were indulgent enough to serve him (though he had always looked older than his age). And everywhere he went everyone had talked to him, gentle and kindly talk, the half of which he never understood. He had certainly fallen in love with England—too much? For England had betrayed him, so they said, with this sickness from the public swimming baths in Tunbridge Wells.

But, coming back, it was Paris that had seemed dead to him. In his mind it was Paris that had stricken him—Ste Colombe that had healed him. For Augustin, the 1940 calendar on the parlour wall marked time stopped; for Paul it signified when life began—the year of his birth. Or rebirth.

That first summer at the end of the war was a coming of age for Paul.

They brought Bernard's body back to Ste Colombe to be buried in the family vault, and the army sent six buglers, and the people came from far and wide for the funeral—men mostly whom Paul had never seen before. He felt awkward at first in the stiff new blue suit he had bought at Croze. Having inherited his father's agnosticism, tinged with a vague Protestantism from his mother, he had never been in the church as a member of the congregation, although he had always admired the building itself. The interior had been heavily restored, but the outer fabric was an almost perfect example of early Romanesque. As one walked down the hill into Ste Colombe, the lovely little square tower with its columned openings appeared to sink slowly behind the houses until it vanished gently into the heart of the village.

He understood nothing of the service, not even knowing when to stand or sit or kneel. But afterward, outside, as they lowered the coffin into the grave, this embarrassment and that of the stares of the people dropped away from him. It was a brilliant day, with a faint breeze that gently stirred the flaxen locks of Father Morine as he shook diamond drops of holy water into the opening. The scent of the massed flowers—wreaths and bouquets and sprays—rose delicately on the air and, as the bugles blared, Paul raised his head in a daze to the high blue sky. It seemed not a lament, but a celebration—almost a triumph.

And afterward he was still dazed as the people came up and, often with no more than a nod to Augustin, shook his hand, embraced him, wept.

"Ah, he was a man . . ."

"We had some good times together, Bernard and me . . ."

"You can be proud . . ."

"Without him, mon vieux . . ."

Augustin had hired a car from Croze and, he and Paul in the back seat, they were driven slowly back to the house. Everyone, it was understood, had been invited. Monique had gone (to Marseilles, they said) and it was not the moment to look for another girl, so that morning Paul himself had gone down to the village and bought a great basketful of round, spiked brioche. He had cleaned and swept and polished and opened the doors between the parlour and the sitting room they never used. Now he ran down to the cellar and brought up a dozen bottles of Meursault—the last dozen.

They waited. And nobody came.

On the north, windowless side of the house, there was a long, still vivid scar on the yellowish stucco where, one night in the middle of the war, the Resistance had raked the house with a Sten gun. A warning to the old man, the schoolteacher. (And Augustin had lit a paraffin lamp and flung open the shutters—"Cowards, traitors, Bolsheviks—kill *me!*" he had shouted into the empty night.) Now, it was a sign to keep away.

So, grandfather and grandson, they waited wordless on the terrace to greet their guests.

At last came Mme. Thibault, their close neighbour, almost dragging her powerfully built husband, surly and saturnine, recently come back from four years in Germany. All that time she had worked the farm alone, except for some help from the Lombards, paid, and from Paul, unpaid (except in eggs and butter and milk). One winter she had caught pneumonia and Paul had moved into her one great room and nursed her day and night for ten days. So Mme. Thibault came, whatever objection her great oaf of a husband might have.

And then Mme. Buisson, Thérèse. With her young daughter, Arlette, but without her husband, also a returned deportee; Charles Buisson was much weakened, they said, had had TB, but worse than that, was sour and embittered. Perhaps especially embittered against Paul, who had worked long and happily for Mme. Buisson, putting up with her piety and her daughter, by turns noisy and sullen, for the sake of her gargantuan meals and her rolling local "r's."

Finally, to Paul a totally unexpected arrival—Father Morine. Yet not so surprising really, for Augustin was a regular communicant and, ignoring the schoolmaster's traditional hostility to the clergy, was a mainstay of religion in the commune. Morine was in his early thirties, handsome in a frail-looking way; his first post had been chaplain to an infantry regiment and in the first month of the war his shoulder had been shattered by a piece of shrapnel—he still moved his left arm awkwardly, often tucking it into his jacket for support. The honourable wound had exonerated him from any taint of politics, and, anyway, he was a man totally involved in his own piety. He had, so they said, a special fondness for the Sacred Heart. The women loved him. His presence certainly eased the atmosphere of the little gathering.

Paul opened the Meursault and handed round the glasses and served the brioche, but they ate and drank little, enough only for the sake of politeness. He talked to Mme. Thibault, whose normally strident peasant voice was subdued today. Augustin said nothing. It was Morine who carried the party with a stream of platitudinous chatter, apparently oblivious of any tension. Looking around the room, Paul, eased of his responsibility as host, was able to observe the guests. Mme. Buisson, in total black, was becoming animated with wine and piety as she listened to the priest; her daughter kept her eyes down. He had never seen her dressed up before with a little hat and gloves—and he was struck by the fact that this little urchin was pretty. Arlette's hair, usually a scraggled mass, was black and lustrous with brushing; her eyelashes were long and delicate; there was a low swell of breasts under the severe gray of her dress and, below the wide hips, her legs were beautifully shaped. Aware of his regard, she glanced up and gave him a direct and open stare and a quick, bewitching smile. His heart turned over. He gulped his wine. His leg trembled and he needed to sit down. Then Morine was addressing him—something about his father —and he answered vaguely.

Paul suddenly had an idea. He went and fetched the General's letter from the drawer in the sideboard where he'd seen Augustin put it. And he read it out loud to them, then handed it round. They all nodded, grave, impressed, and handled the paper with reverence—as though it had been a morsel of the Sacred Heart. Arlette was the last and, as she gave the letter back to him, she looked at him again—her eyes were deep brown with a circlet of tiny gold flecks around the pupil—and he thought he saw a kind of admiration in the glance, as though it were he who was the hero. He turned away, aware that he was blushing, and returned the letter to its place.

They left soon after, dutifully shaking hands all round. Paul walked Morine to the gate—he was grateful to the priest and tried to say so.

"But it's quite natural that I should come," Morine replied with his fragile smile.

"Yes. I see . . ." He was at a loss.

Then Morine said, "You are a walker, I know. I always walk up to St. Remi early in the morning before mass and again after supper—in the cool of the evening. If your work permits, perhaps you would care to accompany me one day?"

"Thank you, I should like to very much," Paul said, surprised to detect a certain honesty beneath the politeness of his response. They shook hands, and, in the brilliant sunlight, he watched the small black figure until it disappeared behind the deserted barn. A priest. What on earth did they have in common—except that they were both crippled?

Augustin attacked him directly as he entered the parlour.

"Why did you show that letter? You filled me with shame. Do you think it's fitting? Do you imagine I am proud to have a son who . . ."

Paul turned away his wrath with soft words. He remembered his father's injunction—"Take care of the old man." He listened with pity—Augustin, too, had been betrayed, betrayed in his love for a son who had died for a cause that was all he detested.

As Paul went into the kitchen, his grandfather cried, "And I suppose I am to make the dinner again?"

"It's only chicken—I'll put it in the oven myself, now."

Upstairs he went to the attic window and looked out, not over the fields and the hills beyond as he usually did, but down to the village, where the little rose-coloured church rose above the red-tiled roofs with their weather cocks and lightning rods, and the smoke from the chimneys leaned gently in the light breeze. They too would all be cooking their dinners—Morine's housekeeper in the presbytery, Mme. Buisson—whose farmhouse lay on the near outskirts—for her enfeebled husband and her pretty daughter.

Paul went to his table, but he sat for a few moments before picking up the pen. He and his grandfather were alone up here on the hill in their little hamlet of La Roche, although he had hardly been conscious of it before. But down there was a community—people who were glad to see him. He had a strange feeling of elation. Perhaps he had found a friend, however bizarre—perhaps something more.

"Arlette," he murmured aloud—and smiled.

Perhaps the war was over.

He woke up in a shock of fear, half-sprawled across the table in the dark. He sat up abruptly and automatically pulled the ancient pistol from the drawer. Then he heard it again—the crackle of faraway gunfire and the flash of war in the night. He struggled to his feet, to the window, still half-caught in that thirty-year-old dream of horror—the advancing Americans bombarding Croze, the Resistance attacking the Germans in the rear, too optimistic, too early. The men dead, the vicious retaliation, the savage burning of the village of Massury.

He steadied himself at the window—and suddenly the dark was illuminated with explosions. Red, green, white, blue, orange—the fireworks of the Fourteenth of July—and moments later the crackle of their bursting. Rockets and stars and wheels —he watched them expand and dart across the sky from the distant Mont de Mars as if alive, then diminish and die.

He laughed and the laugh turned into a yawn—not of fatigue, for he must have slept away the evening and half the afternoon—of hunger then.

He shut the windows and turned on the lamp on the table and put the gun back in its place. Electricity had come to Ste Colombe three years after the war and he'd had a man especially from Croze to wire the house, but he often missed the smell of the paraffin lamps and candles snuffed out as one went to sleep. Still, it had been wise for the twins.

He glanced down at the page—a fresh sheet—on which he had written:

> A writer cares for nothing above his art—it is his wife, his mistress, his children. It is his house—in which he spends his life preparing for the coming of the bride. . . .

He frowned—shouldn't it be the bridegroom? He turned out the light and hobbled to the head of the stairs and hung up his stick. No, *bride* was correct—but what if she never came? Or came and . . . He stood quite still, looking down into the dark, confined well of the staircase. She *had* come—the rites had been performed, the marriage consummated, the progeny brought forth. And then—bereft. All he wrote now was a grieving—grief for a work whose lineaments and shape he had no memory of and could not recreate. All he bore now was the peculiar heaviness of loss. He descended the stairs carefully, his leg was painful and stiff from being so long in one position.

He looked around the large, rose-tiled kitchen, the little corner where Monique used to sleep, the old range he never used but had not bothered to have removed. He had prepared nothing for supper. Why? From some kind of superstition; somewhere in the back of his mind he'd hoped, that if he made no preparation, Hélène would come—yesterday or today.

He picked up a basket and went out to the garden. He took some potatoes, pulled a few carrots, cut a young cabbage with his pocket knife. The distant revels illuminated his labours.

But what is a writer who has lost his art?

He took a lettuce, then stood and raised his head.

When they were small, he had allowed Agnès and Hélène to stay up late to see the fireworks on the Fourteenth of July. He would wrap them in blankets and sit them on the chaise longue on the terrace and let them eat bread and cheese while they watched. For a long time they were persuaded the celebration was for his birthday, which occurred on the previous day.

"It's all for you, isn't it, Papa?"

"How lucky you are, Papa—so beautiful!"

They were quiet, obedient little girls, not much given to imagination, so he took a special pleasure in this obstinate expression of their childish love. He didn't disabuse them of the notion.

Augustin had always opened a bottle of champagne for Paul's birthday, and Paul had kept up the custom, though switching the day to the Fourteenth, so that he could sit in the cool of the evening with his daughters as the sky lit up with its golds and sapphires and rubies and diamonds, and slowly drink his Veuve Cliquot. So perhaps the girls' confusion was natural, for they always gave him his presents on the Fourteenth. Invariably, from Agnès something beautifully embroidered, and from Hélène nearly always pencils.

In the kitchen, he put the basket of vegetables on the table —but he realized he was not in the least hungry now. So he went slowly down the outside stairs to the cellar and fetched a bottle of champagne. He settled himself with a blanket on the chaise longue; it creaked under his weight—always well built and still strong in shoulder and arm, he had grown heavy with age. Only his legs were frail. As fireworks splashed the heavens with colour, he gently swizzled the champagne bubbles with his finger. Yesterday he had been fifty—an elderly man by rural standards. Today? Today was an anniversary of a different sort.

"Grandfather—I've been invited to lunch at the Buissons tomorrow."

Augustin was pouring the champagne into long, thin glasses —he despised the *coupe*. He said, "Then of course you must go."

"You wouldn't object?"

"If you mean because it is the Fourteenth—no. It's not a festivity about which I am enthusiastic." He set down the bottle, handed Paul a glass, took the other and stood up. He waited for a moment, looking down at the liquid that was still audibly hissing. Then he lifted the glass. "To your coming of age, Paul." He drank.

"Thank you, Grandfather." Paul rose slowly, trying to think of an appropriate response. All the graceful things he might have said—"May my manhood be as worthy as your own," for example—were sour on his tongue. He looked out at the garden, the hill rising behind the house.

36

He turned back to the old man. "To peace," he offered.

As they sat down, Augustin drew from his pocket a small package wrapped in white paper and sealed with red wax. "This is for you."

Paul opened it with care; inside was a gold fob watch and gold chain. "I . . ."

"It belonged to my uncle and godfather, Augustin, after whom I was named." He smiled dryly. "He was a man of peace."

"Thank you, Grandfather, I—I shall treasure it." He examined it—it was a beautiful object, the initials A.G.M. inscribed on the back. He was uneasily aware of the watch on his wrist —unbreakable, waterproof, shockproof—which had been part of his father's effects. What on earth was he going to do with this fragile thing?

"And now we must talk about business."

"Business?"

"Bernard's estate. It is time for you to take charge of your own affairs. Naturally, he left everything to you. I have all the papers here." He touched a thick brown envelope that lay next to the champagne bottle. "I think you will find it all in order."

"I'm sure, I—thank you."

"You will of course want to verify them for yourself. But perhaps you'd like me to explain in simple terms what—"

"Yes—yes, I would. Please."

"For a successful businessman, your father appears to have been somewhat improvident." He cleared his throat and touched the tip of his moustache. "Of course he—and Emily —lived in a highly extravagant fashion. In my day, we saved and invested in property. Of course I inherited this house, but by the time I was merely maître-assistant I had already purchased the little apartment in Nice for our retirement. . . ."

In talking of business, Augustin seemed to lose his customary clarity—or perhaps it was Paul who simply failed to grasp the simplest statements about money.

"I hope you will not be disappointed, but the assets of the estate amounted only to a little over one million francs, which includes—"

"A million!"

"A useful little sum, but hardly what might have been expected. And of course—"

"A million." It seemed an enormous fortune.

"My dear Paul, I do wish you would not interrupt. Of course, this amount includes an evaluation of the contents of the apartment, so it is not as much as—"

"The Paris apartment?"

"The Champ de Mars is in Paris, so I understand. Really, Paul, you are being exceedingly slow this morning. Frankly, I find it astonishing that your father did not own the apartment. My advice to you would be to get rid of it at once—as it is, the rent, the charges, the local taxes are a constant drain on the estate, not to speak of the wages of old Clotilde which I understand cousin Edouard has been paying. I have taken no steps myself but . . ."

Paul murmured his responses. He was moved, shaken. It was like being handed back his boyhood on a plate. Would it be the same—the pink carpeting, the velvet, the marble mantelpieces, gilt sconces, his old yellow bedroom? And Clotilde.

Mme. Thibault had come in to cook and serve the birthday lunch—trout and roast veal and green beans and salad and a Camembert, which Augustin had somehow miraculously procured, and a raspberry tart. Paul hardly noticed it, was hardly aware of his grandfather. He was in another world. These possessions so abruptly thrust on him made what was absent suddenly present, what was lost, found, what had been dead, all at once alive and about him. His mother embroidered—it seemed unlikely, yet he remembered her sitting there beside the window in the sun, her fingers making little birdlike swoops and darts. And she used to sing—not at the piano or anything formal like that—but wandering about the house. He remembered his father saying once, "A song before breakfast, grief

before supper." But Paul had thought it wouldn't count for her
—she never took her breakfast before ten. And they'd had a car
—a big, open car, yellow and black. Once on a Sunday they'd
driven down to the Black Bear at Fontainebleau and on the way
back his father had pushed the car up to 130 kph and Emily's
hat had blown away—he could almost hear her laughter in his
ears, could almost see the little cloche hat sailing and swirling
in the wind behind them.

In the kitchen after lunch Mme. Thibault presented him
with a tie of peculiar ugliness—mud-coloured blues and greens
and browns with a vivid white stripe.

"It's beautiful," he said. Impulsively he embraced her.

"Of course you won't be able to wear it until next spring,
which is a pity."

"Of course not." A year's mourning was still the rule.

Mme. Thibault touched his arm. "I hope everything will be
all right for you, Paul," she said and he was surprised to see a
tear in her eye. "You are a good man."

Upstairs the attic was baking and Paul was heavy with champagne and red wine and two glasses of *marc*. He sat in a kind of
trance, the sweat prickling his skin under his shirt, not attempt-
ing to work. After a while he took out the letter that had come
this morning.

"Bonjour, Monsieur Paul," the postman had shouted when
Paul opened the door. "There is a letter for you. An important
letter. From Paris."

"Come in, Postman." *Postman* he was called—like that—few
people knew his name.

"I came early, because it is important. A registered letter.
From Paris. You will have to sign for it." It was eight o'clock
and Postman hardly ever came before eleven—he walked
twenty-five kilometres a day on his rounds and often didn't
finish till sunset. His inquisitiveness had got the better of him
today, Paul guessed.

"A glass of wine?" Paul asked, but was already pouring.
"Where do I sign?"

"Patience, young man, patience. Let me see." He took the glass, "Santé," and drank it down like water. He thumbed slowly through his book. "It's from Molphey, Edouard. A relative, no doubt?"

"A distant cousin." Paul smiled—he would have liked to have given Postman more information, but had none to give. "I have never met him. He lives in Paris."

"Ah, Paris. Then that is the one."

Edouard had written to him after his father's death—a short, simple letter of condolence, the only one Paul had received. In fact, he might have met him long ago at the apartment, although he had the feeling all those cousins and uncles were from his mother's family.

After two more glasses, Postman had departed frustrated, for Paul had not opened the envelope which bulged heavily at one end. Instinctively he felt that its contents would somehow interfere with his morning's work, so he had slipped it into his pocket for later—until now. The paper was thick and creamy, of prewar quality, a pleasure to touch; it was headed *Pascal, Pierre*—P.P.—the small publishing house where Edouard was an editor.

July 12, 1945

My Dear Cousin,

When I saw your father shortly before his death, he gave me the enclosed objects and charged me, if anything were to happen to him, to send them to you on your twenty-first birthday. It is with a deep sense of sadness that I now fulfill this, his last wish. At the time of her arrest, Emily was able to slip them to Clotilde, which explains how they have come to survive.

At that time also I was able to persuade Clotilde, whom no doubt you remember, to move down from her maid's room into the apartment itself which I felt on no account should be left empty. She has been living there ever since, although she is not now in very good health. After your father's death, I took it upon myself to continue her wages.

Perhaps you will let me know if I can be of any further help. I imagine that before long you will wish to come to Paris to dispose of matters relating to the apartment—who knows? perhaps you will decide to live in it yourself. I look forward with great pleasure to seeing you at that time and reestablishing family ties.

Meanwhile, may I take this opportunity of sending you my very good wishes on the attainment of your majority.

With all friendly greetings,
Edouard Molphey

Paul set aside the letter and shook a small tissue-wrapped packet from the envelope. He had already guessed what it contained and yet, when he saw the two rings nestled in the paper, he was somehow surprised. They were tiny—a plain gold band and a ring set with six diamonds and beautifully enameled in red and white, green and blue—and he recalled the smallness of his mother's hands, the fingers so thin that when she held them up to the light they seemed as translucent as alabaster.

He laid the rings away carefully in the drawer beside the heavy old revolver. And then suddenly he was seized with a frightful anger. His hands trembled violently and when he looked up, out at his dear countryside for calm, he saw only a writhing mass across a black desert. He snatched the revolver from the drawer and staggered to the window, his leg jumping and quivering so that he could hardly stand. He raised the gun toward the shimmering distorted village and fired and fired again—*click-click, click-click.* "Traitors! Cowards!" he shouted.

There was a sound behind him. He swung around to face the enemy.

"Is everything all right, Monsieur Paul?"

His sight cleared—it was only Mme. Thibault, standing at the door, drying her hands on her apron.

He lowered the gun. "Yes—yes, everything's all right."

She stared hard at him, nodded gently. "Bien." Then she

41

turned and disappeared, closing the door softly behind her. Long ago, above the lintel, someone had nailed a notice— *A Place for Everything, and Everything in its Place.* Paul laughed.

He went back to his table and put the gun in the drawer, the thought crossing his mind from nowhere—*next time I shall load it*. He looked down at what he had written, that morning—but he knew that he could write no more today. He wiped his face with his handkerchief, then went downstairs.

He took an old ash stick from the rack—because he was going for a long walk—God knows how long—and he didn't trust his leg anymore.

He crossed the lane in front of the house and cut down through the meadows and, skirting the village, entered the woods.

Later, he could remember very little of that walk—except standing on the top of the Mont de Mars and seeing far away the smoke puffs of a steam engine and, even farther away, the clean silver glimmer of the great river.

As the sun was setting he found himself at St. Remi. After a while he became aware of the presence of the priest beside him.

"Bonjour, mon ami."

Paul nodded, not wanting to speak. He leaned all his weight on the stick. He was tired now, but his mind had cleared. The great red globe almost visibly descending calmed him and he knew somehow that when it was gone, the summer twilight would restore tranquillity, give him back his country.

The sky was cloudless. The sun was bloody.

"It is like a great dying heart."

Paul jerked his head, frowned.

"I'm sorry," Morine murmured.

The sun had touched the hill now—a dead tree on the crest was black against its scarlet.

They remained together silent until the last brilliant slice disappeared suddenly, in the twinkling of an eye.

"A cigarette?"

"Cigarette? No—I—yes, perhaps I will. I didn't know you smoked."

"Nor does anyone else—or so I fondly imagine," and Morine smiled as he lit their cigarettes. In the flare of the match his face was smooth, unmarked, untouched—and Paul felt at that moment infinitely older than the priest, who was at least ten years his senior.

Since the funeral they had met four or five times thus. Once in a moment of expansiveness—or weakness—Paul had mentioned that he was writing and, after that, Morine had talked almost exclusively of literature. He was half shamefaced, half eager about it—but his judgment was interesting and his reading wide beyond his faith; he had admitted a fondness for Michelet as though he were confessing an act of forbidden lust. Paul had lent him Baudelaire and he had devoured it with avidity. Yet the simplicity of his faith was unmoved and he sometimes made observations of a pious banality that made Paul wince— once the setting sun had shone through a brief rain shower, making the drops glitter golden, and Morine had compared it to the grace of God falling to Earth.

It was hard to obtain books at Ste Colombe. "One day I hope to be sent to a town—with libraries." There was a trace of regret, but no bitterness when he said, "Of course, when you have finished your novel, you will go to Paris."

Paris—he always wanted to hear about Paris, a desire that taxed Paul's memory. But tonight, in a calmer mood of remembering, Paul did talk a little, easily, slowly, as they smoked their cigarettes, then strolled down to the village.

"An apartment in Paris," Morine said in that tone of quiet awe he usually reserved for the Sacred Heart. "You will live there, and be happy and famous."

Despite a lingering feeling of melancholy, Paul smiled.

"And yet you are sad," the priest said as they shook hands in the dusk outside the church.

"Perhaps, a little."

43

"It is only the past we need be sad about," he said, suddenly urgent, "the future is glorious!"

The future is glorious. Perhaps, thought Paul the next day as he put on his new blue suit; at least, if not the future, the day. He'd risen at dawn and worked the whole morning through—writing, clear-headed, with a new rapidity. Now, as he dressed for lunch at the Buissons, he felt released—devil-may-care. He wore Mme. Thibault's tie and ignored Augustin's slight frown as he saw it. There was nothing to mourn. The future was glorious.

He walked down to the village without the stick. His leg was strong. His mind was lucid. His heart was in the right place. He was hungry.

And as they ate slowly through that immense meal—*oeufs en gelée,* salmon with mayonnaise, great thick Charolais steak, a dish of mushrooms, quail bestrewn with grapes, *fromage à la crème,* fruit salad, *petits fours* and brioche—words, which that morning had come so readily to his pen, now came as easily to his lips. "The Brain," he had been nicknamed in the village, and his amiable silence had been respected—but now he talked well, feeling his way at first here and there, but with a new fluency until often he had them all in a roar. He even cracked smiles from Charles Buisson (for which Thérèse later thanked him—"You have made him forget himself"), and when they learned that the day before had been his birthday, Charles fetched up the champagne from the cellar. Paul thanked God that due to some odd accident of heredity (his father being of medium height, his mother minute) he was a big man and could absorb all the alcohol they thrust on him without losing his wits.

They drank until dusk, and all the time Paul was aware of Arlette, demure, half-smiling, darting a glance at him covertly now and again, lightly brushing against him as she placed a new dish on the table.

Then they ate again. And afterward, all the "young people" —Arlette, her cousin Jean-Claude and her friend Ursule D'Ornay and *her* sister Béatrice, and Paul—walked down to the ball at Ste Colombe.

He danced.

As a child, every Thursday, from the age of six he had had dancing lessons, his mother herself taking and bringing him back—until on his tenth birthday he had quietly said, "No more." He remembered her pleading—"Mais, Paul!"—weeping, but he had remained adamant. And he saw again his father —for once at home—sitting smoking his pipe, a whimsical smile on his face, until eventually, "Let him alone, Emily—it's more important that he knows what he wants than that he knows how to dance." And Emily, in a sudden rage at such betrayal, had picked up a vase and hurled it at Bernard, who, almost casually lifting his left hand, had caught it and set it down. And they had all burst out laughing.

And now miraculously, after ten—eleven—years, the steps came back to him. He could not manage the twirling, hardstamping peasant dances, but the waltz was a dream—a dream of feather-light elegance, rising and sweeping and turning like a light barque on an ocean of love. And the girls in his arms. They all danced well, but none as well as Arlette, deft footed, smiling open eyed now, smiling at him, soft mouthed, entranced and entrancing. He drank only a glass or two—to quench his thirst—but the smell of the marquee, of the old boards, tobacco and wine and sweat of the young bodies intoxicated him.

He was exalted.

During an intermission he took her out in the full moonlight, into the shadow of a barn and talked, told her of what he was, of his writing, his life, his hopes for a new world, a new place.

"You mean, Paris?" she whispered.

"Paris!" He laughed. "Yes, Paris!"

"You will go away and forget us."

"Never! This is my home! Here are my roots! This is my love!"

Later, they kissed. A kiss of dreams and soft wings. And her lashes fluttered on his cheek.

They danced again—and again.

And then he took them all home, as the moon set. And the others vanished into the house, into the night, and for a moment he was alone with her and she said, "Je vous admire beaucoup, Paul."

"Et moi, je t'aime—tu es belle comme la lune."

"You are as beautiful as the moon."

He awakened with a smile on his lips, the taste of a new kiss.

He blinked slowly—an old dream. It was full daylight now.

He groaned softly. He was cold, frozen stiff on the ancient chaise longue. Not even a blanket.

In the last few weeks he had got in the habit of sitting out on the terrace late into the night, drinking slowly, remembering, regarding the moon: old moon, new moon, hunter's moon, crescent moon. A foolish mooning.

A hot, humid August—but not hot enough to warm his bones in the morning on the terrace. What would Hélène say if she came and saw him thus? But Hélène hadn't come, wouldn't come now.

He reached down to grasp the leg of the chaise and ease himself up, and his hand knocked over the empty bottle—it rolled to the edge of the terrace, fell onto the stone staircase, then bounced tinkling down every stone step to the bottom. That ought to bring Mme. Thibault out, if anything did. He peered through the thick leafiness of the vine on its trellis—but there was no sign of her this morning.

They always greeted each other—as he walked to the school and she came out to clean her vegetables on her terrace—with a nod and a "bonjour," but there had been a distance between them for a dozen years now. Ever since that early evening in

January when he had heard a terrible wailing scream and had hobbled out of the house just as she ran into his garden.

"Paul, Paul—come quick, I beg you—oh, what a horror."

Still in his shirtsleeves, he'd followed behind her into her barn—and there, by the light of the naked bulb, was M. Thibault, suspended by a rope from the high beam, tongue protruding, eyes fat and staring. He must have jumped from there —for the head lolled and clearly the neck was broken. Paul took hold of the hay cart and, using all his strength, hauled it under the slowly twisting body. He mounted and tried to unknot the rope at first, but it was iron fast.

"Get me a knife, woman."

"There's one in his pocket," she whispered in a strangled voice.

But it was blunt, and, as he sawed and hacked, the body swung and jumped, as though he had stabbed it. It fell at last into his arms; he carried the dead man into the house.

"Not on the bed," she cried. "Not on my bed!"

So he laid the corpse on the table. In the sideboard he found the bottle with the wooden devil on a ladder inside it and poured two large glasses of *marc*. They drank it down cleanly, but she would not let him touch her, comfort her.

"What am I to do?"

"You must wait here, Mother. I'll drive down to the village and fetch Father Fley and call the gendarmes at Croze."

"What a way to die! He was a wicked man—but what a way to die. And he won't even have a proper burial. My God, my God—and what will people say."

And Paul had nothing to answer. "I'll fetch help," he said.

"Help—what will help the poor fool now?"

He crossed the lane and, without bothering to go up to the parlour to get his jacket, brought the car out of the garage. A few months before, he had bought the new Renault to ferry the twins from the *lycée* on weekends, but hadn't yet mastered the gear shift properly and, as he backed it jerkily into the lane, he crunched the rear lights into Mme. Thibault's garden wall.

There was no one he could call to stay with her while he was gone—La Roche was too tiny a hamlet to have a public phone. In the winter he and Mme. Thibault were the only inhabitants —and M. Thibault, until now. He drove with a cold caution that Hélène always made fun of, but the sweat in his eyes half-blinded him.

Paul had not been to the presbytery since Father Morine's desperate flight. Even now he hesitated for a moment—and then he pounded at the door.

Father Fley answered it himself at last. Unshaven, like Paul in shirtsleeves, a thick leather belt buckled around his baggy trousers—"Well?"

"You are needed. Thibault has hanged himself."

"That doesn't surprise me." He glared at Paul for a moment. "Come in."

"No, but you must—"

"Come in!" He held the door, slammed it as Paul entered and led the way into the dining room.

"Marie!" he bellowed. He motioned Paul to sit down, took a glass from the cupboard, filled it and his own from a half-empty litre bottle and sat down himself.

"Oui, mon père?" Mlle. Nocent's trepid face appeared at the door. Some said Fley slept with her, but she was of such ugliness that it was hard to believe—yet perhaps that was the attraction.

"Get on the phone to Dr. Mullet—and then to Sergeant Grosjean at Croze, not one of his minions, I don't want them calling up the paper to earn a few francs."

"Why—what has happened, Father?"

"Thibault has committed suicide. Tell them to get over to the house at once."

"Lord have mercy on us!"

"Too late for Thibault. Get on with it, woman." Then, when she had gone, to Paul: "I suppose it was suicide? Drink up."

"It certainly wasn't an accident." He sipped the wine—it was surprisingly good.

48

"I wasn't thinking of that."

"Then what? Murder? Who would have wanted to murder Thibault?"

"I can think of a dozen." Fley had laughed, showing his brown, broken teeth. "You, for instance."

"Me?" Paul felt a prick of exasperation—what warped fantasy of the clerical mind was this? "Do you imagine that I am Mme. Thibault's lover?"

"Mon pauvre vieux. It is not of love I talk." He stared closely at Paul, as though about to say more, then he shrugged. He raised his voice, "Marie—is it done?"

"No, Father—there's some difficulty with the line."

"Well, we can't wait. You'll have to follow on foot. Bring your nightclothes—you'll be sleeping there tonight. Well, Molphey, will I drive or will you?" He stood up.

"I'll take you."

"Frightened of my driving, eh?" He laughed—he'd had more minor accidents in a year than the rest of the commune put together. "Then you'll have to bring me back."

"Agreed."

"Good." He put on a heavy jacket of bright red and green plaid; he was already wearing a beret, once black, now green with age. Paul thought that the contrast between this shabby, careless figure and the polished and immaculate interior of the house was deliberate.

"My God, you can't drive any better than me," Fley growled as the car rabbit-hopped the first few yards.

"It's new," Paul said, irritated at the note of apology in his voice. He disliked the priest for many reasons, some of them sound—he was lazy, obtuse, coarse, quarrelsome, uneducated, drunk, and wrong about nearly everything—but some of them, Paul acknowledged to himself, not so rational. At the back of his mind he always compared Fley to the gentle Morine, then flinched at the thought. However unpleasant Fley might be, at least he was honest—and tonight Paul was glad of his company, any company.

"I think Mme. Thibault is worried aboout the burial."

"Why?"

"Isn't there some rule about not burying a suicide in consecrated ground?"

"I don't believe in all that nonsense."

"And the archbishop?" said Paul, trying to put a little sarcasm into his voice.

"I bury who I like in my churchyard."

They drove in silence up to the Thibaults.

"When I'm done here," Fley said as he got out, "I'll come across to your house. It'll be some time."

"I'll wait."

This time, with the utmost care, Paul backed the car into the garage, leaving the gates open.

He went into the house, put on a jacket, wrapped a scarf around his neck and climbed up to the attic. He didn't turn on the light, but instead struck a match and lit the candle on the table. At night he often worked by candlelight—the life of the flame giving substance and movement to the shadows. That afternoon he'd written:

> Where are the companions to make my flesh real? Where is that birthright of trusting humanity which is surely mine? Where are my brothers who speak to me as I am, not as I appear? Where are the words to strike my heart?

He opened the window and took his post there, unaware of the chill of the January night, watching the house opposite. He saw the jerky little figure of Dr. Mullet get out of his black sedan and run up the steps—Mullet, sometimes of overwhelming toothy charm, sometimes of superlatively offensive arrogance. A man of moods. The few times he'd come to the house, when the girls were ill, he'd invariably tried to persuade Paul to go hunting with him.

Then Mlle. Nocent, with a small cardboard valise in her hand, darting glances left and right.

Then Grosjean, the gendarme, fat as his name, self-important, blowing white plumes of frosty breath and rubbing his hands as if going to a feast.

Then an ambulance, and Fley suddenly appearing on the terrace. "Go home, you fools—we don't need you, unless you can raise the dead!"

After a long time, Mullet and Grosjean left together, the sound of their cars receding until the night was totally silent again. Few thoughts passed through his head. He was glad the girls were away.

The cloud cover was low and there was a feeling of snow in the air. The smell of it. Scattered over the countryside were half a dozen pinpricks of light and twice the headlights of a car descending the long hill above Croze—but it was too far to hear them.

A draft guttered the candle, then snuffed it out. He turned away, and in the darkness he saw Thibault again, stiff, swollen, cold. He shut the windows and went downstairs. It was cold there too and the fire almost out.

He put dried bracken in the stove and kindling and four small logs and opened the damper wide.

Then he sat down and waited for Fley.

Arlette had been confined to bed since the middle of October, and now it was almost Christmas Eve. A difficult pregnancy, Mullet said. But even before that she had not wanted Paul in the same bed, not allowed him even to touch her. She detested her state, was ashamed of her swollen body —and her belly did seem incredibly big for such a small frame to bear. But he thought her more beautiful than ever, more than ever he wanted joy of her. If she did not want it, he blamed himself—he'd had little joy to give her in all these dreadful months.

He would come back from school to find Thérèse sitting beside her—and they seemed to have the same look of challenge in their eyes.

"Look, my hair is falling out. Look," she accused him, brandishing a little tuft of dark hair.

And as he moved toward her—"No, don't touch me, you have chalk on your fingers."

It was hardly his house—Thérèse was always there, bustling, pursing her lips, making tisanes, frowning. She stayed until ten every night, refusing a lift in the vilest of weathers—"there must be *someone* in the house"—and came just as he left for school. At least he was permitted to make breakfast.

"The coffee is detestable this morning—what have you put in it, salt?"

In January Thérèse was coming to sleep in the house—"as a precaution"—although the baby was not expected till February. His one consolation was that she cooked him lunch and supper.

When, after their three agonizing weeks in Paris—"our honeymoon"—they had returned to Ste Colombe, Arlette was already suffering from morning sickness. The sight of food revolted her, so she said. Yet, when that was past, he was surprised to find she knew nothing at all about cooking—she could not fry an egg without breaking it in the pan, she didn't know the difference between an onion and a shallot, between chives and chervil, she either oversalted or left it out altogether. When he attempted to show her, she would get angry and whisper furiously at him in the kitchen, whisper because she was afraid of Augustin. When he took his final departure in June, she said, "Thank God that old fool's gone."

Later she said, "I wish the old fool were here—at least he could *talk*."

And it was true, Paul knew—he had lost his ability to amuse. It was as if, with the loss of his manuscript, he had lost all his words—written or spoken, could talk only in the arid accents of the classroom.

"Do you think it's a pleasure for me to have you standing there like a sick dog—have you nothing to do? What about your precious book?"

And he would go up to the attic and sit, lick the nib of the pen and dip it in the ink:

Today in my village the bells rang out for peace over a dreamless people. But dreams there are . . .

He looked out of the window over the last of summer, the autumn, the beginning of winter, but he could remember no more. Did he no longer believe that there *were* dreams? He would take off his shoes and pace softly up and down, because once when he had descended after fruitless hours, she said, "How do you think I can get any rest with you tramping back and forth above my head? I must have rest. Dr. Mullet said I must have rest."

Sometimes when he came home, he would find her friends Ursule and Béatrice D'Ornay and often two or three boys. He thought of them as *boys*—though they were hardly much younger than he. He liked their laughter, their high spirits, even their teasing of him, "Oho, silence, here is the great writer!"—because it amused Arlette, made her happy. Only Béatrice, he noticed, would not join in the taunting.

Sometimes Morine came, and Paul would walk a little way with him down the lane and try to draw some comfort from the few words exchanged. Yet the priest seemed ill-at-ease—as though his former enthusiasm for Paul's book had become shameful and Paul's loss a failure of grace that could contaminate. Perhaps it was no more than the traditional hostility between priest and schoolmaster—yet the soft voice and averted eyes troubled and disappointed Paul.

"My God," Arlette said once, "dull as he is, I'd have rather married a priest than a schoolmaster. At least he can smile."

But gradually Morine came less often—he had not been for three weeks now—and the girls too were less frequent visitors.

Perhaps Arlette's bad spirits had put even them off, thought Paul. For she complained now almost all the time.

"You never think of me—you think only of your wretched writing. Is your book more important than your wife?" Then she had added sarcastically, "If there ever was a book!"

And then suddenly he was shouting at her—an orgasmic rage; he was aware only of the blood in his head, the jerking of his leg, the violent trembling of his whole body. Then he was being pulled away, pushed out of the room by the strong arm of his mother-in-law. He caught a glimpse of Arlette's face, white to the lips, then he was in the kitchen being shaken, berated.

"Madman, monster, maniac!"

He stumbled upstairs to his attic. He sat, but could not for a long time control the convulsive shivering; to his disgust he found he had an erection.

He wanted to weep, to cry out to the night. But he could not. And he could never remember what his words had been —perhaps some of those Augustin had used, when he'd announced his engagement to Arlette: an obstinate, narrow-minded, self-seeking, featherbrained peasant, without aptitude, ignorant, coldhearted, hard as nails. "I know," Augustin had ended with absolute calm, "because I have tried to teach her."

After that, she would flinch when she saw Paul. He was obliged to sleep in the old living room. There was no one to whom he could turn for help. No one.

Murmurings from the other room always ceased on his entry, and mother and daughter would stare at him blankly. Living communication had vanished—like the *Signals of a New World*, it might never have existed. The only sound had been Arlette's sobbing all through the night after Mullet had told her to expect twins.

Paul turned on his truckle bed and looked at the luminous hands of his father's watch—2:00 A.M. It was Christmas Eve now. Silence—the utter silence of rural winter. Silence, to which it seemed he was doomed forever.

There was a sound—a groan. He sat up in the bed. Was it his own? No—again from the next room. A moan, then, "Paul —Paul!"

He sat quietly drinking tea with Mme. Thibault in the parlour. Every now and again she got up and went to the kitchen to check on the pans and buckets of boiling water on the range— the first time he had even seen it lit—or to refill the teapot. At the same time she would slide another log or two into the green-enamelled parlour stove.

They didn't talk very much—he had shouted out to her, tooting on the horn of Augustin's old Citroën, before he began his mad dash down to the village to fetch the midwife. Mme. Bouquin had taken a maddening amount of time tidying herself up, filling her bag with aprons and instruments—surely she should have had it all ready—wondering where she'd left the scales. She was slightly cross-eyed and was supposed to be a witch—when the vet had failed with a sick cow, often she would be called and would shut herself in alone with the animal and faint murmurings would be heard. Sometimes the de-spaired-of beast would get well. People were a little wary of Mme. Bouquin.

"Plenty of time, plenty of time," she had said with a faint smile at his restless shifting, "These things don't happen in a moment, Monsieur Paul."

He was still Monsieur Paul to her and probably always would be, though lately some had begun to call him Monsieur Molphey—which, before, had been Augustin.

When he had returned with her—driving with care because it had begun to snow—Mme. Thibault was already there, the range lit, water beginning to boil, a pile of clean towels on the table. Paul had driven off again immediately to fetch Thérèse. Then later he was sent down to the village to phone for Dr. Mullet. By then the snow was thickening and Mullet didn't arrive for three-quarters of an hour.

Thérèse came in every five minutes, "Isn't he here yet? What can have happened to him? He must have had an accident. Paul, you must go and look for him."

Her authority and confidence had deserted her, she was on the edge of tears, and actually wrung her hands. It was Mme. Thibault who calmed her with gentle words and cups of tea—once ordering her to drink a glass of wine. They would go into the kitchen and whisper together and Thérèse would return to the bedroom, momentarily restored.

"What is it, what's the matter?" he asked.

"It's often more difficult with twins—if one wants to emerge buttocks first, it is hard to turn him because of the other baby. But it will be all right, it is simply harder on the mother."

"Arlette, she—she's not suffering too much?" There were double doors between parlour and bedroom, and no sound could be heard.

"Of course she is suffering, that's natural. For any good thing, one must suffer. But she has broad hips, she is strong, she will survive—that one. Ma foi."

Mullet had come at last, trying to conceal his irritation under a lot of puffing and blowing and slapping of arms. Even from his car to the house, he had become covered with snow. "It's as cold as death out there," he said, flashing a meaningless grin. He accepted and drank a glass of wine gratefully, but Paul saw that his hand trembled.

It was overpoweringly hot; Paul had taken off his jacket and sat in a kind of dream, although he was totally awake. The parlour was its old shabby self—the 1940 calendar still on the wall; he had started to fix it up in the summer, but had stopped because Arlette couldn't bear the smell of fresh paint.

At half-past six Thérèse had come in, her hair awry, tears streaming down her face. "It's a girl . . . oh my poor Arlette, how she is suffering!" She went back with a ewer of boiling water, and, one of the doors being open, Paul heard a cry.

He stood up.

"Sit down, Paul."

"Perhaps—perhaps I should get the champagne."

"Wait. Sit down."

And he had. His dreaminess had gone now, and every part of his being was vibrant. "A daughter!" He grinned and suddenly wanted to clap his hands. "What luck!"

Mme. Thibault laughed. "You wouldn't say that if you were a farmer."

"What?"

"You'd want two strong hands to help you in the fields."

"Oh." He looked down at his own hands; he hadn't worked on the farm at all this year and the calluses had gone, the skin was soft again. And then he laughed too.

Twenty minutes later Mullet burst into the room, his face white, one cheek jumping as if pulled by wires. Gripping his black bag in his hand, he half ran to the little bathroom.

"What is it?"

But he shook his head.

"Shall I bring you hot water?" called Mme. Thibault—there was only cold in the bathroom. But he had already slammed the door. Silence—then after three or four minutes they heard the water running; soon after he emerged, smiling, his hair slicked down, the twitch gone.

"Well, my dear Molphey, another daughter for you. Two out and one to come."

"Triplets!"

Mullet nodded sagely. "The two girls are identical—if the third is an identical girl, that will be a record in these parts. A fertile seed, Molphey—ha ha!" And he showed all his teeth in a wide smirk. "We shall know shortly."

"And the mother?"

"Oh the mother—she is a peasant. No offence intended, of course." And he grinned again. "Well, back to my labour!"

When he had gone, Mme. Thibault raised her right hand and pressed a finger into the inner side of her left arm—the motion for a hypodermic syringe.

"You think . . . ?"

57

She shrugged and laughed. "So it is said. But at least he is not trembling now."

Paul nodded, then forgot it. Triplets—three girls. He smiled.

"You are happy?"

"Yes."

"What will you name them?"

"Agnès, Hélène and—and Emily."

"What if it's a boy?"

"Then Bernard—but it won't be a boy."

He was wrong.

There was a sudden high shriek that pierced the doors as though they had been cardboard. A second later Thérèse burst into the parlour, "Paul, Paul—quick, fetch Father Morine! Oh for God's sake be quick!"

"Why, what is—" His chair clattered behind him as he rose.

Then Mme. Bouquin pushed past Thérèse. "It is a boy, but there is a problem with his breathing and with premature babies—"

"He is dying! Oh go, Paul—in the name of God, go!"

Mullet gripped Paul's arm, "I got him breathing once—I thought it was all right for a moment. And then he stopped," he whispered.

Paul nodded, watching Morine's black form bending over the child in Mme. Bouquin's arms. Thérèse moaned softly all the time; Mme. Thibault was quite still. Arlette lay pale, eyes closed, a tiny white bundle on either side of her—by standing on tiptoe Paul could see a patch of pink, almost purple face.

Morine muttered, made a movement with his hand. The gas heater murmured.

Paul thought the scene grotesque. He felt compassion for his wife, gratitude—gratitude for the delight within him for the two small, breathing babies. But the joy of birth was being

58

drowned in the grief of death. He resisted it—how could he grieve for a being that had hardly lived?

Then it was over.

On the terrace, kicking at the snow, Mullet said, "I'm sorry, Molphey. It was difficult. But we saved two. There was nothing to be done."

Looking down at him, Paul wondered for an instant if that were true—if the drug had not dulled him, might he not have been quicker, cleverer? Then: "I'm sure you did your best. Good night, Doctor."

There was to be no celebration, no champagne.

He drove midwife and priest back to the village. There was a predawn light in the sky as he drew up at the presbytery; he got out of the car and shook the priest's hand.

"Morine?"

"Yes?" He was turning away, turned back.

"Morine—do they really believe it—that the child will go to hell?"

"Not hell, Molphey—limbo." Then with a sudden, unfamiliar bitterness: "He's lucky. Limbo is better than hell." And his face seemed to gleam grey with sweat in the faint light—then he turned, his footsteps silent on the new-fallen snow.

Back at the house, Mme. Thibault helped him move the truckle bed into the bedroom for Thérèse and to prepare two boxes lined with blankets for the children—they'd not planned to buy a crib till the New Year.

"I will be back in the morning, Monsieur Paul."

"Thank you—thank you for your help."

He sat with Arlette for a few minutes. He took her hand—adorned with Emily's rings, gold and blue and red and white and green—almost as small as his mother's. He knew she was not asleep, though her eyes were closed.

"Arlette—I'm sorry."

She opened her eyes and stared at him.

"Arlette. You have—have given me great joy. You have suffered to do it. I—I have made you suffer. But it will be different now. I promise. I shall give you joy—and happiness—and all the things you should have."

Her hand lay listless in his, and then it stirred.

"I'm sorry," he repeated.

"It doesn't matter," she murmured. She withdrew her hand; she shut her eyes.

"Leave the poor girl alone!"

"Yes—yes of course. I'm sorry." He stood up.

"Can't you see she's exhausted?"

"Of course."

"Now don't you make any noise in that attic of yours. To-morrow you will have to drive to Croze and buy a crib and bottles and . . ."

In the kitchen closet he found the mattress on which Monique used to sleep and took it up to the attic with an armful of blankets and his overcoat. It was bitterly cold, but all the same he opened the windows wide. In the dawn light a wind was blowing the snow in wisps and plumes across the meadows. The clouds were thin above and had been quite swept away on the horizon. The sun rose red as a polished apple, and down in the village the mass bell began to ring clear and silver—close over the snow, as though it rang to him.

He shut the windows and lay down and covered himself. There was a great swelling in his breast. He closed his eyes. Then, from below, there came the tiniest of newborn wails—after a moment, joined by another.

The noises of joy together.

He went to sleep smiling.

What is language but to chant together in harmony? That is what language is, my fellow human beings—noises of joy together!

Under it he wrote the word *fin*. He blotted the page with care and laid it on the thick pile of manuscript.

He had done it; he was astonished.

He looked up. It was April, and there were soft yellowish shoots on the trees, and the line of poplars on the nearest hill already seemed bushier, more solid; the long grass in the garden below would soon have to be scythed. He had time for that now. Time.

All winter the spiders had woven their webs on the window panes. Why did they do so, when no prey could be expected for weeks, months? But then, the spider might think, why did this man scrawl his fly traces on the paper day after day where no one could see?

He opened the window with care for the cobwebs. Smiling, he looked out on his smiling country. The delicate spring sun shone. Below him, the pink lane twisted down the hill; beyond, the hills were misty against the pale blue sky. In Mme. Thibault's kitchen garden, the Lombard had long gone, and Thibault himself was now working, his thick hands thrusting in thin stakes—for peas or tomatoes, already. A good thing—a man come into his own again.

All about him the meadow sweet smells mounted like music. And he felt a rising within himself—the strength of sap in his veins. He held out his hands—his fingers were grass, his heart the young spring sun, his feet set to dance, his head dizzying into the white-blue heavens. He clapped his hands . . . and a magpie flew out of the neighbour ruins with a startled cry and Thibault jerked erect.

"Bonjour, Monsieur," cried Paul. "Bonjour!"

"Bonjour," Thibault muttered, then under his breath, but as clear as if he'd been in the room, "un fou."

And Paul laughed. He was right. A madman. He had clapped his hands and startled one bird and a surly farmer, and he had thought to arouse the whole commune, the country to joy—to noises of joy together!

He rubbed his hand over his face. He must come down,

come down. He went back to the table and opened the drawer
—where lay the pistol, the gold watch and the wedding rings
—and took a sheet of the fresh white notepaper he'd bought at
Croze just for this day, this moment. He wrote:

12th April, 1946

Dear Cousin,

You must think me very remiss at not having answered
your letter of two weeks ago. But events here have much
occupied my time.

I was much concerned to hear of the robbery at the apartment—though naturally glad that nothing of value appears
to have been taken—and even more so to hear of the distress
caused to poor Clotilde. It is of course a wise decision to
have new locks put on—though obviously nothing can deter
a determined burglar—and I am most grateful to you for
attending to the matter. I am writing to M. Greuze the
notaire to ask him to defray the expense you must have
incurred, including, of course, the monthly sum you pay to
Clotilde. I think it better that you continue to pay this,
rather than it come from an unknown lawyer, which might
upset and puzzle her. However, I hope to relieve you of all
these burdens very shortly. For I am intending to come to
Paris early next month, to be exact on Saturday, May 4.

The reason for this trip involves two, both serious and
joyful, matters. First—on May 3—I am to be married! The
bride is to be Arlette Elisabeth Buisson, daughter of a prosperous farmer at Ste Colombe. What can I say more—except that she is very beautiful and I am very happy? But
you will certainly meet her and can form an opinion for
yourself!

The second reason for my coming to Paris is that I have
written a novel. I imagine every "first" novelist thinks that
he has written a masterpiece, so perhaps I may be excused
from a similar view of my own work. If I say that it has my
whole heart and soul in it, that is perhaps to say no more
than that it is readable! I hope you will consent to read it
and, on this matter also, form an opinion for yourself. Noth-

ing of course would please me more than to be published,
under the family auspices, by P.P.

With friendly greetings,

your cousin, Paul.

PS: Would you be so kind as to alert Clotilde to our arrival?
She need prepare nothing more than a bed.

He sealed the letter and stamped it and put it in his pocket.
As he went down the stairs he tried to whistle—but he had
never been able to carry a tune, and all his mother's melodies
had gone from his head. Perhaps in Paris he would remember.

In the parlour, Augustin had just come back from afternoon
school and was hanging up his hat and raincoat.

"Hello, Grandfather."

The old man nodded slightly. "Bonjour, Paul." Paul sensed
how tired he was—this last year of teaching seemed to have
taken more out of him than before. He was uneasily aware that
he had neglected him—had failed to "take care" of him—and
was going to neglect him again this afternoon.

"I have cleaned the vegetables for the soup."

"Thank you." Augustin paused. "You are going down there
again for supper?" It was always *down there*—he couldn't bring
himself to mention the name Buisson.

"And to post a letter. There is goat cheese in the cellar."

Augustin sat down with a barely audible sigh. He was visibly
aging now. Sometimes his memory fumbled. Once, a few
weeks before, he had forgotten to shave. Yet he was still dapper. They had wanted him to resign, but he had refused. He
would not be seen to be driven away. He would exact respect
—just as he would obey the law—until the last. He had taken
down the portrait of the Marshal from the schoolroom wall and
rolled it up and brought it home. The poster of de Gaulle he
had pinned to the inside of the closet door, which could be
opened for display if the inspector came, thus falling within the
strict letter of the law, but which normally was locked shut.

"Is there something I can get you? A tisane?"

"Thank you, no." He raised his chin and his pale blue eyes examined Paul. "You are—a little excited. About something special?"

"No, no." Then Paul smiled—he could not withhold it from the old man. "Yes—it's true. I have finished my book today!"

"Felicitations."

There was a silence between them. Paul could not quite bring himself to leave. Augustin was quite still, one hand flat on the green tablecloth, his eyes unfocussed gazing out of the window. Suddenly, a little smile came to his lips and he looked at Paul again.

"I too wrote a book once, long ago."

"You—you did? What about?"

"Oh, it was not a novel. During the war—*the* war—one of the officers in my artillery unit, Gaston D'Orsel, always carried a little book in his breast pocket, in very fine print on thin paper. He would read it assiduously whenever he had a moment. It was *Les Rêveries du Promeneur solitaire*. You are familiar with it, of course. One day D'Orsel gave me the book; he said, I remember, 'Here, Augustin, this will cheer you up.' Later he was killed. Naturally I had read it before, but I read it again— it is at times painfully banal, but it did give me comfort. I lost it on a train. Then after the war we lived in Sallanches for six months—it was when I was not quite well. I decided to write a book myself. Every day I would walk in the mountains, then in the evening I would write my little book."

"And did you finish it?"

"Oh yes, I finished it. Many pages—a great many pages." His attention wandered to the window again.

"What happened to it?" Paul asked after a pause.

"Eh? Oh, I gave it to your grandmother to read. Hélène said it was—painfully banal." He smiled. "Rousseau *manqué* were the words she used. So I destroyed it."

"You *destroyed* it?"

"My dear Paul—in my position, it would not have done. Besides, I am sure she was right—it was a great piece of nonsense. The alpine air is thin and makes one's head dizzy and full of absurd dreams."

"But to destroy it—why?"

"I was not a young man. It wasn't suitable. I was forty—in the army they called me Grandfather, as you do. It was a *folie*. One must not burden oneself with *folies*." He looked at Paul gently. "I am not suggesting that you burn your work."

"No—no, of course not. But . . ." He spread his hands—he was nonplussed.

"Paul, now that you have finished your writing, I will ask you once more—for the last time. Will you not, after all, consider sitting for the examination? Your name is still down as a candidate. There is still time, almost a month. If we worked together intensively, you might have a chance, a good chance."

"No, Grandfather, I can't—you know I can't. I shall be married."

"Paul, I beg of you"—the old man stood up with a momentary struggle—"I beg of you for the last time—give up this disastrous idea of marriage!"

"I can't. I do not want to."

"You are young. You should not be burdened with a wife now. What have you to offer her? Nothing. You have no profession, no qualification beyond your *baccalauréat*, no knowledge of the world, no job, no means, you have—"

"I have my father's money."

"That is not to be spent! That is not to live on! It would be gone in the twinkling of an eye. How can you take on such a responsibility—a wife, children before you can turn round. What is a writer? Nothing! Nothing at all, nothing honourable, nothing decent—until he is dead perhaps!"

"Grandfather—please don't continue, I—"

"And she—what has *she* to offer *you*? Less than nothing. She will feed on you, take your money, ruin you and—"

"I can't listen to this."

"She is as empty and frivolous as your mother—and she will

hurt you just as Emily wounded my son, she will destroy something in—"

"Grandfather!" he shouted.

The old man stared at him, touched the back of his hand to his lips. He sighed. "I am sorry, Paul. I should not have said that."

"I accept your apology."

Augustin lowered himself to the chair. He looked away.

Paul went to the door and opened it, then turned. As though aware of being looked at, the old man lifted his head a little, and put one finger to the pointed tip of his moustache.

Paul could not bring himself to speak. He shut the door softly and stepped out into the fading afternoon.

As he walked down to the village, he gradually became aware of the letter in his pocket again, the hope in his heart—and of the fact that he was hungry.

After the night of the ball it had been difficult to get Arlette by herself.

He went to the farm almost every day after lunch and helped Charles Buisson in the fields—and he needed help badly. Two of the upper fields had been let go during the war and he was trying to reclaim them for crops again; the vines had been neglected, and gorse and even bracken had encroached onto some of the best grazing ground. And Buisson himself was not fit for much heavy work—he would spend an hour hacking at a hedge, then have to sit exhausted for another hour to recover. He was a small, fiery man and attacked the land as though he hated it. Gradually through the summer he became stronger— but was still grateful for Paul's strong arms or, at least, didn't refuse his help, which amounted to the same thing. He'd hired one of the Lombards with great reluctance—the one with the club foot, who never said a word. Once as all three were attacking a swathe of brambles and nettles, Buisson had stopped and looked at the other two and had begun to laugh—the first time Paul had heard a true deep laugh from the man.

"What is it?" he asked.

"Look at you—the pair of you—my two speechless cripples!"

The Lombard ceased all motion; he turned slowly, slightly lifting his scythe, and stared. Buisson's laughter stopped abruptly—and in the bright metallic heat of the afternoon, there was a coldness, a breath of night and mortality. And then Paul forced a laugh and, after a moment, the Lombard went back to work without a word.

The scene lingered in his mind, and he recognized a truth in it—he was thought of as a cripple. And an atheist, though he'd been careful to utter no blasphemy. An educated man—"The Brain." Finally, a stranger—which he would remain even though he lived to the end of his days in Ste Colombe.

So it was not merely Arlette he had to court, but the whole family too—and, in a way, that was easier. At least they were there and he could make them smile, lighten Buisson's gloom, flatter Thérèse's cooking. But Arlette was hard to catch, except in his dreams. If she was not feeding the pigs or milking the goats or churning the butter or running errands for her mother, she seemed always in the company of her friends—particularly Ursule D'Ornay, blond and blue eyed and as palely passive as Arlette was dark and vital and full of fire.

Then one rainy August evening he went to the farm for supper—it had rained all day and no work had been done and everyone was grumpy. Arlette was not there. She had been sent to bring in the cows.

"You'd better go and help her," Charles had growled.

Later—years later—he wondered if it had not been planned. But then, the thought didn't cross his mind.

He found her almost in despair in the middle of the big meadow. She was hitting a cow under an old oak tree, while the others waited patiently by the gate. At every blow, the cow would lumber slowly around to the other side of the tree, then stop.

"Oh Paul, I'm so glad to see you. This wretched beast, she will not move—would you believe it, she is afraid of the rain!" And she gave the cream-coloured rump another angry whack with her stick. She was soaked to the skin, her black hair hanging lank to her shoulders. She looked like a vexed child come too late for the cake. And Paul laughed.

For a moment he thought she would hit him—the stick raised, her eyes furious, the mouth a white line. And then she laughed too. And he simply took her in his arms and kissed her.

He was brought out of his daze by a brilliant flash of lightning and a shattering crack of thunder above their heads.

"Oh!" She clung to him.

It was almost black and the rain had turned into a torrent, so they could not see ten yards across the field.

"We can't stay under this tree—come."

"Oh no, Paul!"

"Come on." He caught her by the waist and dragged her into the open. Then suddenly she was no longer reluctant.

"This way, quick!" They ran hand in hand to the top of the field where there was a bank, with a gully behind it, sheltered by an overgrown hedge. "In here!" She lay down and rolled into the gully, and he followed, though not so easily. It was dry and leafy and still smelled of summer dust. In the false night, he saw the white of her teeth as she smiled and the gleam of her eyes looking at him.

"No one will ever find us here," she whispered.

The thunder cracked as he touched her, and the lightning flared again and again, and the rain beat violently all around and about their shelter of gentleness, of warmth, of the choking quiet of desire. He could not believe her body, her freedom, her openness, the readiness of her mouth, her hands, the firm, soft, risen breasts, milky smoothness of belly and thighs.

It was he who drew back at last, not she.

"Tell me about Paris," she murmured.

And, smiling, he began to tell her. He talked about the apartment, the car, restaurants, the one nightclub he had been to—painting a picture of opulence and gaiety which he hardly recognized himself. But she wanted to know too about the details of domestic life: did they have dinner, when did they eat, what did they eat, were the bedrooms heated, how many bathrooms, did they drink champagne all the time?

"Hardly ever. My father disliked it. Bordeaux mostly."

"Not Burgundy?"

"My mother thought it was too heavy." And they laughed.

She was impressed that he'd been to England. Had he seen the king? No, he'd spent only a day in London, but he had seen the palace and the changing of the guard. And he, in his turn, was touched that she had never been farther than Croze —a town of no more than three thousand inhabitants.

He talked until the storm was only a rumble in the distance. And when they emerged from their hiding place, the sun struck crystal gleams from leaf and grass. The recalcitrant cow was docile now, and the small herd, washed clean by the rain, trotted home eager for milking.

After that, Arlette did not seem to be as occupied in the house as before, and it became an understood thing that the two of them fetched the cows in the evening.

The summer was idyllic and, as it gradually passed into autumn, he sensed the natural opposition of the Buissons to his attachment melting away. With Arlette he was balanced on a narrow edge of passion, and sometimes in the night he would lie awake feverish with desire for her—but he never went as far again as in the hollow under the hedge. He knew very well that, despite the bonhomie, in that community the lines were carefully drawn. He was aware too that he was being examined, probed—they were curious, anxious, that he had no plans for a job, but he had the advantage of talking about a world of which they knew little. People had been starved so long for books, he said, they would buy anything now. His cousin

Edouard would certainly get him a job in publishing. But it was only when he casually mentioned his inheritance that their ears pricked up; and when Arlette began to talk of the apartment, it was taken for granted that it too was part of the *héritage*. A man of property—that they could understand. It was a relief. A step in the right direction.

"It has three bathrooms and two WCs," Arlette said excitedly, and they all laughed; but they were impressed. The Buissons had an outhouse in the kitchen garden—a simple hole in the ground with a stack of newspapers in the corner; there was a well in the courtyard, but their only running water was a cold tap in the pantry; the only heat was from the range in the kitchen where they ate, lived, and where the parents slept in a big bed in the corner. The upstairs bedroom, which belonged to Arlette, was reached by an outside ladder. In winter it was glacial.

But they ate well. Besides the pigs, Thérèse raised chickens, rabbits, geese, guinea fowl and turkeys, and goats for the cheese. At Christmas—the Christmas at which Paul formalized his engagement—she wrung the necks of a dozen assorted fowl. And there was always beef: great roasts cut in thick slices, steaks, hashes, cauldrons of *boeuf bourguignon*. And veal—stewed, stuffed, cut fine in *belles escalopes*. And after the hunting season opened early in September, there was hare, rabbit, venison, pheasant now and again and, rarely, wild boar.

It was then, at the opening of the season, that Charles had asked Paul if he owned a gun.

"I—I have a revolver," Paul said tentatively, not understanding.

And Charles had laughed. "No, no—a shotgun. You can't hunt with a revolver!" The thought amused him immoderately, "Thérèse, you hear that? This young Molphey and I are going to shoot wild boar with a pistol."

Paul said, "I've no doubt I can get hold of a shotgun. Is it tomorrow the season opens?"

"Sunday, mon vieux. But can you shoot?"

"Naturally."

Charles eyed him. "Are you sure?"

And Paul smiled easily—it was, he knew, a test. "Of course. There's no problem. I will arrange it."

The next day, he asked Augustin to drive him into Croze— the Citroën had been taken off its bricks and put back into service and Augustin drove with a curious mixture of extreme sedateness and occasional gay recklessness, sweeping down the wide-curving hill into Croze with a smiling abandon.

To Paul's surprise, the old man was delighted at the idea of buying a gun—he discussed the various models at a technical length which impressed the gunsmith and bewildered his grandson. And, against the advice of the gunsmith, they bought a three-barreled model—the third barrel rifled.

"Of course, the old fellow is right in a sense," said Augustin, "you cannot use the gun as a rifle with any accuracy—it is a hybrid and, like all hybrids, bad." He gave Paul a hard, sharp glance. "But—but although you might not use it once in ten years, if you happen to be faced with a wounded and unamiable stag, he will not be stopped by lead pellets. Only a bullet will bring him up short."

"Grandfather, why don't you hunt?"

"One does not hunt alone. If one is killing what's in front, one has no time to watch what is behind."

"You mean—you think . . . I see." And Paul thought of the scars on the house—better a bullet in the wall than in the back. "But the war is over."

"The war is never over."

And Augustin drilled him in the use of the gun as though it were a military weapon—with the same precise clarity of in- struction he employed on Racine, or in teaching Paul to drive the car. Paul was touched by the old man's care in these things —it was as though he were conscientiously fulfilling some kind of last duty to prepare his grandson for the manhood he had so recently attained; just as earlier he had trained the young man in the domestic arts—to cook, to sew, to chop wood, prune the

71

fruit trees, name the plants and wildflowers, even to make a bed.

Shooting came easily to Paul, although he never attained the smooth swinging expertise of Charles Buisson who seemed able to hit whatever he wanted without appearing to aim. That autumn they often hunted together, and the sport seemed to revive the farmer—his cheeks were ruddy, his movements quick, he was tireless, never needing a rest, darting about, rubbing his hands, shouting to the dog Eve and, at the end of a morning, with the heavy bag slung over his shoulders, striding briskly while Paul, his leg jumping with fatigue, could hardly stagger.

One day in late November they went deeper than ever before into the heart of the great forest that took up over half the commune. Paul had come to the house at dawn and they had eaten bread and goat cheese and drunk white wine in the chilly kitchen. Arlette was not up—lazy dog, Charles said. She would not come down until it was warm. Thérèse fed logs to the range, but it wasn't hot enough to boil water for coffee, and Charles was impatient—he wanted to be away. Some of the other men in the village had seen wild boar at a certain spot the day before, and Charles was determined to be there first.

They went through the village and up the road to St. Remi, Eve darting from side to side in front of them. The sky was lightening, cocks were crowing, and smoke was already beginning to meander from the chimneys of the farmhouses they passed.

"Wild boar—it's seven years since I shot a boar," said Charles. "In my father's day they were plentiful, but there are few left now and they hide themselves well away from the tracks. Oh, he is cunning, your wild boar." He laughed—he was excited and Paul had never heard him say so much at one time. "In the old days the wolves would keep them down, but when the wolves were exterminated, the boar proliferated—

when I was a lad we weren't permitted to enter the forest alone until we were eight or nine and knew how to run or nip up a tree."

"Wolves?" said Paul. "But surely that must have been a very long time ago?"

"Not so long, not so long," he chuckled, pleased at being able to give information to "The Brain." "My grandfather Hector remembers when they shot the last wolf at Ste Colombe—1888, it was. He was given one of the teeth and still keeps it on his watch chain."

Suddenly ahead of them, almost at the top of the hill, but just around a bend, there was a deep growling.

"Eve—what is it? Here, girl, here!" Charles began to run, Paul behind him.

They both stopped abruptly. Father Morine was jumping and dancing in the road as Eve growled and snapped at his trouser legs. It was a bizarre sight—the little black priest skipped and hopped, as though jerked by puppet strings, and the white dog leapt and pounced, snarling and worrying—and the two hunters laughed.

"M. Buisson, if you please, call off your animal."

"Eve—here, girl, heel, heel!"

The bitch backed off slowly with diminished growls, but the hair still rose on the back of her neck. She was not taking her eyes off the priest.

"Bonjour, mon père!" called Charles heartily.

"Thank you. Bonjour, Buisson. Er, bonjour, Paul."

"She hasn't injured you, I hope?"

"No, no—it's nothing. Just my trousers." There was a rip in the black cloth from knee to ankle, exposing a section of startlingly white leg. "Why does he attack me?"

"She—a bitch, father. You must have cats in that presbytery of yours."

"Are you all right, Morine?" said Paul, guilty at his laughter.

"Quite all right—a matter of a few stitches, I imagine. It's true, I do keep a cat—three, to be exact."

"Ah, in that case, all's explained." And Charles grinned as though it explained not only the dog's assault, but the priest's nature. "I'm sorry," and he gave Eve a perfunctory slap.

"It is nothing, I assure you—nothing." He smoothed his hair and tucked his bad arm into his jacket.

But there was something, Paul knew. Was it the destruction of his morning's peaceful meditation that caused the strained, blanched look on his face? Or fear?

In his courting of Arlette, Paul had neglected his evening walks with Morine, and, as they shook hands all around, he was sorry for it.

"Good-day, Father."

"Good-day."

"Good-day."

They turned into the forest, Eve behind them now, somewhat chastened. After a few yards, Charles began to laugh again—soon he was laughing so hard he had to halt. Paul watched amused, as the farmer took out an old handkerchief and wiped his eyes. "What a spectacle!" Eve stood, one ear raised, scenting that somehow she was being congratulated.

As they began to walk again, Charles sighed. "All the same, un pauvre type." A poor fellow, a sad chap.

"Why do you say that?" Paul asked, curious.

"It's obvious. He is still a young man—and no woman. Imagine that, Paul—never to have a woman in your entire life. What a prospect! No wonder he is lugubrious. What has he to take to bed—a missal?"

"Or a cat."

"A cat. Very good!" Charles smiled broadly and began to hum.

They saw hare and rabbit and once a pheasant, but Charles forbade Paul to shoot. "We're after boar—we must surprise them," he said with conspiratorial geniality. "Eve will find them if anyone can—a good bitch."

But Paul remembered that when Charles had returned from

Germany, he wouldn't allow the dog in the house, had kicked it and, in the yard, thrown stones at it. And Arlette, who had raised and loved Eve from a puppy, had to hide her from her father's inexplicable dislike. But then he had found her to be a good hunting dog—an incomparable pointer and a splendid retriever—and since then Eve was always at his heels, had quite forsaken Arlette.

Later, as they penetrated silently deeper into the heart of the forest, Charles's geniality was stretched fine, and he began muttering that they were all liars, there was no boar. It was an extraordinary autumn day—still and quiet, with the faintest of mists which seemed to belie the dangerous life hidden and lurking beneath the trees. All Paul's senses were alert—he heard Eve among the leaves ahead of them, saw the glittering webs stretched between the little branches—and yet he walked in a quiet dream of peace.

And it was thus that he met the boar.

Eve had dropped behind, rooting and barking at a burrow, and Charles had gone back to stop her—"Quiet, you stupid bitch, we're not after rabbits today." Paul was half across a small clearing, when suddenly the whole underbrush ahead of him seemed to heave and the thick, hairy, low-slung animal stood before him, red eyed and snorting with little tusks protruding above the snout. They both stopped dead—man and beast—looking at each other, not ten yards between them, their hot breath white in the cold air of the autumnal glade. Only the cloven hoof was restless on the rough turf.

"Move, Paul, move!"

But he could not. His leg jumped and trembled but otherwise he was quite still. Slowly, slowly he raised the gun like the most delicate of consummations, and at that moment the boar charged with incredible speed from a standing start. He fired from the hip and the great animal jumped, stumbled, turned half-left and fell dead at Paul's feet.

He almost fell too from the great thump on his back. "Magnifique, mon vieux—magnifique!" Charles let out a roar of laughter and triumph and Eve barked furiously—and dog and man pranced together around the slain prey.

"What a shot—straight between the eyes. Paul, you are something. Not bad, not bad at all." He seized hold of the gun and raised the barrel to his nose. "Ahah—the rifle. Perhaps you are not such a fool after all. And I thought I should have to drag *you* home!"

Paul forced some kind of a smile; his leg was weak as water, and in the chill winter air the sweat was clammy on his body. If he moved, he would fall. He watched Charles, all business now, unsling the sack from his shoulder and remove a length of rope and two buckets, one inside the other. With deft movements he roped the hind legs of the boar, then began to pull.

"Come on, give me a hand."

Paul laid down the gun, breathed deeply, took a tentative step—all right. He took hold of the rope and together they lugged the animal under a gnarled and twisted oak at the edge of the clearing. Charles flung the end of the rope over a stout branch and they heaved until the body was suspended a short distance above the ground.

"Bien!" Charles placed a bucket under the head, took out his knife and with one quick, hard slash slit the boar's throat. The blood leaped, gushed steaming into the bucket. The two buckets were only just enough for all of it. As the last drops fell slowly, faintly rippling the crimson surface, the great carcass twisted gently, revolving left, then back again to the right, the smile of the wound answering the farmer's grin.

Paul turned his back and leaned against the tree. A spot of blood had fallen on the back of his hand—he rubbed at it absently. There was a dull ache in his upper arm—the gun's recoil must have wrenched a muscle. He was aware of each tiniest corrugation of the tree's bark. Somewhere in the distance the dog was yapping.

Suddenly Paul leaned forward and was sick—a rush of vomit pattering onto the dry leaves.

76

"Paul!"

"Yes?"

"Paul—are you all right?"

"Yes . . . yes." He raised his head—the dog's barks were close at hand now. He took out his handkerchief and wiped his lips and his face and his blood-smeared hand. He turned round; he regarded the dangling corpse with equanimity; his head was quite clear. "Yes—I'm all right."

"Good, because we must hurry and get the cart." Charles set a fast pace and at first it was difficult for Paul to keep up, but gradually his strength came back and, instead of concentrating on the path ahead, he was able to pay attention to what was being said.

". . . not any kind of decent life. Not for anyone. If I had a son, I'd send him to the town to become a mechanic. As for the girls—well, they all want to be hairdressers or typists. I say that's good."

"Yes—I suppose so."

They had come out of the forest and stopped for a moment on the top of the hill, looking down at Ste Colombe. All the mist had cleared away and it was a peculiarly perfect morning of pale autumn sunlight. Now and again came shots from other hunters in the distance.

"You're fond of Arlette?"

"Yes—yes, I am." Paul looked at the farmer—there was a close, grim set to his face as he stared at the landscape.

"Then take her. Take her off my hands. Take her away from this stupid, miserable existence—where one does nothing but work. For nothing—nothing at all. Take her away. Take her to Paris." He turned his head to Paul—anger, challenge, and contempt in his expression.

"Thank you." Paul smiled and held out his hand. "Beau père."

After a moment, the farmer nodded slowly and managed a faint smile. They shook hands. "Then it is arranged." He gave a quick bark of a laugh.

"Then it is arranged."

They started down the hill, Charles all at once jovial. "Ah, and this is where our poor little priest did his jig. Eve, my clever bitch, how you made him dance, eh? We won't forget that, will we. . . ."

But Paul didn't listen. He glanced up at the birdless sky, down at the village where the rose-stoned church tower sank graciously behind the crowded roofs as they descended. In the hedges the holly berries were blood red, and the ivory-coloured mistletoe hung in thick bunches from the occasional oak that leaned over the lane like a blessing. It seemed to him this joy would last forever.

The flies swarmed thick on the south wall beneath the attic window, as they always did in early September. Paul fancied he could smell autumn in the air—in a few days he would be back at school, the summer forgotten except in the lingering inattentiveness of the children in the classroom. He could even now hardly remember it himself—there had been nothing to mark off day from day, no visit, no call, no letter, nothing even to differentiate this summer from the thirty-three others he had watched come and go from this window. Although nowadays of course there was always somewhere the noise of tractors or the monstrous combine harvesters that sometimes squeezed down the lane or the chain saw of some industrious farmer cutting his wood early for the winter. The landscape had not much changed—telephone poles along the roads, a march of pylons across the valley, here and there the stark white roof of a new barn or cow shed. In the village there were now TV aerials among the weathercocks and lightning rods. But these slight blemishes vanished as the sun lowered in the sky and struck a rosy glow from hamlet after hamlet like soft and ever-renewing flowers in a country that had hardly changed for centuries.

That day he had written:

> The controlling characteristic of the writer is total attention
> to life—which is in itself the love that is the only true con-
> nection between man and man. . . .

But the phrase seemed empty as though he had learned it by rote, familiar as if he had written it many times before. And perhaps he had—perhaps if he searched among the old scraps and pages he would find the very same words inscribed in faded ink a quarter century ago.

There was a languor in the air. It was not the sultry oppressiveness of the heart of summer—that heat was always eventually broken by one of the slow-moving, violent storms, which would start with a darkness on the far hills shot with lightning and warlike thunder, then approach in a solid curtain of rain that marched in measured fashion across the valley, shutting off village after village, house after house, engulfing meadows and trees until it mounted the hill and absorbed the little hamlet with an instantaneous crack of thunder and bolt of lightning that would make the plugs in the wall crackle and burst the lightbulbs and once, as Paul had been standing in the kitchen, had broken a plate he held in his hands.

But the season of storms was over. This was another sort of languor—a languor of emptiness, as though time had stopped.

Four or five of the houses in La Roche had been bought by tourists—a Dutch family, one from Germany, two from Lyons and another from Paris. So in high summer there was much hammering and sounds of children in the day, music and laughter on the night air. Sometimes they liked to photograph Paul —and he knew he was a strange object to them, as they to him. Occasionally he invited them in for an aperitif or dispensed *menthe à l'eau* to the children; but he had nothing really to offer them—like him, they all had TV—except sometimes a bit of advice: he warned them all about the ruined barn next door, more precarious than ever and holding on by the skin of its teeth.

And at the end of August, as if at a given signal, they all

departed. And the artificial life they gave the place vanished with them, leaving only him and Mme. Thibault, and the real silence descended. And yet their going left a temporary sense of emptiness, timelessness—the harvest in, the machines muted, the grape picking not yet begun.

He felt the loss—mirror of old departures—yet he knew that feeling too would pass.

His had been the first television set in Ste Colombe. He bought it—like the new green Renault—for the girls: not to fetch and carry them so much, perhaps, as to hold them.

The Saturday after Thibault's suicide, he brought them back as usual for the weekend. The snow had thawed on the roads, though not on the fields; he drove with slightly more than his usual care, but it was not really dangerous. He had made a *coq au vin* for lunch and put off telling them about Thibault until the meal was finished, although neither of them ate much these days and could not be persuaded to take any wine, which made him drink less himself. He recalled their former hearty appetites with a pang. Sometimes now they seemed to him like polite strangers—they were barely interested in his inconsequential chatter about communal affairs. They were both absorbed in the *lycée*, their friends there, Hélène in books, Agnès in some quiet interior place of her own. Neither of them took to the TV—to Hélène it was *banal*, to Agnès *vulgaire*.

They were just sixteen. In looks they were still almost impossible to tell apart—they had the quick, alert darkness of Arlette, mingled with a fineness of feature and bone that came from his mother. Their physical beauty touched him to the quick, and every time they walked out of the school gates to the waiting car, he caught his breath. But in character they were quite different; both had been sober, obedient, rather silent little girls, and Agnès was still that, with an overlay of

Thérèse's piety, which Paul told himself was a passing phase. But Hélène was quite different—she had something of the stern and lucid quality of Augustin; she was diligent, even brilliant, but steely, sometimes almost contemptuous. Agnès would always stoically accept his embrace, but Hélène was brusque about it—"Oh, Papa, you haven't shaved properly again today!"

And yet he could talk to Hélène in a way he never could to Agnès. Often by Sunday evening he managed to break down her reserve; she would get involved in any great argument and he would see something of her hidden passion. And then it would be time to get back to the dormitory.

He told them about Thibault over coffee.

They took it silently, almost indifferently—and, after all, what was Thibault to them, except a surly peasant whose "bonjour" seemed to be wrung reluctantly from some inner part? And yet, when they were younger, they had often followed him about watching him work on the farm; and they had always been fond of Mme. Thibault, who gave them cream cheese to eat and baked them bread and cakes—had, indeed, made their last birthday cake.

"The funeral is this afternoon at four—we will all go, of course."

"I suppose I shall have to wear a hat," Hélène said.

"But, Papa—how can there be a funeral if he committed suicide?" asked Agnès.

"I don't know, you will have to ask Father Fley that question."

Hélène had snorted, but Agnès had merely sighed.

After the ceremony, Agnès had not come back with them in the car—perhaps she wished to pose the question to the priest, perhaps she simply wished to pray. Paul did not ask.

When they returned to the house, Hélène went at once to wash her face.

Paul sat down at the parlour table and poured himself a glass of wine.

"Give me a glass too," she said. She had changed into trousers—"not trousers, *jeans*, Papa"—into jeans and one of his old shirts which she wore without the detachable starched collar.

"This is unusual," he remarked mildly. He was torn between a residual conventional disapproval and a concrete admiration of the liberty of her clothes. Agnès wore only dresses or skirts and sweaters of a uniformly dark hue.

"Anything to get the taste of all that slobber out of my mouth."

"It is traditional to weep on these occasions, Hélène. A mark of respect. We didn't do very well on that account, I'm sorry to say." He slid the glass across the table to her.

" 'A decent respect for the opinions of mankind?' If we'd shown what we really thought, we'd have spat."

"Oh come, surely—"

"Say, Papa, this isn't bad."

"It's a Mercurey I bought six or seven years ago—it has body, which one needs at such moments."

Hélène smiled. "You never weep, do you, Papa?"

"Not in public, at least. Seldom. Not for a long time." He returned her smile.

"But then you've had nothing to weep about for a long time, have you?"

"No, that's true."

They drank in silence—it was a good, strong wine, full of fortitude. He looked out of the window, up the hill where his father had come for the last time, swinging and whistling—a man of fortitude. But he'd not even wept at his father's funeral in that same churchyard, with the bugles blaring.

"Papa—where is our mother?"

He turned his head slowly. "I don't know."

"She isn't dead?"

"I don't think so—but I'm not sure."

"In Paris?"

"Perhaps. Though I think Marseilles more likely. But I do

not know. Your grandmother might, but I doubt if she would tell you—she doesn't tell me."

Hélène gave a quick little nod of her dark head, as if it were of no importance, yet he knew it would be stored in her mind, just as she stored everything, too quickly often for her teachers who sometimes mistook her cleverness for carelessness.

"Papa, if I do well in my *baccalauréat* in June, I should—"

"I think you will do well—very well."

"Yes, I shall do well. In that case, I shall want to go to Paris. To the Sorbonne." In the dying light of the afternoon her watchful eyes seemed enormous—the deep brown of the iris and the black of the pupil merging as one.

Paul gripped his wine glass more tightly. "Yes." He cleared his throat. He had hoped for Lyons or, perhaps, Dijon, but . . .

"If there is any problem about money, I can—"

"No—no, there's no problem about money." There was still something remaining from Bernard, and when Augustin had died five years ago, he had left Paul everything he possessed, including the small apartment in Nice where he had spent his last days. And Paul had been provident, frugal—another legacy from Augustin, perhaps.

"Then I may go?"

"Yes, you may go. If you do well." He drank a mouthful of wine—all of a sudden it tasted less full, less rich. He forced a genial, judicious tone. "It is, after all, the best place. You will be—be happy." He shied away from her frown and began to ramble. "I remember our apartment when I was a boy, we used to—"

"Apartment?" Momentary interest. "Where was it?"

"In Paris—oh, the seventh."

"The seventh? Well, I couldn't have lived there!"

"Perhaps not." He gave a wintry smile, wondering how she came to know anything of Paris. "But it was a pleasant place —on the Champ de Mars. I remember chasing the pigeons there. I wonder why children love to chase pigeons?"

But she was not interested in his reminiscences, nor was he then. Slowly he dried up, and they sat again drinking in silence.

"Agnès is taking a long time," he said.

"Oh, she has probably gone to confession or something."

"And what would Agnès have to confess?"

"She probably forgot to think about the Sacred Heart for half an hour." She laughed.

Paul smiled a little, but he didn't like the mockery. He didn't like the contempt. And, as if sensing it, Hélène said, "I'm sorry—that was perhaps a cruel thing to say. Though true enough."

"Perhaps. Hélène—why—why would you have spat upon Thibault?"

She made no reply and in the gloaming he could not see the expression on her face, only the slow movement of her fingers stroking the stem of the glass.

"After all, he must have been an unhappy man, and harmless, and now he is dead."

"Dead—thank God he's dead!"

"Why, Hélène, why?"

She raised her glass and drank—and the delicate, awkward little gesture reminded him of his mother. He recalled his father saying one day, "Emily, one would always think you had never drunk a glass of wine before."

"Why, Hélène—there must be a reason?" This irrational detestation disturbed him.

"Yes—yes, there is." Her voice was hesitant, even diffident —the voice of her sister. "But I don't know if I should tell you."

Suddenly he wished he had not asked. "Well, you must tell me now."

"Very well. It—it was when we were nine. A heavy August afternoon, just before Assumption. You had given Mme. Thibault a lift into Croze to do some shopping. I suppose Agnès and I were bored, at any rate we went over to see what old

Thibault was doing, not that we were really interested, but it had become a kind of sport in a way. I used to tease him—Agnès tried too, but was not much good at it. The idea was to see how far we could go before the morose brute answered back.

"That afternoon, I went too far. He was cleaning out the cow house—it was dark in there and stank. I said something about a dumb ox being at home among the filth. Agnès giggled, and then I embroidered on it. He didn't say anything, or do anything, at first. Then after a time he put down his spade and went over and shut the door and bolted it top and bottom—suddenly the sunlight was cut off, and we could hardly see him. Then he was on us—I managed to half duck, half wriggle under his arm. But he caught Agnès. 'Filth is it?' he said. 'I'll give you filth, my pretty little maidens, and see how you like it!' And then—"

"Hélène," Paul cried out, "Hélène!"

"No, please, listen. There was this ripping noise and a great sort of heavy panting. Agnès didn't make a sound, but I knew she was fighting. I tried to find the spade, but I couldn't see it in the dark. And he began to groan and suddenly there was a single shrill cry from Agnès. Then I found a milking stool and I hit him with it again and again on the back, but it didn't make any difference; so I hit him on the head and he half rose, then flopped over. I dragged Agnès away and stood on the stool to open the top bolt, and then we ran home. She was covered with muck and there was blood and . . . I bathed her and washed her and put her to bed and gave her tisane, but I thought she would never stop weeping . . . perhaps she never has."

"Hélène—why didn't you tell me?"

"I promised I never would—she made me swear that. And then I was afraid—I was afraid I'd killed the brute, you see."

"Oh my God."

"But the next day there he was of course, plodding about the yard as though nothing had happened. And Agnès was better, at least she'd stopped sobbing, and you'd accepted that she just had a touch of fever."

He had no memory of it at all. None.

"So you see why I'm glad he's dead?"

"Yes." He held out his hand across the table and she joined hers to his.

"I hope he's in hell, if only it existed."

"Yes."

"Agnès is praying for him now, I expect. She'll probably spend the rest of her life trying to forgive him."

They sat hand in hand in the darkness, until at last they heard Agnès mounting the stone steps.

"Don't tell her I told you, will you?" she whispered.

"No—no, I shan't do that."

He let go of her hand, and they stood up. He turned on the light just as Agnès entered the room.

That night he couldn't sleep. After the twins went to bed, he sat up alone and finished the wine, but it didn't help. There was a tightness in his chest, as though his heart had stiffened or filled up with blood that would flow no further.

He prowled softly about the house, careful to make no noise. In the bedroom he stared for a long time at the crescent moon, until at last it was fleeced by slow clouds and buried. He went to the bathroom and shaved in cold water with the utmost care. Then he cleaned the vegetables for tomorrow's *pot-au-feu;* he peeled the turnips and carrots and potatoes, stripped and washed three leeks, put them all in a large bowl of water, depositing the peel in the special plastic bucket he had bought for the compost heap.

In the sideboard drawer of the parlour he found the package of cigarettes Fley had left behind on the night of Thibault's death. Fley had known of course (for Agnès would have confessed her "sin" to him) and had hinted as much that same night. And Paul, exasperated, had dismissed it as chatter, fantasy, although he knew Fley never said an idle word. But it was too late, far too late to make the faintest difference.

He sat on in the parlour, slowly smoking the remaining cigarettes; and at last he must have dozed, for when he became conscious again after a series of flitting half dreams, half nightmares, the room was icily cold and dim with beginning daylight.

He went down on his knees and relit the little stove—cleaning out the ashes, laying a scrunched sheet of newspaper, a handful of dead bracken and a layer of tiny twigs, kindling sticks and a cross-hatch of small logs. The stove was old, the green enamel casing almost black with time and cracked in two places, which he had carefully wired up—but it drew well and quickly, and soon the small mica windows were creaking as they expanded with the heat.

He was cold to the bone, but it was too early for coffee—perhaps some hot white wine with sugar and a clove was what he needed. As he went out onto the terrace, dawn was breaking, though the greater part of the valley was invisible under its sea of floating mist. Instinctively, he turned and looked up the hill behind the house—it was still night there, black with a tinge of mauve. He began to tremble and his leg buckled with weakness so that he had to cling tightly to the iron rail as he went down the stone steps to the cellar.

He took down the key, unlocked the old oak door, turned on the light and entered. Then, as he stood there on the dry earth floor, amid the vinegary smell of long-spilled wine, the fleshy odour of stored potatoes, the dustiness of the cut bracken stacked in the corner, he remembered.

One summer's day, when the girls were just about one-and-a-half years old, he had put them to play on a blanket spread out on the grass, and had set himself to pick all that remained of the red currants—he would use some of them for a tart for supper and the rest he would make into jelly. Sometimes the children would moo or coo—they were not quite up to walking yet, but each could totter a few steps, then would fall, and they'd both giggle softly at this extraordinarily amusing event. Apart from that, there was the absolute silence of the early afternoon when the farmers were at table and their machines were still.

Then Paul paused—there was a curious sound, in the far far distance, a kind of faint drumming. He looked up the hill and it seemed to him the sky was darker there. He put down his basket—the children were absorbed in patting their hands together—opened the garden gate and went into the meadow. As he mounted the hill the noise grew louder and when he reached the crest it filled the air with a continuous menacing thunder. The sky was a rich thick purple and the north valley beyond was entirely blotted out by a solid wall of—of what? It was not the usual curtain of rain; he'd not seen this before, nor the sky quite that color. As he stood stock still, staring, he recalled that a week before there had been typhoons reported on the west coast of France, for the first time in living memory.

Then he was running for dear life back down the hill. As he came into the garden, his foot caught on a root and he fell with a shock that knocked the breath out of him. He staggered up, hearing himself mutter, "My babies, my babies," then he caught them up and rolled them both tightly in the blanket. He took them down to the cellar and put them on the floor. "It's a game," he said, "a game—we're going to play house down here —be quiet and good and I'll fetch your bears."

He ran back up and started to close the metal outside shutters over the windows—he was clumsy and they clanged and banged and the bars slipped out of his hands. He had almost finished—the parlour shutters were the last—when he glanced back over his shoulder. The great white wall had entered the garden, obliterated the plum tree—and the sky was as black as night. He left the shutters loose, crossed the terrace and stumbled down the steps as, with a rending crash, the storm struck the house.

He crouched in the cellar, clutching the bundled girls close to him. In the dim light he could make out their solemn faces, their great black eyes staring up at him. "It's nothing," he murmured, as the furious crashes sounded all about them, "nothing." It sounded as though the house was falling—and above all, the drumming, drumming of doom.

And then it was over.

He stood up slowly, still holding them tightly, and opened the cellar door and stared. The garden was white—a white that suddenly sparkled and shone in a ray of sun. And then he smiled—it was hail. But what hail! He stooped down and picked up a piece—it was as large as his fist. He carried the girls up and sat them on the terrace step and collected two saucepans full of hailstones for them to play with. He went up to the garden—the damage was appalling. The plum tree was almost stripped of leaves and fruit, the tomato plants and the beans were smashed to the ground, the red currants in his basket were a pulp beneath a layer of hail. He came back and gave them each one of the hailstones covered with red currant juice to suck.

Five of the eight panes of the parlour window were shattered; a score of roof tiles had been broken or displaced and the old Citroën, which he'd not put in the garage, was dented as though someone had been at it with a sledgehammer. Hailstorms were not uncommon, but he'd never seen one of anything like this ferocity. The crops would be flattened, the vines ruined—even beasts in the field could have been killed by this. The sun shone and all the meadows glistened and sparkled just as after the heaviest of winter frosts—but this was a disaster.

And then, as he turned to the twins sitting on the step, solemnly licking their hailstones, he laughed.

"Come on," he said, "we'll have some iced lemonade." He picked up four of the larger hailstones and, with an old deftness learned from a magic set he'd had when a boy, he juggled them. The girls took the ice from their mouths and stared at him, then stared at each other, then back at their father—and they all began to laugh.

Fourteen years ago.

Paul's whole body began to tremble. With an enormous effort, he took two hobbling steps and sat down on the little stool that years ago he'd put beneath the wire-mesh larder hanging from the ceiling so the girls could reach up and get the meat or butter or the cheese kept cool away from the summer's heat.

The naked bulb burned his eyes; he lowered his head and put his face in his hands. Above, his daughters slept in some kind of dreaming peace. He had protected them from all imaginary menaces—but he had done nothing, known nothing about the real dangers. Softly, with slow, wracking sobs, he began to weep.

The post office was on the small central square of Ste Colombe which was dominated on one side by the church. Next to the post office was the grocery, the bakery, and the village's only café. On the north side were several small houses, one of which was inhabited by the strange, solitary Lombards —easy to tell theirs, plain-faced and peeling paint, while all the others had roses on the wall and window boxes filled with geraniums, not yet in bloom. To the south, there was a row of plane trees, pruned in exact rectangular shapes, a line of ridiculous green boxes which was a special pride of the village. Beneath them was a space for *boules;* but no one was playing this afternoon. Now and again one of the women would putter down on her mobilette to fetch the evening's bread, thick *pains* and great, round *couronnes* with holes in the middle. Apart from that, and the occasional sound of voices from the café, the square was remarkably quiet.

As Paul dropped his letter to Edouard in the postbox, the church clock struck five. He hesitated—it was early yet. Despite the argument with Augustin, he was still elated, and needed to tell someone of the completion of his book. Arlette, he knew, would be full of praises and delight—but to her his writing was not work, like milking a cow or digging a ditch or making the wine; it was a mark of cleverness, like a bright child doing an intricate puzzle, but of no practical import, at most a magical wand that might secure for her the city, security, success, money . . . perhaps. No, just at this moment, he wanted a different sort of appreciation. Then he nodded to himself and, smiling, stepped across the stretch of beaten pink gravel, and knocked at the presbytery door.

Lately he had done his best not to neglect Morine. In fact he had dutifully gone to see him once a week for instruction in his duties as a non-Catholic husband and father in a Catholic family. Morine had been taken aback when Paul had produced a Protestant baptismal certificate—a pleasing compromise between faiths which must have amused his parents, who believed in none—but he had recovered manfully. Nevertheless the document had caused difficulties—the pastor in Paris had to be asked to vouch for its authenticity, the archbishop had to give his acceptance, Paul had to swear to bring up any children in the faith, and it meant that a nuptial mass would not be possible—a bitter blow to Thérèse, although Arlette didn't mind so long as she could have her bridesmaids, and the wedding feast, and the ball and the traditional nighttime hunt for the hidden couple.

Morine had mentioned only once, lightly, the possibility of his conversion.

"Of course, it would be a great advantage if you were a member of the faith."

"Surely one doesn't take up religion for advantage?"

"No no—no, indeed not." And the little priest had smiled wanly. "I was merely thinking of your grandfather, such a devoted member of—"

"My father did not see eye to eye with my grandfather."

"Ah—what a lamentable thing these conflicts of generations. And yet"—tentatively—"your father was buried here."

"He had no choice. But I do."

"Oh quite—yes, quite." And he'd never touched on the subject again. And yet, perhaps because of this, for the first time Paul felt a certain distance between them—or perhaps because of the scene on the hill when Eve had attacked his trousers; Charles had told the story with relish and it had caused a good deal of amusement in the village (though not to Thérèse who refused to allow the dog in the house anymore and was foolish enough to tell Morine why).

But today when he was ushered into the immaculately gleaming dining room and blurted out his news in the first sentence—the distance vanished.

"But Paul—this is a marvel! We must celebrate. Marie—Marie!"

"Yes, Father?" She must have had her ear to the door, she came so speedily.

"Marie, we will have a tisane and the brioche you bought this morning and the brandied cherries."

"Yes, Father."

"Or—or, hold. Paul, perhaps you would prefer wine?"

"No—no thank you."

"But, yes, of course—what am I thinking of? Marie, we still have a bottle or two of the Auxey that Father Berzey sent me, I think?"

"You always take your tisane at this time, Father."

"Marie, please allow me to judge what is suitable. I—"

"But I want nothing," Paul said. "Really—nothing for me."

"Are you sure?"

"Absolutely."

"Besides, Father, you gave the last bottle of Auxey to the old widow Richard. I will bring the tisane."

"Later—later then, Marie." When she had gone, Morine said, "I am afraid Marie is not always altogether truthful. I am certain there are two bottles remaining."

"Well, if you drink as little as you did at my father's funeral, they will last you a long time." Paul smiled.

"You're right. But one has to make a decision. Drink is a

92

great temptation of ours, you know—particularly in these parts, where my brethren in more fortunate parishes are inclined to reward small services with a gift of a dozen or so of their superior produce. And the peasants of course always expect one to take a glass. Little by little, without hardly knowing it, one could easily drink too much. It starts innocently enough with the communion wine and then . . . well, I have seen it happen all too often. Alcoholism is, alas, the vice of priests—just as drug addiction is that of doctors. But doctors, of course, can marry."

Paul smiled at the gravity of this speech. "I'm sorry," he said, "but what has drunkenness to do with marriage?"

"Not with marriage. Precisely, not with marriage. But lechery and drunkenness are not unconnected. If the individual faith is not strong enough to keep the flesh in check, then wine, taken in sufficient quantity, will dull the appetite."

"Really? I thought it only ruined the performance."

Morine smiled. "You are joking about a serious matter—but I forgive you. It is your day. You have finished your book—tell me about it. You are going to leave us."

"Well, certainly I shall take the manuscript to my cousin in Paris, and if it is successful—"

"You will not return—except once a year at Christmas perhaps, to visit us provincials. And it will be a success, of that I'm sure. And you will stay in Paris and make a new life. And you will have great happiness with your beautiful wife, and you will have beautiful children—"

"Beautiful Catholic children."

"—beautiful Catholic children. You are lucky, my friend." And, although he smiled, there was a pensiveness about him —a regretful, almost bitter, undertone to what he'd been saying which puzzled and touched Paul.

"But you haven't told me about your book—except that you were writing it, have finished it?"

Paul looked at him—*un pauvre type*, as Charles said? A man of untroubled piety—the crucifix above the sideboard, the

93

pierced heart of Christ over the mantelpiece—as Thérèse was pleased to think? What was Morine's vice—reading matter on the Index, a simple love of books? Very well. Paul made up his mind.

"Would you like to read my manuscript?"

"Read it—I? My dear friend . . ."

"But of course. Why not? Between now and my wedding it will be doing nothing but gathering dust in my attic."

"There is nothing I could wish for more, but—"

"I'd value your opinion."

"Is it true? Would you?" And Morine laughed a shy laugh of pleasure. "Then I accept."

The clock beneath the Sacred Heart struck six.

Paul stood up. "I must go."

"So soon?" Then at the door, he said, "I shall miss you, Paul."

"I shall bring you the manuscript tomorrow."

As he made his way across the square, skirting the well, he heard a wistful echo—"tomorrow." Dusk was falling, and he shivered slightly and quickened his pace away from the presbytery's melancholy toward the Buissons and a kitchen full of strong smells and broad laughter and rough wine, of life, of love—of food. He was famished, and already half-regretted his promise to the little priest.

"Paul, I should prefer Grandfather to take me," she said, frowning as she carefully pinned the large white summer hat into place.

"But, Arlette, surely it's more suitable for your husband to accompany you at such a moment? Don't you—"

"I shall be in quite safe hands with Grandfather." She stepped back a pace from the wardrobe mirror and examined herself.

"No doubt, but that's hardly the point. I should have thought—"

"Grandfather is an excellent driver." She pulled down the brim of the hat, then pushed it up again.

He opened his mouth to continue his protest—but what was the use? If Grandfather had consented—then Grandfather it would be. "Very well then," he muttered.

She turned slowly from the mirror to face him. "I knew you would be reasonable." And she gave him a radiant smile. His heart melted; she was utterly beautiful in the white hat, the white summer dress and the white gloves she was slowly fitting to her fingers. He moved toward her.

"Careful! You mustn't disarrange me." She held up her cheek to be kissed, then, taking her bag, went to the door. "Dr. Mullet said I must have plenty of rest—and *calm*. If what he suspects is true."

"Well, we'll soon know," he said with a touch of impatience at all this prevarication. "Provided Mullet isn't off hunting somewhere."

"*Dr.* Mullet," she said with a frown. "Besides, it's not the season."

"Yes. Yes, I know." And as he followed her into the parlour and out onto the terrace, he heard Augustin starting the car.

"Au revoir, Paul—à bientôt."

"Au revoir, Arlette." Then, as she started down the steps. "Arlette!"

"Yes, Paul."

"You look ravishing."

She smiled faintly and continued on down. She had an air both of sanctity and provocativeness—a marvelously seductive mixture. Perhaps it was the white dress that did it—a child going to first communion. She had made it up from her bridal gown. In seven weeks of married life, Paul had discovered she had few of the accomplishments of the housewife—except that she was an expert needlewoman.

He would descend from his attic, full of the numb anguish that had possessed him since their return from Paris and which sometimes he felt would altogether bear him down, and sit in the parlour or on the terrace in the late evening sunlight and watch her sew. Her hands were slightly larger, more practical than Emily's, yet the remembered motions were the same. They soothed him, and yet at the same time disturbed him with old memories of the Paris apartment—old memories that would slowly become infiltrated and then invaded by the more recent experiences, until his calm was quite swept away by the new pain, so that he would have to get up and find something to do in the garden or the kitchen or go back to his attic and try again.

He went to the end of the terrace and pushed back the vine and watched the black car beetle slowly down the hill—Augustin was driving in his most sedate fashion. Although he had never withdrawn one word of what he'd said about her, the old man was in some way sympathetic to the girl, and she to him. He, too, would watch her sewing and he would always be the first to refill her glass at table. And for her, it was "Grandfather" says this, "Grandfather" does that—"Grandfather," "Grandfather." When Augustin made the coffee in the morning it was invariably excellent, while Paul's was usually "too bitter" or "too weak." And it was Augustin who had immediately diagnosed her morning sickness and insisted on taking her to see Mullet and that the proper tests were made—the results of which they were to be told this afternoon. "Grandfather says that your grandmother Hélène also was ill in the morning."

Perhaps it was better this way—Augustin's concern appeared to satisfy them both. And Paul knew that he was not very well up to managing at this point. He seemed only to be going through the motions of life—he had no dreams, no juice, no nightmares even. But he had no need of nightmares. He lived from day to laborious day. He did not really believe Arlette was pregnant—she just liked the idea, it was interesting, a romantic compensation. And in a way he was grateful that they both had something to turn their attention away from himself.

When he and Arlette had come back from their "honeymoon," he had told Augustin the news quickly and briefly. And Augustin had said nothing, asked no questions—had not even hinted that he might then sit for the examination after all. Anyway, it was just too late for that—until next year. Next year—Paul could not believe in that either.

And yet all the same he waited anxiously. He took a basket to the raspberry canes and began to pick, from time to time popping a berry into his mouth and crunching the seeds. *The bells rang out over a dreamless people . . . today . . . in my village . . . for peace.* He knew he should go down to see Morine—or arrange to meet him at St. Remi in the evening. He would help, *he* would remember—the only man who'd read the manuscript. And yet to disturb the priest's gentle, almost blushing enthusiasm for the book—like a lover astonished at the declaration of love—to disturb that, would be a rejection of hope, a confession that he, Paul, had lost, not just the words, but the spirit, the particular vision, that he had lost his youth.

He looked down and saw that he had crushed a raspberry between his fingers. He wiped his hand on his trousers. His leg was trembling. "Courage, mon vieux!"

He limped back to the house and put the basket in the kitchen. He sat at the parlour table and poured himself a glass of wine—he was tempted to drink a lot of wine these days. As though he were a priest. But he didn't touch the glass, nor did he look out of the window. He simply waited.

When he heard the car returning at last, the gears grinding up the hill—as had another car two years ago announcing a death—he stood up and tossed the wine off in one swallow and went out onto the terrace.

He didn't trust himself on the steps.

The car door banged.

She mounted slowly, languidly, her face shaded by the hat, Augustin close behind as though he thought she might fall.

"Well?" said Paul.

She raised her head and looked at him, but said nothing. Behind her shoulder, Augustin gave Paul a quick nod.

"Oh, my dear!" He came forward as she reached the terrace and took her gloved hands in his. "I am so glad."

"Are you?" she murmured so softly he scarcely caught the words. She seemed wan, withdrawn. "I am so tired." She sighed and cast her eyes down.

"Of course, my—"

And then she screamed and wrenched her hands from his grip.

"What is it—what?"

She spun around and half fell against Augustin, who staggered, then clutched her.

"What? What's the matter?"

"He's got blood on his hands—oh, oh!"

"Blood?" Augustin raised an eyebrow at Paul.

"It's not blood, Arlette—it's raspberry juice. I've been picking the raspberries."

"Oh, how could he?"

"My dear," said Augustin firmly, patting her back. "It's merely the juice of the raspberries Paul has been picking."

"Raspberries?" She stiffened, swung around; then she held out her hands. "My gloves, look at my gloves—you've ruined my gloves!" She burst into tears. "No—don't touch me!" As she ran past him, he lowered his hands—then he started to follow her into the parlour.

"No, my boy—no!"

Paul stopped uncertainly and turned.

"Don't be distressed. It is often like this. It is a difficult moment. They are hysterical. It is normal."

"But she seems so—so unhappy."

"It only seems so, Paul. She will recover. She will come to herself. It's better to leave her alone."

"But—but it's good news, joyous news."

"Of course. And she will see it, but later. Just at the moment it is a shock—a change. All change, especially in one's body, is a shock. That is perfectly natural."

"Yes. I see—I suppose I see."

"I doubt it. It is not something that will ever happen to us." His head was cocked a little to one side; suddenly he smiled. "But you are right—it is an occasion for joy. And I suggest we celebrate it in the appropriate fashion."

"In the appropriate . . . how?"

The old man laughed. "Champagne, Paul, champagne." And he clapped his hands, as if to summon a waiting sommelier with ice bucket and napkin.

"Yes—yes of course. I'll get it."

"No, no—allow me. Sit down, sit down and contemplate the prospect." And he ran briskly down the steps to the cellar.

Paul lowered himself onto the chaise longue—he felt a great weight of tiredness, and of bemusement. He gazed across the garden at the ruined barn opposite, as if it were trying to tell him something important, though he had no idea what. There was no sound from the house—but perhaps that was a good thing; she would be resting, coming to terms with—with joy. He rubbed his lips slowly; it was a long time since he'd smiled.

"Two bottles, Grandfather?"

"One for later—when she is herself again. I shall put it under running water in the kitchen."

He came back with glasses and opened the champagne in his own particular, neat manner—drawing the cork but at the last moment holding it down, with only a crack open to allow the aeration to escape, so that then the wine could be poured smoothly without fizz or froth.

"To a new Molphey."

Paul hesitated. "To a beautiful child."

"An *intelligent* child. We cannot put too much on that—*that* mother." He smiled faintly, bleakly. "We must bank upon the father."

"Father." The word sounded strange applied to himself. But it was going to be true, after all. Papa. It may have been the warmth of the afternoon or the champagne but he felt a quiet, happy gratitude—quite unlike the euphoria at finishing his book. But then this was a beginning, not an ending.

"And you will be a great-grandfather."

"That is of no importance." The old man made a dismissive gesture. "It is you who will bring the child up—it is you who will be responsible. Not I."

"Yes—I—of course."

"So what are you going to do?"

"Well—to do? I shall endeavour to do my best."

"Of course. That is understood. You will certainly not permit your son to be brought up as one of these peasants. But that is not what I'm asking." He frowned and carefully set his glass down on the small glass-topped table. "I mean, what are you proposing to do with *your* life?"

"Oh I shall continue to write."

"To write?" He frowned as though in puzzlement, then his brow cleared. "Ah—your book! Yes, of course. It is a dream we all have. But it is gone, isn't it? Yours is lost, vanished. I am talking about the real world—of wife and family and children. After all, we cannot eat words."

"I have enough to live on until I—I—"

"No, no. One can always gamble on one's own behalf, but hardly when there are others to be considered. Besides, if you gamble and win, you can remain relatively untouched, free— but if you lose, you dream the more of winning, you become an addict, you put more and more upon the table, you become obsessed, enamoured of failure, the willing whore of disaster. Until all about you is in ruins. And you have lost. Very well then, accept it. If you do, then it is of no great moment. But if you do not, your life and your spirit will be dissipated in dreams and those of your loved ones in misery."

"But I can't give up—I must go on. I must."

"Wait, Paul. You are young. Do not press hard. Do not compel others to participate in your sacrifice. Your time will come. One cannot force, one must reflect. And meanwhile one must get on with the business of living. I have observed your misery these last few weeks. You are eating up your own substance—and it is because you have nothing to do."

"But what can I do?"

"Ah." Augustin picked up his glass, sipped. He gently touched his moustache. "Let me tell you, Paul, that I have decided to retire when this trimester ends in a few days. I have more than amply fulfilled my duty and, to tell you the truth, I am beginning to feel my age—occasionally I am forgetful and impatient in the classroom. That will never do—that is the way, justly, that one loses respect. And to lose the respect of others is eventually to lose one's self-respect. And self-respect is the most precious possession that we have." He stared hard at Paul with his light blue eyes.

"Yes—but I thought you were going to stay on for another year at least."

"No. It is not necessary either for them or for me. And also, if I were to stay much longer in this house, I would become *de trop.*"

"No, you can't say that. Why, Arlette is truly fond of you."

"And I am behaving myself?" he asked drily. "Ah, my poor Paul, what little you know of the arts of dissimulation." He paused, then continued in a softer tone. "When Hélène and I were first married we were forced—by circumstance—to live with her parents for a year. At the beginning all went well— my father-in-law was most courteous and intelligent and my mother-in-law Agnès was charming and solicitous. All too charming and solicitous, particularly to me, the stranger in her house. I am not speaking of anything scandalous, you understand; merely of perhaps an excess of hospitality. It was not long before I began to observe signs of irritation in the old man and a feeling of resentment on the part of my wife against her mother. We had planned to stay three years, but after one I decided that we must leave if any semblance of civility in the family life was to be maintained. So you see—"

"But—"

"No no—do not protest. I apologize—all that was by way of a diversion from the main point, which is that next week I intend to inform the board that I shall not be returning to teach at Ste Colombe in the autumn. The post of schoolmaster will therefore become vacant."

Paul looked down at his glass—it was empty. He put it on the table. "Are you seriously suggesting that *I* apply for the post?"

"Why not? You have a respectable *baccalauréat*, you attended one of the more distinguished *lycées* in Paris and you have certainly advanced much in your studies since then. And I don't imagine that there are a great many candidates who would actually *want* to be buried in a rural school such as we have here. No, I should think you've a very good chance of being appointed; in addition to which, I have myself a certain modest influence." He smiled and picked up the bottle and refilled their glasses.

"But, but . . ." He wanted to say the idea was utterly absurd, laughable. "But I have never taught anyone anything."

"It is not difficult. One is not expected to work miracles. You will of course be expected to wear a tie."

And then Paul did laugh. "You want to make me respectable."

But the old man answered him with seriousness. "Clearly. What are you now in the eyes of these people? An agreeable, idle young man of some privilege—someone always willing to lend a hand, but who does no real work. Your knowledge, your intelligence finds no confirmation in usefulness. Nothing that you are—or might become—commands respect here. Buisson is a man of some rectitude, is respected in his own right, but if you are nothing but his son-in-law, you are nothing. Respect is the cement of our society. If you had not allied yourself to such a family, it would perhaps not much matter—you would be regarded as an amiable eccentric. But you have done so. And that makes your situation difficult, even critical. But if you became the *instituteur*—the schoolmaster—you would have a *position*. Not, I will confess, always a very comfortable position. But you will have a *raison d'être* which will be understood. You will have a respect—as will, by association, your wife. You are confronted with a rather clear choice, my dear Paul. Either you raise her—or you debase yourself. And now, of course, you must consider your child."

Paul slowly rubbed his forehead. He knew that all Augustin had said was true—all too true. He had believed, he had hoped, that there were signals of a new world which could, would change all that—that would wake true dreams and laughter and make them real. But he could not remember them now, he had nothing now—nothing except the new life growing in the belly of his wife.

"Think about it, Paul. Reflect. But quickly."

"Yes," he said, "yes, I shall."

"Très bien." He stood up unexpectedly. "Then I shall go and ask your wife to join us—and perhaps you could occupy yourself with the second bottle."

"Yes—yes of course," he said. But he made no move, as Augustin disappeared into the house. He stared out at the late afternoon lengthening into evening. All was calm. Yet there was a murmur, a hint of life—a coursing of blood in as yet unformed veins. Paul raised his glass—still half-full—to the coming night. "To you," he said, "my son—or daughter." And he drank to hope. Perhaps with this beginning, he could begin again too. . . .

"Oh Paul—look, look!"

She was like a child in her excited delight and her innocent awe.

"No, Paul—not at me. *There!*"

He smiled and glanced out of the dining-car window as the train drew into the second stop, a town whose checkered and multicoloured roofs were bright with sun after morning rain.

"Oh, it is beautiful—like a fairyland!"

And he laughed outright then, watching her across the immaculate linen and the shining wine glasses which tinkled gently as the train shuddered to a halt. To him, a fairyland was St. Remi glittering with rime like an ice mountain in the heart of winter; for her it was the urban—even the provincial drabness of the first stop, a small town gloomy with drizzle, had impressed her.

Augustin had picked them up from the D'Ornays' at ten-thirty to catch the noon train. Arlette was bright-eyed and vivacious—justly proud of herself in her going-away suit and the little straw hat pinned to her hair—while Paul was still heavy with the sleepless night. They'd left the ball at one—after several ritually prevented attempts at an earlier escape—but had not been discovered in the principal bedroom at the D'Ornays' till half past three in the morning. By the time the ceremonies were done and the last of the crowd had departed, it was after five. After that, there had been no possibility of—or desire for—sleep. Finally Paul had dozed fitfully for half an hour, only to be shaken into some semblance of wakefulness by an Arlette already dressed and deep in the new day. In the dining room—for the D'Ornays' house was large and, in the village, was generally known as the *château*—he found them all already drinking coffee. Arlette's excitement was a palpable force in the room, only the slow-moving dignity of Mme. D'Ornay restraining her ebullience. The D'Ornays had once been considerable landowners but, although they still retained a couple of the better farms in the commune, they had been forced to sell most of the land after the death of Hippolyte D'Ornay, once alternate senator for the department and highly respected, whose memory, however, was somewhat tarnished by a multitude of debts and bills unpaid for years. The only son, Hémeric had installed himself in Lyons as a lawyer, then moved to Paris; they said he made money, but there was little to spare for the family. The old lady ruled with a gentle authority and now, at the breakfast table, it was her daughters—Ursule and Béatrice, the white and the black they were called, after their looks—who exhibited the bridal modesty more appropriate to Arlette. And it was Béatrice, not Arlette, who, noticing Paul's tie was badly creased, had ironed it back to its pristine beauty.

Now, drinking the cool white Chablis, Paul felt his fatigue falling away, and the rocking of the train seemed to ease the slight tightness behind the eyes which was the only sign of the countless litres of wine he'd drunk the day before. He was content to take pleasure in Arlette's astonishment and in the certain element of new respect she was giving him. She recognized they were advancing into his territory.

And when they stepped down from the train at the Gare de Lyon he felt immediately at home. He took a deep breath of the station smell—steam, soot, wine, iron, cold stone, brown paper, urine—and felt dizzy with joy. He hailed a porter, who smiled knowingly and brushed his drooping moustache at the sight of Arlette clinging tightly to Paul's arm; and Paul grinned, delighted to be so easily recognized as a honeymoon couple.

"Taxi, m'sieur?"

"Why not? But first—the *consigne.*" He had packed the manuscript separately—for reasons both of security and of nostalgia—in the small cardboard case he had brought with him to Ste Colombe six years before. It fitted beautifully, well wedged between two bottles of Charles's oldest *marc*, which was to be his gift to Edouard. He was not going to see his cousin before Monday and, remembering the tale of robbery in the apartment, he preferred to have the case safe in the left-luggage room till then.

He gave the driver an intricate route that took them across the Île de la Cité, looping around Notre Dame and the Palais de Justice, along the Left Bank, cutting down past St. Germain-des-Prés, down the rue de Rennes to the Gare de Montparnasse.

"Look, Arlette, you see there?" He pointed at the station. "Up on the right—years ago a train's brakes failed and it ran right through the station and fell out onto the street just there."

"Were there many killed?"

"An old woman selling flowers below, I think—but no passengers."

"How lucky," she said seriously.

"Not for the old lady."

"Ah well—if you are old, you expect to die."

Paris was its beautiful grey self—the multitudinous tones of grey, of road and buildings and roofs, even of the bark of the plane trees, adding a soft depth to the whole. The purplish grey dome of the Invalides was pencil sharp against the blue sky. They passed the École Militaire and the bottom of the Champ de Mars—Arlette marveling at the Eiffel Tower—and then they were home.

Old Clotilde greeted them with joy—tiny, plump with tight drawn-back grey hair, apple-red cheeks, she seemed hardly to have changed at all.

"Oh, Monsieur Paul!" She embraced him heartily and wiped tears from her eyes with the edge of her apron.

She kissed Arlette too—"Madame, we are so pleased for you." And Arlette blushed—it was the first time, he realized, she'd been so addressed.

There was champagne—"Monsieur Edouard ordered it and said I must be sure to give you a glass as soon as you arrived."

And then there was the news, the edges of the news: the familiar hardships of the war—the lack of coffee, sugar, soap, meat, heating—worse in the city, the robbery, the kindness of Edouard. The real news—the arrest of Emily, the last visit of Bernard—would be kept until later when he and Clotilde were alone. He insisted on Clotilde taking a glass of champagne with them and, as he listened with half an ear, they drank, looking out of the high windows of the salon onto the Champ de Mars below, where the trees bloomed, the bushes burgeoned, the children played in the sand pits, and the dogs frolicked.

Arlette was delighted to find that, by standing close up to the window, one could see the Eiffel Tower.

106

"Ah, Madame, but in the master bedroom—I have put you in the master bedroom, Monsieur Paul, I hope that is correct?"

"Yes," he said quickly, but with a strange feeling in his heart, "yes, of course."

"From there, lying in bed in the morning, you have the tower right before your eyes."

"Is it true?"

And Paul and the old maid both smiled.

"Quite true, Madame. You will both perhaps be tired from your long journey? I have prepared something simple for you tonight if you wish to stay in—pâté, a cold chicken in aspic, a fresh salad, a Camembert—but . . ."

"Oh, I thought we would go out tonight—unless that is, you are tired, my love?"

"Tired? Oh no, not in the least."

"Well then—if it will keep, Clotilde?"

"Oh, it will keep, no fear of that."

"Then tomorrow night, perhaps."

"Of course, no problem."

That night he took her to La Tour D'Argent and they ate truffles sautéed in champagne and slices of pink *gigot* (lamb being a rarity in Ste Colombe) with a prewar Margaux (Paris *was* Bordeaux, Paris was Emily . . .) and looked out on the darkened city. Later he took her to a nightclub, recommended by Edouard at Paul's request, where they danced slowly to a black band. She drank yellow chartreuse and he drank whisky. Arlette had never seen a black man before and, later in the evening, when the saxophonist came and sat down at their table, she was numb with strangeness and admiration. He was American and spoke fluently, but with a thick accent that made his French almost incomprehensible. He asked her to dance but she refused, not knowing the step, she said.

"Then I will teach you."

It was a foxtrot and she seemed to pick it up as quickly as though she had known it all along. Paul watched them and

slowly drank his whisky and ordered another. It reminded him
—which was why he'd chosen it—of his stay in Sussex long
ago; at precisely eleven o'clock each night, Mrs. Trumball went
to bed, and Mr. Trumball mixed himself a whisky and soda.
Totally taciturn but unfailingly courteous, he always offered
Paul one too. Toward the end of his stay, Paul had taken to
accepting, although he did not like the taste; but he liked sitting
silently drinking with the Englishman. At first, he had tried to
make conversation—but they really had nothing to say to each
other, no interest in common, and soon he grasped that this
was an essentially silent ritual, almost like prayer. Occasionally
Trumball would clear his throat or poke the fire, but otherwise
all was quiet and motionless—and gradually Paul came to appreciate the communicativeness of silence, a certain type of
wordless companionship.

As Arlette sat down, he realized he was a little drunk. But,
Morine notwithstanding, alcohol did not diminish desire.
There was a kind of open sensuality, a looseness about his sloe-
eyed wife that made him call immediately for the bill. "Unless
you want to stay . . . ?"

"Stay?" She came out of her dance-induced dream. "No—
let's go home." And she gave him her most brilliant smile.

She woke him with a kiss and coffee and a fresh croissant on
the old silver tray.

"What time is it?"

"Ten-thirty. It's late already."

She sat on the bed and watched him eat—he was ravenous
and ate three croissants doused with jam and a brioche still
warm from the oven. "You make good coffee."

"Not me—Clotilde." She got up and wandered around the
room, touching objects here and there—the Sèvres vase filled
with pink roses, a pink glass elephant on the mantelpiece, a
glassed-in winter scene that snowed when tilted. She handled
them roughly, moved restlessly, and for a moment he wanted
to cry out, "No no!" For it seemed suddenly a kind of blas-

phemy—"Madame" but not Emily, pacing and touching—just as he lying here in his mother's bed was almost a violation.

"What?" he said, "what?"

"Paul, look!"

Behind her, framed exactly in the window, rose the Eiffel Tower in all its sober intricacy. When he was a boy, Bernard had told him exactly how many nuts and bolts and bars had gone into the construction—but he'd forgotten now, only remembering the rare glint of enthusiasm in his father's eye.

"Paul?"

"Yes?"

"Can we go up it?" she asked with such childlike anxiety that he laughed—the air blown clear of ghosts.

"Of course, of course!"

And afterwards—Edouard having kept the car in good order and miraculously finding petrol to fill it—Paul drove her down to the Black Bear at Fontainebleau for lunch. In the afternoon he walked her with increasing briskness through the palace— he saw she was bored with old things, and, before the tour was finished, they unobtrusively left the guide and crept out, depositing a tip at the desk.

Coming back into Paris, a brief spring shower drenched them before Paul could put up the top—so they left it down and were soaked and went laughing up to the house and bathed and changed and then had tea with petits fours which Clotilde had bought that morning. Then, taking Arlette by the arm, he showed her around the apartment. Gradually, although she was there beside him, touching him, fascinated now by every object, every room, he became less and less aware of her and his discourse took on more of the nature of a private musing, so that he was hardly aware of speaking. It was the presence of his mother that was closer to him then. As he stood in his old primrose bedroom he remembered the days of his illness—the long autumn and winter, with the sleep-in nurse who massaged his legs for fifteen minutes every two hours, day after day, week after week, except on Sundays when Emily did it, giving up God-knows what parties and dinners to do so. And her touch had been quite different from the nurse's diligent kneading—delicate and feather-light as her conversation, wafting and tumbling with laughter. He had never had so much of her time before, never so much of her love. And sometimes, in the evening, Bernard in his new uniform as a major of engineers would come and watch, sitting cross-legged on the end of the bed, filling the bedroom with his pipe smoke, and they would all talk together. Paul told them of his silent evenings drinking whisky with Mr. Trumball and Emily laughed so hard she got hiccups.

"Paul?"

"Ummm? Yes, my dear?"

"Do you think perhaps I could have another bath before supper?"

"Of course. You may do exactly as you like, Arlette—it's your house." It would be her third that day—but she was enamoured of the bathroom, the space, the mirrors, the gilt tap that spouted a thick stream of almost boiling water, the bath oil and the last cake of Emily's special soap that Clotilde had preserved. The lingering perfume of that soap renewed the pain of nostalgia. The scent was not appropriate for Arlette, just as the rings did not quite fit her fingers—he'd had the wedding band enlarged, but the engagement ring could not be tampered with, so she wore it on her little finger.

In the huge, ugly old kitchen he found himself asking Clotilde about his own childhood, as though it had happened to someone else, as though it was his last chance. He was astonished and delighted to hear all this history—for it did all seem to have happened in another age—told in Clotilde's soft Norman accent. She seemed to have forgotten nothing, could even tell him his favourite childhood foods—mussels and eclairs and *pâté de foie* and clementines. She talked to him of his parents and gradually he came to realize that, for all his father's long absences and his mother's constant party-going, they had been an exceptionally happy couple. For Clotilde, Emily's refusal to leave Paris when the Germans came was not an act of foolishness or ignorance, but of courage.

"Of course she knew quite well what might happen."

"Did she? Are you sure?"

"Oh yes. Many's the times she said to me, 'And when I'm gone, Clotilde, be sure to pack away all my clothes in mothballs.' She said that, you see, to comfort me with the idea that she would come back—and I did as she said, everything is in tin trunks in my room upstairs—but we both knew different."

"Clotilde—tell me, what did happen?"

She told him quite simply what had occurred that evening when his mother had been taken away. It was spring, just such a time as this; Emily had played—had taken off her rings and put them on top of the piano, which was why they were not taken too—had been playing for a long time, almost an hour, when they came, soft footed, polite, and asked her to accompany them. It was gay music, happy. "I remember thinking that particularly—there's Madame in a good mood, I thought to myself. Not that she was ever sad or droopy, if you understand what I mean, but she was thoughtful sometimes."

"What was the music, Clotilde?"

"That I couldn't say. it was out of her head, you see—but happy, like I said. Joyful. I can't describe it, but I'd know it if I heard it again." And then she went on.

Paul listened in silence, his head slightly bowed.

When she had finished, he stood up slowly, and they embraced and held each other, their cheeks wet, the twilight gracefully muting the harshness of their grief.

That night, after supper, he searched through the record collection. He had an idea of what he was looking for—there was one piece that Emily had played almost every day, "it's good for practice," she'd said—but he did not know its name. He wound up the gramophone and put on record after record —after a while Arlette, who'd been moving restlessly about the room, went out to the kitchen, and he was left alone. He found it at last almost by accident, for he was concentrating on piano rather than chamber music. As soon as he heard the familiar strains, he reached out automatically and turned off the single lamp in the drawing room. As the music swayed—rocking as softly as a cradle—he felt an ineffable stillness at the core of him, and then a lifting so that he raised his arms and stood on tiptoe in the darkness.

And then all the lights went on.

"That's it, Monsieur Paul—that's it! At least, part of it."

He lowered his arms and turned to see Clotilde at the door, her cheeks flushed, and, behind her, Arlette with a frown on her face.

"What is it?"

"The first movement of Beethoven's septet."

They looked at each other and smiled. And then the old seventy-eight ended, ricketing in the hissing final grooves. He lifted the arm and replaced it, but didn't turn the record over.

"Paul?"

"Yes, my dear?"

"Couldn't we have something gay?"

"But of course." He laughed. "Clotilde, is there any kind of liqueur left?"

"Oh yes, there's cognac and almost a whole bottle of Poire Williams and—"

"The poire perhaps?"

"Oh yes, I'm sure Madame will like the poire."

As Clotilde went to the sideboard and poured two small glasses of the transparent liquid from the cut-glass decanter, Paul took off the old record and, after looking through the collection, put on a new one and started to wind up the gramophone again.

"There." Clotilde gave them each a glass. "Will that be all, Monsieur Paul?"

"Oh yes, yes, I think so. Bonsoir, Clotilde."

"Bonsoir, Monsieur Paul. Bonsoir, Madame."

"Bonsoir, Clotilde. Sleep well."

At the door, Clotilde smiled. "Sweet dreams," she said, and then was gone.

Paul raised his glass and bowed slightly and they both drank. "Well?"

Arlette made a *moue*. "It's harsh."

"Harsh?" It was fresh as a mountain stream, sweet as a young summer.

"Oh, it's not bad, I suppose. But what about the music?"

"Ah, the music." He clicked the lever and lifted the arm and put the wooden needle gently down onto the record.

"*À nous, à nous la liberté! . . .*"

"Bien," Arlette said, "that's more like it."

T he opening of school was the most difficult day of the year because it was a beginning without change. For him it had long ago superseded the pain of spring or the melancholy of his solitary celebration of January 1st with oysters and champagne and calculated stupefaction.

He had arrived early, as he did every first day, and unlocked the classrooms and greeted his two assistants and addressed the assembled children with the same short, unvarying speech. He had put up the coloured poster of the new president, pinning it to the inside door of the supply closet, just as Augustin had done. The old chief of state had been plump as a pigeon, the new one was more like a starling hoping to be taken for a falcon —but the change was one of appearance only.

No, there had been no change. And sitting over his soup that evening, Paul had to struggle to push away the invading memories which came ghostlike to sit at his table. It was the time of year, he said to himself, simply the time of year. It was a struggle he could not win, but he could put off the moment. He drank more wine than usual, but was not able to finish the soup.

So at last, slowly, he mounted to the attic. He was physically tired; the first days of the school year always exhausted him, particularly the walk to and from the schoolhouse—the time was not far off when he wouldn't be able to manage that short kilometre any longer and would have to drive. That would be a peculiar indignity.

Outside the day was softly closing down. He sat on in the dusk, trying to empty his mind; but ripples stirred the surface, circular, diminishing, but always renewed by another stone cast into the pond. He wondered briefly if Agnès, his immured daughter, was any more successful at her religious exercises than he at his. He smiled and, reaching into the drawer, took out a box of matches and lit the candle. He forced himself to look down and read yesterday's reflection:

> The unnatural adversity of the writer's life is, one can only say, a deformation he himself seeks out. Is the artist then by necessity masochistic and, if so, what disaster gave rise to this appetite for punishment that may never be appeased?

He lifted the sheet and placed it carefully on top of the pile of useless manuscript. He sighed and closed his eyes for a moment. Then he gripped the table with both hands and, raising his head, looked out at the darkness beyond the sharp point of the candle's flame.

"Paul—my dear cousin—come in, come in!" Edouard took him by the hand and drew him into the small office. "Mon Dieu, how large you are—un bel homme—the last time I saw you you were barely up to my shoulder. Of course you don't remember me?"

"Oh yes—yes I do." Or rather, he remembered the thick-lensed horn-rimmed glasses Edouard wore which gave a strangely owlish look to an otherwise aquiline face. He was a slight man, quick of movement, dapper in a grey flannel suit, his mouth crooked in amusement as though he guessed the source of Paul's recognition.

"And this—this is the work?" He took the battered case from Paul and staggered with the weight of it. "My dear Paul, I can tell at once it is a masterpiece!"

"Oh that's just a couple of bottles of *marc* I brought you—although it *is* long, I'm afraid," he said, suddenly anxious.

"All the better. Well, we will put it here for the moment," and he laid the case on his remarkably clean desk. "Now sit down and tell me—you are just married? How is your wife—is she beautiful? Shall I have the chance of seeing her? And old cousin Augustin—still as fierce as ever? How did you find the apartment? Did Clotilde welcome you properly?"

Paul laughed, happy at the lithe, quicksilver little man and his quickfire questions, happy to be in this workmanlike room with books from floor to ceiling, their paper spines ranging from old burnt sugar to dun to cream to sharp white and the more recent publications grey as the wartime bread. "Which shall I answer first?"

That morning he had awakened early and dressed carefully, choosing a mauve silk tie from his father's rack to add a little lustre to his country-made wedding suit. Clotilde had polished his shoes to a glittering shine and, as he left the house, she handed him one of his father's wide-brimmed Borsalino's and a malacca cane. A hat!—he'd never worn one in his life before.

He kissed Arlette good-bye and strode out to the Champ de Mars. It was a perfect morning, still dewy in the shade, with a breathless tranquillity that seemed to call softly to the coming summer. In the fresh light the Eiffel Tower rose rampant and magnificent. A morning of peace and high promise.

As he strolled along the *quais*, hat in one hand, cane in the other, he felt like a lover about to keep a tryst. And, like a lover, he trembled with joy; city and sky and river seemed of an incomparable beauty, every detail of a piercing sweetness —the plump mammary dome of the Bibliothèque Mazarine, the swordlike spike above the lantern on the Palais de Justice, an ancient barge emerging into the sunlight from under the Pont des Invalides.

Crossing the Pont de Sully he put on his hat and quickened his pace. Paris had seemed empty—little traffic and few pedestrians—but the Gare de Lyon was filled with people and for a moment he was reminded of the scene six years before in May 1940, the milling crowds frightened and battling to get on a train, any train it seemed to him, swirling and surging from platform to platform, with isolated little islands of the apathetic and the lost, children in tears, women aghast, strong men pushing aside the weak, and here and there on upturned suitcases the imperturbables sitting stolidly eating and drinking.

There was a queue at the *consigne* but he waited patiently and at last presented his pink ticket to an official who seemed half-witted or perhaps half-tight and wandered vaguely among the stacks of valises and trunks and boxes and bundles. "There," said Paul, pointing, "there, to your right."

He took the case and left quickly, glad to get away from the station and its memories of fear and flight. He made his way across the Seine and went through the Jardin des Plantes, along the rue des Écoles and across the Luxembourg where already they were wheeling out the immense tubs containing the palm trees. A solitary small boy stood at the edge of the round pond disconsolately regarding his becalmed boat. Kneeling on the gravel and leaning as far out as he could Paul was just able to hook a guy rope with his cane and draw the little yacht to shore.

"Merci, monsieur."

"It's nothing." Paul smiled—the boy was white faced and thin, ill or convalescent perhaps, which would account for his not being at school. "I wouldn't try it again if I were you—there's no wind today."

"No," the boy said gravely, then sighed. "What a pity—I shall have to go home."

"Here." Paul took some coins from his pocket and put

them in the small hand, "Have a ride on the merry-go-round first."

"Mais . . ." The child looked at him in astonishment and doubt.

"That's all right. Enjoy yourself." He picked up his case and, as he moved off, the senate clock struck twelve. He would be a few minutes late for his appointment—but what did it matter? He laughed with pleasure at the day, the boy, the startled and disapproving look of an old man on a bench.

And now, as he recounted the details of the marriage, Edouard laughed too. "How interesting and curious," he said. "Of course, I knew such odd wedding customs still lingered in rural regions, but . . ."

"But not that they would involve people like us?" Paul smiled.

"Perhaps—how foolish that sounds." He paused. "You are happy there, aren't you?"

"Yes—I think I am. I have been, at any rate. You see, it is where I have grown up."

"Yes, I see. I am glad. It has been good for you. You were always considered a delicate child, you know."

"Delicate? Me? But I was always strong—until my illness, that is."

"Oh yes. No, I didn't mean that. Your nature—you were thought to be very sensitive, *fragile* Emily used to call you."

"Extraordinary—I don't think I had an idea in my head."

"But you had dreams perhaps?"

"Perhaps." He hesitated. "But, you know, Edouard, I find it extraordinarily hard to recall my life before I went to Ste Colombe—oh, I have been remembering a little over the weekend, the apartment of course, the objects, Clotilde's tales. And yet, it all seems to have happened to a stranger—to whose mind I am in some way privy, but it is not I. Why I wonder? I was not unhappy—at least I don't think I was unhappy. And yet in some way I seem to have been untouched—except, oddly

117

enough, by England. I remember every vivid detail of my holiday in England when I was fifteen."

"Where you contracted infantile paralysis, if I remember correctly."

"Yes, but . . ." Paul frowned. "Are you suggesting that it takes a—a setback in order to come to a sense of things?"

"Perhaps. A wound perhaps." Edouard touched his glasses —a gesture he'd made two or three times before, as though he were about to remove them and reveal a weakness, and which was, Paul was almost sure, unconscious. "No—I do not believe that. Perhaps you are simply by nature a countryman. Our life here in Paris before the war was peculiarly *déraciné*, contemptuous of roots." He fell silent, sat unmoving in a moment of sadness. "Well"—smiling suddenly—"let us talk of more cheerful things. Your book—what is it called?"

"Signals of a New World."

"Ah—and do we not need them! Perhaps you will show us the way out of all this." He stood up. "You must be hungry— we will lunch. But first—may I take a look at the manuscript?"

"Of course—open the case, it's not locked."

"This, my friend, is a real antique." He undid the latches and opened the lid. He did not move, just looked down; then he glanced at Paul and raised an eyebrow. "A strange manuscript."

"What? What do you mean?" Paul pushed himself to his feet.

"My dear cousin, I appreciate a joke as much as the next man, but this is a little pungent."

Paul stared at the open case—there were the two bottles, but where the manuscript should have been were three cheeses bedded upon a layer of apples. He reached out and put his hand on a bottle—it was the wrong shape, the wrong bottle, the *marc* bottle had a wooden devil inside climbing a ladder.

"Paul—what . . . ?"

He looked at Edouard who seemed suddenly very far away, tiny, opaque and floating behind his glasses. He forced himself to speak, his mouth dry as leather. "It is the—wrong case."

"The wrong . . . then it is not a joke?"

"A joke?" His leg was trembling, shuddering—and suddenly it gave way. Edouard seemed to do a slow somersault, the books on the wall revolved to the left, swung to the ceiling, and far away Paul heard the soft thud of his own body falling to the floor.

For six days the countryside had been completely enveloped in the February fog. And on Sunday morning as he stood at the living room window, it was so thick he could not even see the Thibaults' house across the lane. Somewhere out of the blindness far below came, faint and muffled, the bell for early mass. He stood in his shirtsleeves and listened to the sound until it was done, and then once again there was silence, except now and again for the creaking of the gas stove he'd installed and the soft burbling of the twins in their bassinet. At six he had changed them and fed them and bathed them in an enamel basin filled with tepid water—a task which, since Thérèse had decamped two weeks ago, had been undisputedly his. Only the two feedings in the middle of the day were Arlette's responsibility—and twice already when he had come back from school for lunch he'd found she had forgotten to give them their ten o'clock bottle. After the first week all attempt at breast feeding had been abandoned, with the sage concurrence of Mullet and to the relief of everyone, particularly Arlette—"Thank God, now perhaps I can get some rest."

And rested she had—she slept almost as long as the twins, who after that first bawling week were quiet and amiable. At the beginning Thérèse had encouraged her daughter's languor —"She needs to recuperate, poor dear, she must gather her forces." But gradually the weight of two households and looking after the babies had begun to tell on her indulgence, even on her sturdy physique. Paul had taken to ferrying her from one house to the other, then he had been allowed to make breakfast, prepare the bottles and, under the strictest supervision, to give the babies one or two feedings a day—he learned to burp them and, finally, to change them. For none of this did Arlette show the slightest inclination; she would watch and listen impatiently as her mother demonstrated, then go back to bed and the magazines with which her visiting friends supplied her. Mullet, whose visits were unnecessarily frequent Paul thought, muttered authoritatively about the effects of a difficult birth and "post-natal depression"—and Paul felt a bond of sympathy with his mother-in-law's uncomprehending irritation at such talk. "What does that mean?" she asked and Mullet gave one of his most brilliant smiles and a significant glance at Paul. "Oh nothing, nothing."

And it did mean nothing; for when her friends came—all, with the curious omission of Ursule D'Ornay—she would become gay and there would be almost continuous laughter from the bedroom and, even after their departure, she would remain in good spirits for an hour or two—once even laughing at a mild joke of Paul's. But her merriment and chatter would cease if her mother ventured to remind her of her responsibilities.

So slowly Paul and Thérèse were forced into an uneasy alliance of shared work—for him a pleasure, for her a surrender of control accepted with ill grace.

Then one afternoon he had returned from school to find her white lipped with silent anger, she wouldn't even answer his greeting. He went to see Arlette and as soon as he'd shut the bedroom door, she said, "I hate her!"

"Your mother? Oh come, my dear, she—"

"She says I'm lazy and neglectful—Oh Paul!" And, as he sat tentatively on the bed, she put her arms around him and her head on his shoulder. He felt the dampness of her cheek against his and he was moved as he had not been since the night of the birth.

"Paul, it's not true, is it? Say it's not true!"

"Well—no . . . but I think you *could* show a little more interest in the twins perhaps. I'm sure that's all she means."

"But I do show an interest—it's just, just that I'm not the

120

maternal type. That milky smell they have—it puts me off. I can't help it. And they're so ugly."

"Ugly?" He moved back a little and looked at her.

"Those scrunched little faces—they're horrible."

Paul forced a laugh. "Well, I expect we were all like that once. And after all, they are your children."

She pursed her lips and turned away her head.

"Arlette," he said gently, "you are their mother."

"Am I?" She looked at him, her eyes very dark and large in the winter whiteness of her face. "All I am is a kind of—of vehicle—like a pea pod—when it's fat enough you pop it and *voilà* peas! What use is the pod to anyone after that?"

He restrained an impulse to smile. "But we are people, not peas. We—"

"They look like peas to me."

He wanted to slap her suddenly—he took a breath. "Whatever they look like, they have to be nurtured—and that is usually the job of the mother." He hesitated, but she made no reply, so he went on. "The birth is only the beginning—after all, it is hard to feel very much for an embryo—but after the birth, the love and the care and tenderness a mother naturally feels is what moulds the children, makes them thrive, makes them truly human."

"Then I'm not a mother."

"Why?"

"Because I don't feel any of those things—care and tenderness, et cetera—what you said."

Paul stood up and went to the window and looked out—the sun was setting, a strip of silver in a metallic sky.

"Well, it's not my fault, is it? I can't help what I feel, can I?"

He turned slowly. "No. It's not your fault. I suppose—I suppose it happens sometimes."

"I didn't ask for children, Paul."

"No—no, I know. I realize you had doubts. But I thought —I hoped—when they arrived, you'd be happy."

"Well *I* thought you were going to be rich and famous and

we'd live in your fine big apartment in Paris with Clotilde and a cook and a nurse for the children!"

He winced. "Yes—yes, I see that."

As if sensing her advantage, she went on quickly, "Instead here we are in this abysmal little house—and what am I? Wife of a stuffy country schoolmaster who looks down on my friends—"

"That's not—"

"—doomed to making meals and washing nappies for two filthy little animals and—"

"Arlette! That's enough!" He took an unsteady step toward her and she raised her hand as if to ward off a blow—and a sudden shaft of silvery sunlight struck the rings on her fingers, the diamonds glittering brilliantly. He went to the door, turned, hand on the knob. "Very well, Arlette. I understand now." He nodded. "So be it."

As he shut the door behind him, she called, "Paul—I didn't mean—Paul Paul!" Then he closed the second door and her cry was cut off.

He had been clumsy, he knew, foolish. Perhaps he should have struck her, perhaps he should have . . . He shook his head. It was time to prepare the bottles, time for the babies' feed, for their nightly bath.

It was bathing time that he loved most of all—and they too seemed to relish it; their eyes would be wide open and regard him solemnly when he washed them. Their small, warm bodies were curiously hirsute—black hair ran all down their backs, thickening at the base of the spine, forming a dark down over their buttocks; they even had hair on the backs of their ears and hands—little animals, marvelous little animals.

Looking out on the foggy Sabbath morning, he had a queer, half-guilty sense of happiness. He had had the twins to himself for two weeks now, and the quiet sightlessness of the fog seemed to be a natural expression of the uncomplicated world in which they were enclosed—alone and together, Arlette

122

wrapped in sleep in the next room, the coffee on the stove, the twins dozing, murmuring of their sweet dreams. The purity, the homeliness of that feeling blunted the desolation of those months since Paris when he had moved distracted between his studies, his attempt to reconstruct his book, the care of his pregnant wife, the teaching and the housework. He was still now—unmoving.

As he watched, he saw that the fog had begun to lift; there were clumps of firs that lay like islands in the surrounding whiteness and the black slim finger of a single poplar pointing. The hidden sun was beginning to dazzle. And somewhere he heard a rook caw.

By ten the sun was bright and he fed the girls by the window so they might see the world was still there and be glad. He had developed a method of holding them one in the crook of each arm, so that he could feed them simultaneously. He could hear Arlette moving about, going to the bathroom, coming back and then, through the thin connecting door between the living room and bedroom, he heard her humming. He felt a tentacle of astonished hope. Since the final row with her mother, when Thérèse had left in an insulted huff, Arlette had hardly spoken, let alone sung.

He fed them, changed them, put them on the carpet and sat down cross-legged to play with them—they seemed to like having their feet tickled. He had an idea that they should see the world from as many angles as possible—not just the perpetual bassinet, but from the floor, the table (where he would prop them around with cushions), at the window; soon it would be warm enough to put them out on the terrace or under the plum tree in the garden.

"What in the name of God are you doing?"

"I'm play—" He glanced up at Arlette in the doorway, then gaped. He had become used to her lying in bed with scraggled hair and a dirty neck, but this was something entirely different. She wore a dress of a rich plum-red material she'd bought in

Paris, a dark-red hat, the small string of pearls he'd given her as a wedding present, and over her shoulders was the fur coat that Clotilde had dug out of one of Emily's tin trunks.

"Well what's the matter—have I got a speck on my nose?"

"No—no, you're beautiful." He struggled to his feet. "But where are you going?"

"To mass, of course—it is Sunday, isn't it?"

"Yes, oh yes. But you look more as though you were going to a—to some social event."

"In this abysmal little hole, a mass is the nearest thing to a social event that we've got, isn't it?"

"I suppose so, but . . . well, you look ravishing, almost overwhelming."

"You like it, eh?" She did a pirouette and a waft of perfume floated across to him. She laughed. "Then why don't you come with me?"

"And leave the children?"

"Well, why not? What can happen to them in an hour or so?"

"Oh come, one doesn't leave babies alone in—"

"Well then we'll ask old mother Thibault to take care of them."

"But she goes to mass too."

"Oh shit, if—"

"Arlette!"

"What? *Shit?* I can say what I like in my own house, I should hope."

"No, that's not the way we talk. That's not the way the children will talk."

"Oh no? A lot you know. You think they'll grow up to be priggish little schoolteachers too?"

"It's vulgar and I won't have it."

"Oh sh—*zut!* There, if that's what you want. Well then—what about M. Thibault? He doesn't go to mass."

"Don't be ridiculous."

"Ridiculous? And would it have been ridiculous to get Marie-Claude Bréboux to look after the kids, as I told you when

124

Maman left? Then we could go out, couldn't we? Or is she too vulgar for you too?"

"I . . ." For a moment he was wordless—Marie-Claude was indeed vulgar and there was something faintly prurient, even sinister about her. "Besides, you forget—I am not a Catholic. I don't go to mass."

"Oh my God—you don't have any religion, but you take it as seriously as if you were a monk. What's religion got to do with mass?"

He smiled. "Everything, I would think."

She stared at him, then suddenly she smiled too. "Well, at any rate you're not always telling me to go and see Father Morine."

"Of course not—who does?"

"Maman of course, who else?"

"Why?"

"Because he is so *wise*—if you don't love your children, if you have trouble with your husband, if you can't face your responsibilities, go to Father Morine. Father Morine—that is *amusing!*"

"Well, not that I agree, but what's wrong with Morine? He's a good man."

"A *good* man?" she said sardonically. "You are so innocent—you live here and yet you know absolutely nothing." She started across the room toward the outside door.

"Careful!"

"You're afraid I will step on them? Really, Paul, you are an idiot."

"What do you mean—about Morine? What's wrong with Morine?"

She put her hand to the door and swung it open. "Oh nothing—nothing."

The cold draft of air swept across the room and he bent swiftly to gather up the babies. "Arlette—I want to know, I insist on knowing—"

"Shit!" she said and slammed the door.

He knelt, one baby in each arm, staring at the door. Slowly he got up and put them carefully in the cradle—impervious to the noise about them, they had fallen asleep. He heard Arlette's high heels clacking down the stone steps, the creak of the iron gate. He had done something wrong; he had made a mistake somewhere. If he took the car, surely he could bring Béatrice or Ursule to look after the children, and then . . .

He hurried to the window and wrenched it open and leaned out.

"Arlette—Arlette!" he called.

But she had gone, hidden already by the ruined barn—out of sight. But surely not out of hearing.

"Arlette!" He called again—and then again—although knowing it was futile, too late.

He shut the windows and slowly returned to the cradle. He put a blanket around each little body and tucked it in. Then he stood by them, on guard, waiting.

The June night was so windless that the candle flame burned without a sway or flicker. Paul whistled softly between his teeth as he worked, pausing every now and then to listen for the twins in the room below—an unnecessary precaution really because now that the two-o'clock feeding had been given up they slept tightly and sweetly throughout the night.

Flora and Fauna of the Region—a Curriculum. He had taken up an old idea of Augustin's for a simple adult education course in what lay all about them. The ignorance of the local population was astounding—they had little knowledge of anything that was not immediately useful. Only Mme. Bouquin the midwife was presumed to know anything about the properties of the indigenous botanical life—in her role as the village witch. So her knowledge too, when it wasn't sheer mumbo-jumbo, was practical. More was known of the fauna and its habits, but, again, strictly from a utilitarian point of view—either as game to be shot and eaten or pests to be put down. Even the most intelligent farmer had little idea of elementary forestry or preservation or plantation—all of them ruthlessly cut down their hedges every two years (at least, the "efficient" ones). It would be an uphill job convincing them they had anything to learn—especially from a "foreigner." But Paul was full of hope; he had managed to get his father-in-law on his side, in principle, and Charles Buisson was a man of increasing weight in the commune and was certain to be made a councillor at the next communal elections. And Paul had been conscientiously doing his homework—the table was strewn with half-read botany texts. Unfortunately his mind and interest seemed to stray implacably to flowers and shrubs—a recondite study by any farmer's standards.

Even now, lifting his head, he seemed to catch the scent of honeysuckle. And then he heard a sound—a creak. The gate —could Arlette be back so early from her cousin's? No, and certainly not so silently. He waited, poised; he was not anxious, there were no burglars at Ste Colombe (petty thievery of tools, though, was not uncommon). He heard nothing more, but he had the distinct impression there was someone there. He stood up slowly. He blew out the candle and blinked and went to the window.

He could not see the crescent moon that lay behind the house, casting a shadow onto the front garden, but the sky was clear and spectacular with stars. An owl hooted and then he was almost sure he caught the sound of a step on the stone stairs, hardly a step, more a thin scraping noise. And then, out of the darkness:

"Paul—Paul?"

It was no more than a whisper, but sharp with anguish. He leaned forward and looked down, but saw nothing.

"Paul!" The voice cracked.

"Who's there—who is it?"

"Morine. Paul, can I talk to you?"

"Morine!" He could make out now the blur of an upturned face. "Wait," he said. "Go around to the parlour door, I'll come down."

In the parlour he listened for a moment for the children, but there was no sound. He turned on the light and opened the outside door.

"Morine, what . . ." He stopped.

The priest's hand was raised as if to shield his face from the light—he was hatless and his pale blond hair was awry.

"Come in, man."

"Ssssh!"

"Why? There's nothing to be afraid of." But he lowered his tone.

Morine slipped into the room, as though pursued. "What about your wife? I don't want her to—"

"Arlette's at Amercey—at the ball. She won't be back till late. Sit down. What is it?"

"I . . ." As he sat, he put a hand on the table and the fingers made odd little twitching movements. "I'm sorry to bother you at this time of—so late." He darted a glance at Paul—his face was white and glistened with moisture.

"You need a glass of wine."

"No no, I . . ."

But when Paul put the glass in front of him, he raised it and drank greedily. Paul refilled the glass and sat down.

"Tell me—you're in distress?"

"Distress?" Morine gave a little laugh, then abruptly put his face in his hands and began to sob.

"I'm damned, Paul—I'm damned," he muttered through the choking sobs.

Paul put out a hand and touched the crippled shoulder. "Calm yourself, my friend—tell me what is the matter."

"Friend?" He lifted his face and slowly the shudders that shook his body diminished. "I have no friends—no priest has friends."

"I am your friend, Morine."

128

"Frédéric—my name is Frédéric. You won't be—not when I tell you."

"Frédéric." Paul raised his own glass and took a sip. "You mustn't think just because I've neglected our friendship lately that I—"

"No no—you've had your own problems. I know that."

"You do? How's that?"

"Oh—word gets around," he muttered, "gets around. Gossip. You haven't—haven't heard anything about me?"

"No," Paul said quickly, but with a sudden feeling of discomfort—hadn't he picked up innuendos from Arlette that something was amiss, from Morine's own curious behaviour the night the twins were born? As he watched the priest lift the glass with a trembling hand, he wondered if it was drink. "Come, Mor—Frédéric. It can't be as bad as all that. There's nothing beyond cure—or forgiveness."

"How little you know—how little." He drank the wine in three gulps; for a few moments he stared at the empty glass, then raised his eyes. "I am a murderer, Paul."

"A murderer? In a sense we all are—spiritually."

"Not spiritually—physically." He raised his delicate, long-fingered hands. "I have killed, Paul—with these hands I have killed."

Paul involuntarily glanced at the door to the living room—had he heard a child cry? He cleared his throat. "Who have you killed then?"

Morine seemed to struggle, then at last he got it out. "Ursule—Ursule D'Ornay," he whispered.

Paul took a deep breath, then said with slow deliberation, "Ursule D'Ornay is dead—is that what you are trying to tell me?"

"They are both dead!"

"Both?" he asked sharply. "Béatrice?"

"No. The baby. The baby is dead—I killed the baby, oh God forgive me!" He let out a little wild cry.

"You will have to explain. Ursule had a baby?"

129

"I . . ." Morine bit his lip. "Give me some more wine?"

Reluctantly, Paul poured half a glass. "Now then."

"You'll think that I am—that I'm a . . ."

"Does it matter what I think?"

"No—yes. I don't know. Oh my God, how I have suffered!" He lifted his glass and took only a sip. He seemed to brace himself. "I was in love with Ursule I think almost from the first moment I saw her—when she was a girl. She was beautiful as an angel—and good, good as an angel. She was utterly pure— I know for I heard her confessions. And my love for her was pure too—I swear to you, Paul. And uplifting—it seemed to bring me closer to Our Lord just to see her, to hear her, to . . ." He was gazing down at the table and picking at the cloth with a fingernail. He glanced up.

"Yes?"

"Of course you couldn't understand that." He flushed. "But it's true. It was true. At first. For a long time. Then I began to think that she loved me too—the way she looked at me, the pleasure on her face when I entered the room . . . I visited the D'Ornays quite a lot, three women living alone, you see . . . Then last August they went away to Nice, as they'd always used to do before the war, I believe. Only Ursule came back a week early—because she wanted to go on our annual village excursion. With what is made from the *kermesse* we hire a bus and—"

"Yes, I know."

"Well, this year—last year, I mean—it was voted to go to Lisieux and Ursule very much wanted to come. She has—had a special devotion to . . ." He shook his head. "In any event she came back to Ste Colombe early and we all went in the bus for two days to Lisieux. It was then, after that—I made one of my usual visits and Ursule was there alone and, and we—do you understand?"

"I understand." He thought of them both—both pale, blue-eyed blonds, in the heat of August in the gloomy old house on the hill. Innocents—wrapped safe, they would have been sure, in the purity of their devotion. "Yes, I understand."

"I don't know—I can't explain. There wasn't a moment when I didn't know the sin, the risk we ran. I was torn, we were both torn—between a horror of what we were doing and a kind of helpless elation. Helpless. That is the mark of the Devil—that helplessness, when you are driven beyond reason. It was the Devil that drove me on." His white face was sweating again. He drank more wine and licked his lips. "Of course, it was more difficult when the others returned. But then in September the tenant of their farm on the way up to St. Remi —you know the one—he left unexpectedly, some relation had died and left him property in the Haute-Savoie, I believe. It seemed like a miracle at the time, God forgive me. Ursule used to take the key—and the old man had left some of his furniture there, a big bed . . ." He stopped.

It was cold in the little stone-flagged parlour. Paul thought of lighting the stove, but instead he poured them both a little more wine. "And then she became pregnant?"

"Yes."

"When?"

"I don't know exactly—I think it must have been the end of January or the beginning of—"

"January!" Paul stared at him. "Good God, man—and you tried to perform an abortion on her now?"

"I . . ." The priest bowed his head. "Not now," he muttered.

Paul stood up. "Then when? When did she die?"

"Two weeks ago," he whispered. "The Sunday before last —Pentecost."

"Two weeks—and no one knows?"

"They've said she's gone away—to visit her brother in Paris."

"They?"

"Mme. D'Ornay and Béatrice."

131

Slowly Paul sat down. "Morine—"

"Frédéric."

"Frédéric—you can't keep something like this secret—people are bound to find out."

"Yes. I know. They are already beginning to ask questions. That's why I'm here. Paul, I don't know what to do—what shall I do?" He raised his head and stretched out his hands.

"You'd better tell me the rest of it first."

There was not much to tell—or Morine was in no state to tell it. But Paul could fill in the gaps between the jerky sentences for himself. The first gnawing anxiety when the period did not come, breaking the news to Mme. D'Ornay, the endless discussions of what to do, how to keep it quiet, the growing panic in the household punctuated by long imploring prayers to the Almighty to come to their aid. And then the final decision of these pious people, totally unaware of the danger of aborting a four-month-old fetus, and the last scene played out in the bedroom with the Sacred Heart on the wall—the apparent success and then the hemorrhaging that could not be staunched, the life's blood soaking the sheet, the mattress, dripping down onto the floor. Morine giving the last rites to the girl he'd killed.

"And you just left her there—in the bed?" Paul asked when the halting recital was finished.

Morine shook his head. "No—we, we buried her. And the child too. In the garden—we dug a hole and, oh God, oh God!"

"In the garden . . ."

"It was quite light—the moon was almost full. It took a long time, because of my shoulder, you see. She was so pale—pale and beautiful like the moon, she—"

"That's enough!" Paul said harshly.

The priest flinched. "You think—you think I'm a monster, don't you?"

Paul stared at the ruined man. He tried to feel pity for that dreadful weakness. "No, Frédéric, not a monster." A poor thing, a contemptible thing—a victim of the goodness he so passionately believed in. "What is done is done."

"But what am I to do now?"

"The authorities must be informed."

"Paul—no! I can't—I couldn't bear it!"

"There is no alternative."

"But the shame—the disgrace! How am I to endure that?"

"What about your religion?" Paul said with a quick spurt of anger. And as if struck, the priest hung his head and began muttering: "Oh my Lord, my sweet Savior who through suffering . . ."

"Morine!"

"Yes?" He looked up, blinking at Paul, and the tears ran freely down his cheeks. "Is there no other way? None?" he asked pleadingly.

Paul sighed, choking back his anger. "No. But . . ."

"But?"

"The brother—Hémeric. He is a lawyer, isn't he?"

"Yes. You think . . . ?"

"He has not been informed?"

"No—they are afraid. He is a—a harsh man. He will—"

"That is of no importance. Clearly he must be told. That is the first thing to do. You have a phone in the presbytery? Then you must phone him—now."

"Phone him? No—I couldn't. Marie—Mlle. Nocent would overhear, she listens to everything, I couldn't—"

"Very well, then—the D'Ornays have a phone. Call from there. It must be done."

"But I . . ." His tear-streaked face went even whiter and his hand opened and closed convulsively. "I could not—I cannot. Paul—you wouldn't . . . would you do it? Please, my old friend, I beg you, I implore you!"

Paul hesitated—suddenly it seemed to him the bitterest of ironies that *this* man, this *creature*, was the only person on earth who had read his book or who ever would, the only being alive who knew his innermost heart. What signal had he given Morine—corruption of innocence to crime, of hope to scandal, of dream to nightmare? What worth this man's praise or judgment? "Very well," he said heavily.

"Oh thank you—thank you. I shall—"

"Please. Enough." He stood up and staggered—his leg was cramped and feeble from sitting too long in one position. He limped across the parlour and, opening the door a crack, listened to the quiet breathing of the twins. Then he and Morine left the house and descended to the lane.

"What are you going to do?"

"I'm going to get Mme. Thibault to look after the babies, then I shall drive to the D'Ornays. You'd better go back to the presbytery now."

They stood under the ruined wall of the barn in the shadow cast by the young moon behind them. The priest held out his hand and Paul took it—cold and moist.

"Paul, you are a true friend."

"You must go now."

"A true friend—I shall always—"

"Go."

"Adieu, Paul," Morine whispered. "Adieu."

Paul watched the small black figure emerge into the moonlight, then disappear again in the shadow of the hedge—but he could hear the soft diminishing footfalls for quite a long time. It was the last he ever saw of Morine.

It was more than two hours before he got back to the house again—most of that time spent waiting for a connection to Paris. The three of them sat at the table in the dining room, Paul with the ancient telephone in front of him, Mme. D'Ornay at the head, her plump face thin and yellow now, but her chin lifted, Béatrice with her head slightly bowed, her hands folded in her lap. They gave him a cup of coffee—the wartime stuff tasting only of chicory so they must, he thought, be poorer than he thought. But, otherwise, they sat quite still and did not talk at all.

When the call came at last it was clipped—both D'Ornay and Paul were aware the local operators were likely to listen: a family matter, very grave situation, essential he come with all possible speed.

"I suggest the early train if you—"

"Train? No, I shall motor down—I will start in an hour. You, I take it, are in possession of all the relevant facts?"

"I believe so."

"Who else?"

"No one, apart from the family and one other person."

"It is a matter for the authorities?"

"Certainly."

"But they have not yet been informed?"

"No."

"Very well. Where do you live, Monsieur?"

"The hamlet of La Roche—the new house."

"That ugly stuccoed thing? Yes, I know it. Then I shall be with you between seven and eight o'clock this morning. If that is convenient?"

"Quite."

"Good. À *bientôt*, Monsieur." And he hung up before Paul had a chance to reply.

"He is coming?"

"Yes, he is coming. By car. He will be here early in the morning."

Mme. D'Ornay held out her hand. "Thank you, Monsieur."

He took the hand and bowed slightly. She looked at him, yet did not appear to see him. He could think of nothing to say.

Béatrice accompanied him to the door.

"Oh, Paul," she said, "and a year ago we were all so happy."

"Yes," he said. They embraced.

He let the car run silently down the hill before turning on the motor and putting it into gear.

When he got home, the moon had gone, but the great canopy of the stars was more brilliant than ever. His senses were so highly tuned he fancied he caught the thin cry of the bats.

Madame Thibault was knitting.

"Arlette is not back?"

"Not yet, Paul."

"Oh well. It's so late, I expect she will sleep over at her cousin's." Arlette had cousins all over the place—at Amercey, Gorsin, Martial, Mellecey . . .

"I expect so." Mme. Thibault smiled faintly.

Paul felt himself flush at her ready acceptance of such a lie. "The children," he said quickly, "they were no trouble?"

"Oh no—they are angels." *Elles sont des anges*—had she not put the slightest emphasis on the first word?

"Madame Thibault."

"Yes?" She was gathering up her knitting.

"There is going to be a great scandal," he said impulsively.

"Yes?"

"Not—I m-mean"—he found himself stuttering—"I m-mean in the village."

"Ah, you want to say—Father Morine?"

"How—how did you know?"

"It was inevitable. No one, least of all a priest, should try so hard to be a saint. But Paul . . ."

"Yes?"

"Paul—do not become involved." She had rolled the knitting around the needles, now she put it in her basket and stood up.

"Why—why do you say that?"

"You must not judge us too harshly. You have your own difficulties." She went to the door.

"I don't understand."

"No. You are an innocent too." She smiled. "Good-night."

"Good-night, Madame Thibault."

After she left he simply stood there for a long time. His mind darted hither and thither in obscurity—Morine, Arlette, his book . . . It was beyond his grasp; everything seemed to be slipping away.

At last he roused himself and went slowly into the girls' room and looked down in the darkness at his babies. Which was which? He could tell them apart now because one had a small mark on the lobe of the left ear—and he called her Hélène, but really she might be Agnès. Their quiet breathing was broken by a snort—a kind of little piglike chortle. And the other one answered with a bubbling sigh. A small conversation in the middle of the night.

He drove the old Citroën into the Buissons' spacious courtyard and switched off the engine. He rested his forehead on the steering wheel for a minute. He was desperately tired and cold, too, although the evening was warm, almost sultry—it was the time of year when the weather often came up from the south instead of down from the north, bringing with it the hot breath of Africa and the slow, majestic sweeping storms culled from the heart of France which left the air humid and heavy. He raised his head and tried to breathe deeply; the farmyard smells of horse and cow were thick about him, the mustiness of hay, a faint cloacal whiff from the outhouse in the vegetable garden—he couldn't properly catch his breath.

He got out of the car and went into the big kitchen. Charles and Thérèse must have heard the car draw up, but they both sat unmoving at the table—the faint dusk giving them a false air of placidity.

"Good evening," he said.

They looked at him in silence—and then there was a little whimper from one of the small bundles on the big bed in the corner. The sound brought them to life—like a switch released in a clockwork dummy, he thought. Charles grunted and held out his hand and Paul limped over and shook it, and Thérèse got to her feet and came around and they embraced quickly, uneasily.

"How were the twins?"

"Oh fine, fine. They were no trouble—they're angels. Already they're getting used to their grandmother again. Sit down, Paul, sit down—you must be exhausted. And hungry —there is soup. Would you like some soup?" She had got into her usual bustling rhythm.

"Yes, I would. Thank you." He was famished, had eaten nothing all day and had drunk only a cup of coffee at breakfast and a glass of cassis at midday.

Thérèse went out to the pantry where she did the summer cooking, and Charles poured him a glass of wine, then cut several thick slices from the loaf that lay on the table.

They touched glasses.

"*Santé.*" Paul drank his wine down in one draft and Charles gave him some more. They did not look at each other and, when Thérèse returned with the soup, the couple sat in silence watching him eat. Since Ursule's death and Morine's discreet disappearance, Paul had become painfully aware of being peered at all the time by hidden eyes. The watchers—and the listeners—were everywhere in the village, and no news, however ghastly, no tale of disaster or disgrace ever seemed to come as a surprise. The body of the commune had some kind of preternatural sense of evil in its members and took a veiled but savage delight in their wounds. Death and infidelity, drunkenness, bestiality, impoverishment, suicide, murder—all these were its cruel food. And the silence of the Buissons—and his own—was the silence of victims.

"Coffee, Paul?"

"Please."

It was good coffee—the real thing, strong and thick, heavily sugared. Charles got up and fetched the bottle of *marc* and filled two small tumblers to the brim; then he rolled a couple of cigarettes and handed one to Paul.

"Well?" he said.

"She didn't go to the ball at the Mont de Mars at all."

"But we saw her leave." Thérèse's voice was anxious but accusatory. "We *all* saw her leave."

"What we saw was Jean-Claude driving her off in his car."

Paul picked up the matches and lit his cigarette; he blew a slow stream of smoke across the table.

She'd been, he'd thought, particularly gay—and had been all morning. She had risen before him and made breakfast and had even, for the first time, spent half an hour playing with the children. And, as she'd moved about the house, she had sung a little—"*à nous, à nous la liberté!*" Knotting his tie in front of the mirror, Paul had smiled—smiled to combat the prick of tears in his eyes. Hope, painful but irrepressible, made his fingers tremble as he inserted the gold stickpin, and he drew a single drop of blood from his thumb. She'd given him the stickpin the day before, his birthday—it was of twisted gold with a small pearl at the top. And somewhere in Croze she had found a bottle of vintage champagne. They'd drunk it sitting on the terrace in the twilight, and that night they'd made long, sweet love.

He tried to sing with her, but couldn't catch the tune, and she laughed at him, and he laughed too. She was gentle and merry and, oddly, thoughtful—she insisted on carrying the children down to the car and her suitcase as well, for she would spend the night after the ball with her cousin Rose Daveney at Martial.

"No, Paul—what would happen if your leg went on the steps and you fell with the babies?"

"Perhaps you'd like to drive the car too?" he'd said, pleased and astonished at such solicitude.

And she'd laughed and begun to hum again as they drove down to the Buissons' for the gargantuan Fourteenth of July feast. Jean-Claude was there and also Hector, Charles's grandfather—he of the wolf's tooth. He was a tall, thin old man, dressed entirely in black, his features lupine with age; he ate voraciously, wolflike, and drank heavily, and, later, he smoked cigarette after cigarette as the four men played belotte—a game of mind-numbing banality which Paul had forced himself to learn. But that afternoon he almost enjoyed it—enjoyed, at any rate, the slightly drunken warmth of the day, the continual glasses of white wine, the sunlight falling in thick bars across the haze of tobacco smoke, the lingering smell of food, Charles's sly teasing.

"He's a lucky one, my son-in-law—he hardly knows how to play, yet he wins all the time!" And it was true, Paul had hit a streak where it seemed impossible for him to lose. "You should have seen him in front of that boar the first time we went hunting, eh, Paul? Just stood there, wouldn't move, fired with his eyes closed as like as not—and, bang, into the eye right through the brain. That's luck, eh?"

Paul smiled and nodded and almost succeeded in forgetting the hidden malaise that hung in the air. In other years Ursule D'Ornay had been one of the party—and her absence now was felt more strongly, at least by Paul, than her delicate, pale presence had ever been. People whispered of her in secret in the night, but no one spoke openly. Hémeric D'Ornay had succeeded in burying the whole affair, but it lived on like slime beneath the surface. When Paul had tried to tell Arlette, she had refused to listen, would not mention the name, had banished the memory of her best friend—just like the rest of the village, which had totally ostracized the D'Ornay family.

Paul sighed. "She never went to Martial," he said.

"But Jean-Claude—"

"Jean-Claude took her to Dandin."

"To Dandin? But she doesn't know anyone at Dandin."

"He left her at the café."

"Oh." Thérèse exchanged a quick glance with her husband. The café at Dandin was where one caught the bus to Croze—every morning at eight, every evening at six, Sundays and holidays included.

"Did he say"—Thérèse slow, hesitant—"did he say why?"

"Because she told him to drop her there."

Paul had found Jean-Claude in the garage where he worked. He was a large, good-looking but rather slow young man, though people said he was quick on his feet, a good dancer. His hands being covered with grease, he had extended his wrist for

Paul to shake. She had, he said, changed her mind as soon as they left the house and directed him to Dandin. Why? "Oh, one asks no questions of Arlette—one just does as she says." Why did he think she was going to Dandin? "Oh, to take the bus—why else does anyone ever go there?" Was there anyone else in the café when he left her off? "Oh no—no one, no one at all." But the young man's full lower lip had trembled and there was a suspect eagerness to his reply.

"No one at all?"

"Oh well—yes, a couple of old ladies with brown paper parcels and old M. Flagy who'd been visiting his granddaughter for the holiday."

"Did she take the bus?" asked Paul abruptly.

"Yes—I mean, I imagine she did."

Paul knew he was lying. Jean-Claude might be timid, but he was inquisitive too. He would have driven a little way, turned off, and doubled back on foot to observe. But why not say so?

"Are you in love with Arlette?"

"But she is a married woman! And I am her cousin." He blushed and slowly rubbed his greasy hand on his overalls. Arlette used him, of course, perhaps partly because he was a good dancer, but mainly because he was a mechanic and always had access to a car. Naturally she would have flirted with him —although Paul didn't think it would have gone further than that, not with Jean-Claude—and, equally naturally, he, good-natured and slightly dim-witted as he was, might have imag-ined himself enamoured of her, might *be* enamoured of her.

"So you saw nothing?"

"Nothing, Monsieur—Paul. Nothing. I swear!" But he looked away, shifted his feet awkwardly.

Paul could have pressed him, but it was not necessary, and he had another source now.

M. Flagy had a house on the outskirts of Croze, where long before the war he had been a prosperous grocer. Inside the high walls which entirely surrounded the house there was a good acre of garden immaculately kept—fruit trees in neat rows,

141

apple, cherry, plum, peach, apricot, quince, with an espaliered fig tree against the south wall, a rare patch of lawn, red-currant bushes and raspberry and black currant, vegetables in serried ranks and great blocks of flowers, roses and marigolds, red-hot pokers and foxgloves. As Paul sat on the terrace under the trellised vine and drank his small glass of cassis, it was a world entirely away from the world, a very old world of timelessness and silence. And M. and Mme. Flagy were very old too—and tiny. He was entirely bald with an immense grey moustache, and she was bent almost double with arthritis or rheumatism. But they were both bright-eyed and absolutely alert.

M. Flagy knew at once who Paul was and his courtesy was too innate for any surprise. As they sipped their cassis beneath the canopy of young green leaves that threw patterns of light on the flagstones, he said simply, "I met your wife yesterday on the bus, with that cousin of hers, young Vernaie of Jeandeaux. How very kind of her to go all the way to Nice to visit your grandfather. What a pleasure it is when one is old to receive visits from children and grandchildren."

"And great-grandchildren," Mme. Flagy murmured with a smile. "Although Louis really prefers to go and see them himself—he was always a great traveller."

"You exaggerate a little, my dear; most of my travelling was done in the army—after the war, you know." He brushed his moustache with one finger. "Yes, they sent me to Africa and then to the West Indies—I acquired a taste for the heat."

"When Louis retired we thought of moving to the south, to the coast by the sea."

"It's true, but it would not have worked. No, one must stay in the place where one knows who one is. Would you not agree, M. Molphey?"

Later, standing at the door in the wall, about to leave, Paul said, "The war you referred to—which war was that?"

"Ah! I shall be ninety-six on my next birthday, so you can work it out for yourself, my dear sir." He caressed his moustache again. "Françoise, you see, does not care to talk about the war—although I tell her that no one recollects it now except us."

As they shook hands, Paul took a last look at the garden as it lay in the sunshine, peaceful and triumphant. He left the car at the gate and walked slowly into Croze, illuminated by a kind of happiness—and trust. Neither M. nor Mme. Flagy would mention his visit, he was sure. He was equally sure that they were not without an inkling of why he had come. He had received his answer without even posing the question.

The station was little used these days and there were rumours that the whole branch line would soon be closed down. By his accent, the clerk was not a local man, but he remembered the young honeymoon couple who looked so happy, although he'd thought it odd there was no one to see them off. Perhaps, he said hopefully, they were eloping?

"I happened to be in Croze and I thought I would merely verify that they caught the train."

"Oh yes, they caught it. And you would be . . . ?"

"The lady's brother. And what time would they have arrived in Nice?"

"Nice, Monsieur? They were not going to Nice—Nice is for old people. They were going to Paris—Paris is where you go when you're in love, eh?" He winked and would probably have nudged Paul if the bars of his cage had not prevented it.

"Thank you." As Paul left the ticket window, he heard the clerk mutter, "The brother—my eye!"

Paul recounted an abbreviated version of his detective work.

"Guy Vernaie, Mon Dieu!" Thérèse's face was pale and her mouth drawn tight. "It's not possible."

"Of course it's possible. Anything's possible with that young cockerel."

"It's your family, Charles!" she said sharply.

"Family! My great-aunt's grandson is my family? Nothing to do with me."

"People will say it is."

Charles stared at her wordlessly—it was true, but it was a

fine point: the disgrace would fall chiefly on Thérèse. Charles's portion would be ridicule.

"And it's your daughter," she said, pressing home a useless advantage.

"I hope I can be sure of that."

"Charles!"

"And who brought her up while I was away slaving my guts out?"

"You spoiled her, you always spoiled—"

"Hold your tongue," he said roughly. "Get us some coffee." When she had disappeared into the pantry, he turned to Paul. "Well—what are you going to do?"

"I have telephoned to my cousin Edouard in Paris—I think Arlette might try to get in touch with him. Not now, but later. It's a possibility."

"What about your apartment in Paris—surely she will go there?"

"It was not mine. I broke the lease this year."

"Not yours? But you . . ." He stared at Paul for quite a long time. Then he shrugged. "Like that, eh? Well, how do you propose to find her?"

"I am not going to find her. If she has gone, she has gone. I cannot force her to come back."

"So that is all you will do—nothing?"

"What would you do?"

"Me?" He gave a little jerk of his head to indicate the shotgun hanging over the door. "If any wife of mine ran off with another man, I would kill her. I would kill him too."

"Why?"

"Why? You have to ask? Because she is a whore, a piece of filth, a—"

"Shut up, Charles!" Paul used his most schoolmasterly tone.

"Don't you talk to me like that in my own house!" The farmer's body tensed and his face seemed to sharpen, and Paul saw that he was on the edge of the fighting rage that had more than once led him into trouble.

144

"There's no good us quarreling. You don't believe what you say. One would have to be demented to kill for such a reason."

"And you are not demented?" Suddenly Charles laughed. "No—you are hardly even angry, are you, my poor little schoolmaster!"

"I don't believe . . ." Paul clenched his hand to stop the fingers trembling. "I don't consider I have a very good right to be angry."

"Of course you have the right! My God—your wife runs away with another man and you say you haven't the right to be angry? What is the matter with you?"

"It's not so simple as that. Or perhaps it is. I was not what she wanted."

"What she *wanted*—shit. You were a good husband, weren't you? Too good. You're a decent man, you have a job, money, security, you gave her children, looked after her—you didn't get drunk, you didn't beat her. In the name of God, what more could she want?"

"She wanted to get away from here. She wanted to live in Paris, she wanted gaiety, wanted to dance, she—"

"Pah! That's all very well—but those were mere dreams."

"And who gave her the dreams?"

"Dreams are dreams—it doesn't matter where they come from. Any fool knows one does not live by dreams. And she'll find that out, the poor little idiot. When Guy gets tired of her, what'll she do then? She'll be penniless, without any qualification—all she's fit for is to bring home the cows. She'll come running back to you with her tail between her legs."

"I don't think so, Charles." He hesitated—he hadn't mentioned the other visit he had made in Croze, the visit to the bank. It was not, after all, their business. "No, I think you're wrong there."

"You think so? Maybe—maybe you're right." He began slowly to roll himself another cigarette. "Probably she'll take to the streets like the whore she is."

"Charles—how can you say such a thing?" Thérèse turned on the light and put the coffee pot on the table. "Why—I expect she, she just wanted a little holiday. Ma foi. You know how feather-brained she is—she just didn't calculate the consequences. Oh no, I'm quite sure she'll come back." She sat down, poured the coffee and pushed the box of sugar across to Paul.

Charles licked the cigarette paper, stuck it down and rolled the cigarette between thumb and forefinger caressingly. "Maybe. But I'll tell you something, Thérèse. She'll never set foot in this house again."

"Charles!" Her apron was clutched in her fists. Under the naked bulb, her face was stricken, scored with bitter lines of age, although she was only just past forty. "Charles, she is our daughter."

"No daughter of mine." He struck a match and the brief flare lit hard, sharp points of light in his eyes—like little glitterings of satisfaction.

Paul stood up. "I must go. It's late. The twins . . ." He moved around the table and touched his mother-in-law on the shoulder. "I'm sorry."

Thérèse raised her face to him. "She's a decent girl. You believe that, don't you, Paul? She doesn't mean any harm."

"No, mother, she meant no harm, I'm sure of that."

Charles gave a little shrug, then he stood up too. "Come on. I'll give you a hand with the girls."

They carried the twins out to the car and put them on the back seat and Paul fixed the wooden slat he'd made to stop them tumbling to the floor.

From the open door of the farmhouse came the sound of sobbing. And then a cry. "My baby—oh my baby!"

Charles drew on his cigarette. "You should have beaten some sense into her."

"Perhaps." He got in the car and started the motor. He leaned out of the window and shook hands, then drove carefully out of the gate. In the mirror he saw the figure of the farmer outlined against the light from the kitchen—cap on head, hands in pockets, unmoving.

At home, he gave the children their final feeding and changed them—there would be no bath tonight. Reluctantly he went into the bedroom. He had spent all day in confirming what he already knew—this was merely the last, but necessary, verification. The room was neat and ordered—some odd scruple had even led her to make the bed. There was nothing in the drawers, not even a hairpin, and the mirrored wardrobe was empty; she had taken everything, her summer hat, the red dress, the fur coat. How had she managed to get it all into one suitcase —or had she spirited some of the things away some days before? He'd forgotten to ask the clerk how many pieces of luggage they'd had with them. He felt under the pillow in some faint hope that she might at least have forgotten one thing—a handkerchief, the rings.

Why now? But he knew the answer to that too. After the birth of the twins, he had not only terminated the lease but had also instructed the notaire to have the contents of the apartment auctioned off—goods and chattels, objects, paintings, furniture, clothes, memories. The cheque he had received at the end of June and deposited in his bank at Croze was for almost as much as Bernard had left him in cash—everything he had grown up with and taken for granted had been of great taste and much of it of considerable value. The oils in the bedroom had included a Manet and a Sisley, the old plates on racks around the dining room had been Renaissance, the strange object on the salon chimneypiece was a medieval triptych . . . "A fortune," he'd said to Augustin—and this was another. Arlette had taken exactly half. As he made up the bed with fresh linen —it was his room now—he felt a kind of admiration. She had saved him embarrassment. The bank manager had been most interested in the house they were to build, freely offering advice, services, a mortgage. Mildly Paul had revoked her authority to write cheques on his account. They had shaken hands and smiled all round.

And Paul smiled now too a little. It was not Guy Vernaie who would desert her—she had used him for her escape, just as she had used Jean-Claude for her convenience—but Arlette who would rid herself of the mountebank and set herself up in something: a bistro, a *salon de beauté*, whatever it was, a hard-headed little business in the great metropolis.

He dumped the dirty sheets in the hamper in the kitchen. He stood there, listening. The house was silent.

He moved slowly, limping, out onto the terrace. "I am a young man," he murmured to himself.

It was not late. The garden was quiet, solemn in the dusk. Perhaps, if he lived long enough, he would be able to make a little paradise of it, like the green and coloured bower of the Flagys.

He looked up the hill. The sky was opalescent. Sharp against it were the haymakers—cart, horse, man on the stack, men on the ground. Fat Robert, lazy, late and indigent. Precise black silhouettes, they moved silently in some kind of soundless, ordered dance.

And he could have danced with her.

He watched—until the light faded and the men were gone.

When Fat Robert died—in the middle of a meal which he'd begun with six dozen snails—Paul let the field to the surviving Lombard, much to the disgust of two or three farmers, among them Charles. But since Augustin's death the field was Paul's to do with what he wanted—and what he did *not* want was agricultural machines grinding about on top of the hill. It hadn't been easy to persuade the Lombard to take the field, and the farmers would have been even more disgusted if they had known the derisory rent. At the end of nine years he had renewed the lease at no rent at all, merely on the under-

standing that the man would do the heavy work in the garden
—the digging and the picking and the more difficult pruning.

And, with the help of the Lombard, Paul had completely
remodelled the garden, terracing it to avoid its awkward slope,
making brick paths and steps from level to level. He'd had built
high walls on the north and south sides and planted a fig tree
against the latter, and a low wall had replaced the barbed wire
barrier separating the garden from the field—for he wanted to
be able to look up to the hill. He'd removed the plum tree with
its smashed and damaged branches, which had never really
recovered from the hailstorm, and planted two dozen assorted
fruit trees in four symmetrical rows with a lawn beneath them.
He possessed the only lawn mower in the commune and, apart
from the daily walk to and from the schoolhouse, mowing the
lawn was his only form of exercise. There was a lilac tree in
each of the four corners and he had trained a wisteria on the
south wall of the house, "that ugly stucco thing," and box and
lavender lined the walkways. In the centre, occupying one entire level, was a solid block of flowers—thick, vivid stripes of
orange and pink, scarlet and yellow. The vegetables were in
the one flat patch that ran straight from the kitchen door to the
hill wall, rows of lettuce, peas, beans, cucumbers, tomatoes,
carrots, onions, shallots, garlic, cabbage, cauliflower, beets,
Jerusalem artichokes, leeks, potatoes, flanked by strawberry
plants and raspberry, red currant and black currant bushes.

Although it had the logic of easy access, it was a garden
without style. Yet it had a certain grace—it was what he
wanted. As he drove in the gates on his way back from the
station, glimpsing the garden quickly, he thought really that it
was his only unblemished, and unshared, achievement. Unshared because neither of the girls had appreciated it, although
Agnès had been adept at bottling and preserving and jam making—and had been busily occupied in doing so until her departure ten days ago. It was a skill, like her excellent cooking, that
the nuns would certainly find good use for. By the time she

was nine or ten she had already been quicker and more competent at every household task than he, and yet—yet there had been a lack of domesticity, of warmth, as though every task was a duty, willingly and unsparingly undertaken, but without joy or pleasure. Perhaps she would find that joy in the service of Christ; perhaps all this time she had merely been working for the wrong master—although, he thought wryly, Christ would be unlikely to exclaim over the perfection of her mayonnaise or the excellence of her pickles or her raspberry tartlets. But then for her last few years Agnès had been apparently indifferent to praise, would greet it with, at best, a gentle smile. Her last few years—he sighed, recognizing that in his thoughts she was already in some way dead.

And then he laughed suddenly. "How can she be alive when her heart is above her head on the wall?" Arlette had once asked ironically. Arlette? Hélène. He paused with his hand on the bottom stone step and his hand on the rail. Why had he made that confusion—why now? Because—and he clutched the rail tighter to steady himself—because of course this morning Hélène had reminded him of another indelible occasion. Sitting beside him in the car, with her suitcases in the back, she had hardly been able to stay still and, as they waited on the platform for the train to Paris, her bright-eyed vivacity had been as bridal as her mother's all those years ago. When, with the usual futile parental caution, he had murmured about possible disappointment, the limitation of expectation, she had simply said, "Papa, chéri," and kissed him on the lips as she always did and mounted the train and in two minutes was gone. Gone to Paris, gone to the little "studio" Edouard had found for her, gone to study, to love, perhaps to find her mother, who knew? And although she had promised to come back at All Saints and Christmas—and she would—he knew that her heart had left this place, indeed in a sense her heart, no more than Agnès's, had never been in it.

As he came to the top of the steps Paul was pleased to see the Lombard in the vegetable patch. In his black hat, long coat, trousers bound with string beneath the knees, he stood as still as any scarecrow.

"Bonjour, m'sieur," he called, and, after a moment, the figure turned and nodded.

Paul went to the kitchen and took a bottle from the refrigerator and filled two tumblers with cold white wine. Holding them in his hand, with the bottle tucked under his arm, he paused and looked around—Agnès had left the kitchen immaculate, but now there was an indefinable grubbiness about it. The tile floor needed mopping, the deal table could do with a scrub. He was out of practice; he would have to get used to living alone again. He frowned slightly—for he found the thought did not entirely displease him.

Wondering, he went out to the garden and handed a glass to the Lombard. They drank in silence. The man seemed unchanged from the days during the war when Paul used to look out on him working in Mme. Thibault's garden, ageless with his three-day stubble and his hair without a touch of grey, although he must be in his sixties at least. His face was expressionless, though the deep-set black eyes were always watchful; Paul felt that he was aware of, and somehow in tune with, every living thing in the garden—from the smallest ant to the first withering leaf on the pear tree. Here was one person who needed to be taught nothing about the "Flora and Fauna of Our Commune." Paul smiled at the memory of his dismally failed attempt to educate the locals—on the first evening four people had attended, on the second only one. He was at best an adequate teacher—in him, Augustin's logical lucidity was reduced to arid strictness—but all the same he was puzzled by his failure until slowly he came to realize that it was because of his one faithful pupil, Béatrice D'Ornay. It was his first hint of the ostracism from which she suffered—no, not the first hint, but the first to strike home, because he didn't listen to gossip and, anyway, since the departure of Arlette, few people talked to him.

Although he disliked the arrangement, he had been forced to

leave the children with Thérèse during school hours—telling himself that at nine months they were not impressionable. And he had mornings and evenings and weekends with them; but that did not leave him much time for anything else, his abortive course being the exception. Nevertheless he had called several times at the lonely old mansion on the hill, but Mme. D'Ornay had always refused to see him. In fact she had seen no one since that week in June when Hémeric had come down and, by pulling God knows what strings, had killed the scandal— Ursule, a suicide, shamefacedly interred in some secret place, Morine spirited away by the archbishop, no mention of baby or abortion, no charge of murder or of manslaughter, no publicity. A masterly performance, but it hadn't fooled the village —which had rendered its own cruel judgment.

Paul only realized exactly how harsh the judgment was when, early that November, the old lady died. It was a morning of steady, icy rain when she was buried and, apart from Fley, the new *curé*, only Paul and Béatrice and Hémeric D'Ornay attended—and it wasn't the weather that kept the villagers away.

As they stood uncovered at the graveside, Paul watched the son—now the master—of the house. He must have been a good fifteen years older than his sisters, but he could have been any age. He was a large, pale man, very blond—an unpleasant parody of Ursule, for he had none of her lightness; indeed, Maître D'Ornay was impressively ponderous, as though all the weighty affairs with which he had to deal had added their heaviness to him. The day he had come to the house to question Paul, his manner had been overbearing, almost accusatory. As the funeral ended, he dismissed Paul with a curt nod and a handshake, as though he would have liked to consign him to the same obscure corner of the earth where his dead sister lay.

Paul embraced Béatrice; the following week he went up to the "château" to call on her. To his astonishment he found her in the middle of packing. In her quiet, almost shamefaced, way, she told him that her brother had consigned her to the farmhouse at St. Remi, the rentals of the land attached to it to be hers to live on. Paul was shocked—the income would be barely enough for a mouse to survive on, and there seemed a peculiar sadism in banishing this innocent creature to the very house in which Morine and her sister had made their frantic and pathetic love. And at that moment Paul had a luminous idea, which he was never to regret.

"Béatrice—you know my situation. Every day, during school hours, I am compelled to leave my children with my mother-in-law and then to fetch them in the afternoon. This is not an ideal arrangement from her point of view, nor from mine. I need someone to look after them at the house during the day. It seems to me you would be the suitable person for such a task—would you undertake it? Of course there would be a small consideration, but chiefly it would be a great service to me—and to the children."

She had demurred at first—her brother might object, she'd had no experience with babies, what would the village say? But it had not been difficult to persuade her to agree. "I accept," she had said in a surprisingly strong voice and had given Paul a smile which illuminated her whole face.

So she came, and all was changed.

She would bicycle up in the morning and back again in the evening, promptly at six. Even on the few occasions when the children were ill, she never stayed the night. Little by little she began to tell him of her life in the village. She was utterly and completely ignored: when she went to buy bread or groceries, the other customers would fall silent; at mass no one looked at her; in the village no one greeted her; nobody ever called at her house, not even the tradesmen's vans would stop. Nor did they exempt her dead mother from this punishment; the flowers Béatrice placed on her grave would be scattered or trampled by the next day.

The girls thrived; at eleven months they could utter noises that sounded a little like "Papa," and they were adept crawlers, particularly liking to unlace Paul's shoes as he sat at table. On their birthday, Christmas Eve, Béatrice baked and iced a cake for each of them and they were delighted—the candles had to be blown out and relit again and again. While they slept after lunch, Paul and Béatrice hung the parlour with mistletoe and holly and set the tree in a pot; they stuffed two sabots with sugar almonds and raisins and a clementine and a red apple and little lavender bags in the shape of rabbits which Béatrice had made and two small squirrels which Paul had painstakingly whittled from lime wood in the winter evenings.

Later they wrapped the presents, including two small coral bracelets sent by Augustin from Nice. Paul had written to him at Arlette's desertion and hinted that he would be more than welcome to make his home at La Roche once more. Augustin had replied: "I accept with increasing pleasure the old man's lot of solitude. A little sun, a little wine, a short daily promenade are all my needs. The idea that old age and childhood have some peculiar affinity is one that I would prefer to leave others to test. I am content to remain in memory and affection, as always . . ."

It was the first of five happy Christmases which Paul and Béatrice were to spend together. Yet that afternoon, beneath the happiness, Paul was on edge. For he had come to a decision. As it began to grow dark, he took a stick and walked down to the village.

He had to wait a long time after he knocked on the presbytery door, but it was opened at last—not by Mlle. Nocent, but by the new *curé* himself.

"Who are you?"

"Molphey, schoolteacher."

"Well, what do you want?"

In the dim light of the hall, he could hardly make out the priest, but he could smell him—wine and old sweat. "I should like a word with you, if you have a moment."

"A moment? Don't you know it's Christmas? What priest has a moment at Christmas?"

"I have a particular reason for coming today—at this season."
Evidently he was not to be invited in.

"Oh well, get on with it then." The words were slurred—
the man was half-asleep and probably half-drunk too. Paul hesitated—this is what he had come for, he hadn't thought it
would be easy.

"I wanted to talk to you about Mlle. D'Ornay."

"Mlle. D'Ornay?" he said loudly and the name rang across
the square. "Oh yes, I know her. Mousy little thing. Don't tell
me she's in trouble too?"

Paul felt his underlying anger seeping to the surface, but he
kept his tone even. "Any trouble that Mlle. D'Ornay has is not
of her doing, Father, but that of your parishioners."

"What about my parishioners?"

"Surely you must be aware of what is taking place under
your eyes. Mlle. D'Ornay has had an unfortunate history, but
she is entirely an innocent party and yet—yet here, in this
parish, she is treated as an outcast as though she had been
guilty of the most vile of crimes."

"So?"

"It seems to me that the time has come for something to be
done about it."

"You do, do you? Why now?"

"It is Christmas, a time, so I understand, of joy and love and
forgiveness."

"And what do you want me to do? Make Christians of them
all?" His laugh came harshly out of the darkness. "You're a
fool, Molphey."

"For Christ's sake, man—you could at least talk to them. I
thought, a sermon—"

"You've come to the wrong man. Yes, I could *talk* to them.
And a fat lot of good it would do. Any influence I have here is
because I understand them and don't try to change them—
which I couldn't in any event."

"But surely you could point out to them that what they're
doing is—is wicked."

"Wicked—that's a fine word. And what d'you think would happen if I did? They'd treat her all the worse—and me in the bargain. You can't change peasants."

"So you won't try?"

"No."

"Then there is no more to be said." He started to turn away.

"Molphey."

"Yes?"

"My advice to you is to stick to your own patch—you're in enough trouble as it is."

"What do you mean? Are you threatening me?"

"I'm not threatening you, I'm telling you."

"What exactly are you telling me?"

"Your association with that woman won't do you any good."

"I believe I can take care of myself."

"It's all the same to me whether you can or can't—or what happens to you. But it'll be the worse for her, and it'll rub off on you."

"I see." He gave a light laugh. "Good-night, Father. Merry Christmas."

"Goodnight, schoolteacher."

Before he had gone two paces, the door slammed. He regretted not having brought the car then. His leg was weak under him as he took the hill and once he stumbled and half fell. At the crest he stopped and leaned against the stone slab set for the pallbearers to rest the coffins on their way down to the church. The sharpness of anger had left him and he trembled in the bitter cold. Disgust dragged him down and he wanted to shout and curse—but he hadn't the habit, didn't know the words. Instead, as he took the lane to the house, he tried to clear his mind, to put a jauntiness into his step, to prepare his smile for the pleasure of his children's birthday, to disguise with gaiety his grief at this most lamentable of worlds.

He said no word of his expedition to Béatrice. It would have wounded her immeasurably, and he knew too that she would certainly leave if she felt that she was in any way harming him.

And, as time went on, Paul had to admit that Fley was right. He did not share completely in Béatrice's ostracism—the villagers continued to return his greetings, the schoolchildren remained respectful—but gradually he became as isolated as Augustin had ever been. Even his parents-in-law were uneasy in his presence. His duties as secretary to the council were hampered at every turn—his suggestions were hardly considered, automatically quashed. And on every issue he found Fley's brutal hand behind the opposition. Paul wanted a small sum set aside to buy an old car and pay the retired hedger and ditcher to drive the old ladies on the outer reaches of the commune back and forth to mass on Sundays and to Croze twice a week for shopping or to visit relatives; Fley wanted the money for a basketball court for the young people. Fley won. He prevailed in every instance, mainly because he was genuinely popular—an adopted orphan himself, he had been brought up on a farm not twenty miles from Ste Colombe and he did perfectly understand his flock. But he was also ill-educated, narrow-minded, foul-mouthed and mulishly obstinate. Paul detested him and everything he stood for.

As time passed this anticlerical contempt became only deeper, while Béatrice's unobtrusive and unquestioning piety remained intact. She was a good woman, not beautiful like her sister, but with a delicate, shy charm under which lay a great deal of common sense. For five years they were each other's only human company; yet, even apart from religion, they had little in common. Even their shared interest in nature was of a different kind—hers, oddly, was scholarly and scientific, while his was rather aesthetic and domestic. They did not talk very much; he would give her the news of the village—marriage, deaths, births—but he told her almost nothing of his life. She would tell him what the twins had done that day and, later, what they had said.

The children were their true common ground. Béatrice had a gift, a way with them which was true and loving. Even when she began reading them little devotional stories, he did not

157

express his disapproval. She was, ironically, doing for him the duty he had sworn to do himself and, he reflected, the girls would have to know the devotional myths and the apparatus of religious observance—the Virgin above one bed, the Sacred Heart above the other, the crucifix in the corner, the whole superstitious lore—the better to reject it when reason prevailed.

"Papa," Hélène said one day when she was five, "when I am grown up, you will take me to paradise."

He saw Béatrice look up from her sewing. He said seriously, "And where is paradise, Hélène?"

"Why—there!" she said, surprised, pointing to the north. "You know, the shining place with gold on all the roofs."

"Ah—Paris?"

"Yes—paradise."

"Very well. I will take you—when you are grown up." He smiled. "We will go dancing together."

But in the end he had let her go alone. He bent down and picked up the bottle and refilled the Lombard's glass and his own. He was beginning to grow bald and the sun was hot on his head. Soon he would have to take to wearing a hat.

It was shortly after the conversation about paradise that Béatrice told him that, when the children started school that autumn, she would not be coming back.

"But why?" he had protested. "Of course they will not be at home so much, but they need you, Béatrice—they love you."

"I know, Paul. But in September they will be joining the community—with their father as schoolmaster it will be difficult enough. They need no extra burdens."

"Burdens?"

"You know what they say about us in the village as well as I do—it is stupid and unkind—but they say it and their children will believe it."

"So what? What do we care? We are used to it."

"I don't care for myself. But if we give them cause for scandal now, it is the girls who will suffer—it's not just that they will

158

be tormented and teased, but they will be torn by a conflict of loyalties. They will grow up without faith or trust in anything."

He argued on and off for hours, days, but she was not to be moved. And he knew that in a sense she was right. All that summer she showed no sign of sadness—she was as good and happily gentle with the girls as ever. It was only on the last day of August when she got on her bike to ride down the hill for the last time, that there were tears in her eyes.

"Adieu, Paul."

"À bientôt, Béatrice."

But it was a long time before he saw her again. He had lost her.

And it was perhaps then that he lost the children too—or perhaps it was only then that he became aware of the natural cycle of loss. They were not outwardly much affected by Béatrice's leaving—they were never boisterous children and, if now they were a little quieter, a little less gay, it could have been put down to their starting school, the daunting realization of a wider world. And perhaps he had tried to protect them too much. He worried a lot. Every day as they walked to school together, their hands in his, he hurried them past the ruined barn—gripped by the fear that the wall would collapse on them. His efforts to have the building torn down or repaired —he had even offered the owner, a recalcitrant businessman in Lyons, to pay for it himself—had come to nothing; the council had even succeeded in preventing it being publicly condemned. Perhaps he was a fool—the wall never did fall.

Shortly before Agnès left for the convent, they invited Béatrice to a farewell dinner. It was the first time she had set foot in the house for twelve years. Although approaching forty, she was little altered, except for being more talkative—a change probably due to the three young orphans she'd finally been permitted to take in as foster children. Paul had fought long and hard with the Board to get her that permission against the opposition of almost the entire commune (much of it expressed

159

in vicious anonymous letters, some of which were certainly written by the "good women" of the parish). Only Fley, maybe because of his own orphaned childhood, had for once held aloof.

Agnès had cooked an exquisite little dinner and Paul brought up his Pommard and champagne to go with the raspberry soufflé. The meal was astonishingly lively—the girls responding to a streak of gaiety he had never seen in Béatrice before. Hélène, as usual, had talked the most—about Paris, mainly. Béatrice had reminded her of her equation of the city with paradise and then asked her in whose house she was going to live.

"Oh, I'll be on my own. But that's all right. Cousin Edouard has found a nice place for me. Cousin Edouard will look after me." Then she glanced at Paul as if in sudden doubt. "But you never told me—what is he like? Is he like you?"

"Me? Oh no. No, he's not at all pompous—very quick, urbane, kindly. He is a successful man."

"I think she means," Béatrice said mischievously, "is he handsome?"

And as she and Paul laughed, they both saw at the same moment that the girls were blushing.

"Ah, Paris," Béatrice said quickly, "Paris is a dangerous place. Do you know how to scream, Hélène?"

"To scream? Well, I suppose so. I've never tried."

"Oh but you must try, you must practise. Would you like me to show you?"

"Yes."

So Béatrice threw back her head and uttered a piercing yell that caused Paul to knock over his glass.

This time they all laughed.

"Now you must try, my dear. No, you can't do it when you're smiling. Oh dear me, no, that's not loud enough at all." At Hélène's third attempt, Béatrice was satisfied. "Good—that will bring them running. My father taught me how to scream when I was a very little girl."

After the meal was over and while the others cleared the

table, Paul took Agnès out onto the terrace. It was her next to last night. Sitting side by side in the quiet bower beneath the wisteria and the vine, Paul thought that if he had taught Agnès to scream perhaps she would not have had to suffer that terrible afternoon with Thibault. He felt awkward—he had never found it easy to talk to this daughter. Searching for something to say, he began to speak about his own life, about his own going away from home at just such an age as hers, about what he had found, about his dreams, and what he had lost. After what must have been a long time, he stopped. He had completely forgotten her.

"I'm sorry, Agnès. I didn't mean to burden you with all that."

"It is not a burden, Papa—it is a gift."

Looking at the outline of her face in the darkness, he was for a moment stung by his neglect of her. But, he said to himself, she would be safe now, in good hands—she was going to a place where she would never need to scream. Unless, he reflected, it were with boredom.

Now, standing silently drinking in the garden which his daughters had never loved, Paul thought that departure was a kind of consummation. He could easily have gone to Paris with Hélène, seen her safely installed in her studio, shown her round, taken her dancing. No matter that Paris was no paradise to him, Ste Colombe wasn't either. So why did he stay? Because he belonged? No one else thought so; he would always remain a foreigner even if he lived to be eighty—and he was little respected, largely ignored, and not liked at all. He had become solemn and sometimes, as Hélène had said, rather pompous. Surely, once, he'd had the trick of affection and laughter and friendship—he had lost that too, but, if he went somewhere else, might he not get it back? Maybe, but then he would lose the garden. And hadn't he unfinished business here?

He took the Lombard's empty glass and they shook hands. The man nodded—as if to acknowledge a long conversation they'd had together—then turned and let himself out by the gate in the wall. Paul watched him limp slowly up the hill until he disappeared over the skyline. As he picked up the bottle and moved toward the empty house, Paul thought that at least the garden would not leave him.

All Saints. He closed the parlour door behind him and stood for a moment without moving. He was cold and wet—and tired. He tired easily these days, and the outside steps were a struggle, particularly when they were slippery with rain. Yet he'd not had an exhausting day. He'd woken as usual at six and lain awhile half-dreaming of the baby days when he'd been aroused by infant murmurings and cluckings. He'd made coffee, worked a little in the attic. Later he'd driven Mme. Thibault down to mass—which he generally did in winter or when the weather was bad. In a strange way he rather enjoyed these little trips to the village. He'd gone into the café and drunk a couple of grogs. Things were changed now—they didn't lower their voices when he came in, and today Postman, long since retired but still the commune's most articulate atheist, had even invited him to take a hand at cards. He'd refused, but one of these days soon he would accept. As he waited at the church door for Mme. Thibault, everyone greeted him, several shook his hand; he only had time for a quick word with Béatrice, for she was busy shepherding her foster children— three retarded adolescent girls from the big home over at La Salle. Then he was caught by Mme. Bouquin; the elderly midwife had become garrulous, slightly senile perhaps, and liked nothing better than to rehash her more difficult births: "Oh we had a hard time, didn't we, M. Paul? And on Christmas Eve, too. And three of them—why, I thought our Dr. Mullet was going to faint. Ma foi." Then, suddenly earnest, as though recollecting her other role (though she had passed on her witch lore to her niece and was no longer active herself): "Too beautiful to live, I said, and I was right, wasn't I? At least about the little boy?"

Paul hung his raincoat on a hanger in the kitchen, spreading an old newspaper to catch the drips.

Then the usual huge lunch at his in-laws and the usual rigmarole about the girls. He'd not been hungry, but they ate as enormously as ever; they did not seem any older—Thérèse had a bit of grey in her hair and Charles was completely bald, though, if you didn't know, you couldn't have told, because he never took off his cap. A disinterested observer, Paul thought, would have put all three—mother, father, son-in-law—at much the same age. Even Jean-Claude, very fat now, greedy, the loose lip more pendulous than ever, did not seem much younger. He was still a mechanic, still unmarried—did he carry a torch for Arlette even now? Improbable; he earned well, had no dependents and enjoyed his role of *vieux garçon*— perpetual bachelor—too much to think about the lost opportunities of the past. He was complacent and too lazy even for conversation—he was only invited so that he could play cards with them after the meal. But in fact all he did was to go to sleep in front of the television set—a large colour model which he'd given the Buissons for just that purpose. And they watched too, with a kind of abstract avidity, swallowing program after program of mindless and amateurish trash with neither comment nor complaint. He watched the flickering reflections of the screen on their faces—these were the signals of a new world now. He left early.

He shivered; the room was cold. Awkwardly he knelt down and laid and lit the stove. It caught quickly and, leaving the door open, he warmed his hands at the blaze. As he stood up, he realized his hat was still on his head. For a moment he couldn't think what to do with it, then he hung it on the back of the chair behind the stove. He bought a new hat every Christmas, but they hardly lasted a year; this one was crumpled and stained by rain and sun, sleet and snow, but he wouldn't

163

use an umbrella, feeling absurd with his cane. He poured himself a *marc* and drank it quickly. Then he went upstairs.

Sitting at the table, he pulled the morning's page toward him:

> A writer's work is not the expression of his life; his life is the remnants of his work. Life is put at a distance, enhanced, forced, fought, shaped, put off, charged—and so *dis*charged into the work. And inasmuch as the work is whole, enriched, ordered, alive and vibrant, so is the life random, drained, disordered, untouched, unlived. The work is the rape of life, the life is the abused, abandoned body. The work is *found*, the life is lost.

But the work, too, had been lost.

They had run out frantic into the street, but there were no taxis to be found.

"Midday," said Edouard, "an impossible time. Come, we'll take the Metro, it's quicker anyway."

Paul sat frozen, his mind fixed on that other case in the *consigne*—only vaguely aware of the stale urine and tobacco smell of the station, the clanking of the train, the posters swaying by: DU . . . DUBON . . . DUBONNET. They got out at Austerlitz and as they half-ran across the bridge, the sky was beginning to cloud over. At the Gare de Lyon the queue was enormous; when, after three-quarters of an hour, they reached the front, they were confronted with the same half-witted official, who was drunk now and truculent.

"You expect me to search for another case like that? And what about all these people waiting? What's your beef? You handed in your ticket and you got your case—what am I supposed to do about that? And how do I know it's *not* your case —I've only got your word for it. If you don't think plenty of people have tried that one on me before, you must think I'm a half-wit."

"You are!" shouted Paul at the end of his tethered patience.

"Oh I am, am I? And you can go fuck yourself for all I care.

And anyway, I remember you, you damned playboy, *you* pointed the case out to me this morning." He raised his voice for the benefit of the spectators, " 'That's it, that's it!' he says, waving and pointing at me he was, and so I gave it him and off he prances without a thank-you. And now he's changed his mind—made a mistake he said I did. I been here seventeen years, and I've never made a mistake yet. 'This here's filled with apples and cheeses and *eau de vie*,' he says. Some of us would be glad enough of alcohol and cheeses and apples, some of us would be quite happy with that. But, oh no, that's not good enough for monsieur le marquis here. What does he expect? Gold?" He threw back his head and got his laugh and even a few claps.

"Monsieur," said Edouard, putting a restraining hand on Paul's arm, "you must excuse my cousin's distress which may have led him into unintentional discourtesy, but this is a matter of great importance—and the contents of that case are indeed more valuable than gold."

"More valuable than gold?" the man said sceptically.

"Yes. Monsieur, you are evidently an intelligent and experienced official. It seems to me that the solution would be to examine the used receipt slips to see whether or not there is one that matches the sticker on this case."

"You think that, do you? Well, that's as may be." The man was partially mollified by Edouard's manner. "But that's a serious matter, that is—that's a matter for the supervisor."

"Could you then call the supervisor."

"Not a chance. He's out to lunch."

"And when will he return?"

"Your guess is as good as mine."

"Two o'clock?"

"I wouldn't bank on it."

"Nevertheless, we shall come back at two—and report."

"Suit yourself." Then, as they turned away he called out, "These things happen, you know. It's not my fault."

Paul refused to leave the station, so they ate an inferior lunch at the buffet and then sat and drank brandy, which Edouard insisted on. "Perhaps, after all, we should have eaten the apples and cheese," he said; and then, as Paul stared at him blankly, "Cheer up, cousin. We will find it. I fancy our Norman friend is just as anxious to retrieve his case as you are yours."

"Norman?"

"I think he must be Norman, don't you—Camembert and apples, and I imagine those bottles contain calvados? He must be visiting some relative in the south—a sizable town, I'd guess. He wouldn't take apples to someone who lived in the country. No, an old mother or aunt, probably. Even if he has already departed, I'd be surprised if he didn't attempt to reclaim his property on his way back."

But Edouard was wrong.

By means of judicious tipping they persuaded the supervisor to let them search the *consigne*, while he himself found the receipt which matched the sticker on the case Paul had in his possession, which was no proof of anything as they didn't know the number on the other case, which too was gone.

And so began three weeks of nightmare. Everything that could be done was done—advertisements were inserted in both Paris and provincial newspapers, a reward was offered, officials were lavishly tipped. Paul moved between a total confidence that the manuscript would be retrieved and an equally absolute certainty that it would not. He would stand for hours at the window of the apartment, looking out on the children playing, the old men walking their dogs. Then he would go out and march dementedly all over Paris, invariably circling back to the Gare de Lyon, like a vulture after dying prey or a lioness in search of a lost cub. He would come back late and fall into a dead sleep. Sometimes he made love mechanically to Arlette; he drank a good deal, but could hardly eat. He was barely aware of the others—of Clotilde, kind and concerned and consoling, of Edouard, cool and judicious and gentle, of Arlette melodramatically anguished, seductive, offended and bitter. He couldn't pay attention to all that.

One morning he awoke at four with a brilliant idea—he had not tried the *objets trouvés*, the Lost and Found. At six he was there at the Gare de Lyon; at seven, he was explaining the situation and wishing that he had brought Edouard.

"But, Monsieur, as far as I can ascertain from what you tell me, the case is not *lost*. If it is not lost, then how can it be found?"

His temper broke at last and he shouted. He went away. He was not stable, he knew that. He was not convincing. He would sit at cafés drinking and people would stare at him and he'd realize he was muttering, talking to himself. He could not remember what he said. He couldn't remember what he did.

Once, Edouard asked him if he had put his name on the manuscript. He could hardly remember—but no, no he hadn't. He'd just put the title and started writing.

Then one morning, for no reason, he awoke clear-headed, sane, and knew that it was all over. He would never find it. They packed up and that afternoon took the train back to Croze.

At the station, Edouard embraced him and said, "Paul, if this is the way it is, then you must rewrite it. It can be done, it has been done. You know all the famous cases as well as I— Carlyle and Lawrence and—"

"Yes. Yes, thank you, Edouard. I will try."

"You must. You must not give up. It is important, Paul." And Paul thought—although he might have been wrong—that he saw a tear in his cousin's eye, and he was inexpressibly touched. He waved until the small, immaculately dressed figure on the platform disappeared from sight, and it was a long time before he rolled up the window and sat down. He had never seen Edouard since. Nor Paris.

He pushed back his chair and got to his feet. Picking up the page, he placed it on top of the pile with the others. *The work is found, the life is lost.* He sighed.

He wondered for a moment if all the other annual accumulations of manuscript said exactly the same thing. It was always at this time of year that the thought crossed his mind, when autumn had indubitably taken hold. The yearly memorial cycle of mourning was almost complete; but there was one more part of the ritual to be done.

He left the attic and climbed three steep steps to the old hayloft which had been part of the original farmhouse. The light from the small dormer window was dim but sufficient to show him the little suitcase, sitting on an old tin trunk in the corner. He had kept it, perhaps with the superstitious idea that one day the Norman farmer would come to reclaim his property—the calvados was still there, though the apples and cheeses were long gone. "My God, Paul, I can't stand the stink of them anymore—if we don't eat them now, they'll be good for nothing." And at lunch he'd watched her cut the crust from a slice of the camembert, clamp it onto a piece of bread and start to eat it. And it had seemed as though Arlette were eating *him.* Suddenly he'd gotten up from the table and run into the WC and vomited.

He could smell the vomit now—and the stink of the cheese. He went over to the window and opened it and took a deep breath. Leaning out, he let the rain fall on his head and wash his face. He looked down, half expecting to see the Lombard standing in the garden, a timeless monument impervious to the elements. But the Lombard was long gone—under his own patch of earth now—and the garden showed it. Half the potato crop had gone undug, the beech hedge was ragged and too tall to prune, and there was a patch of nettles under the wall. It was feeding upon itself—paradise going to seed and running wild. It was beyond Paul, and he'd found no one else to help him. Charles had happily rented the meadow and turned it to pasture. One morning the cows had pushed through the rotten gate and trampled all over the garden, smashing a peach tree and a quince—so the orchard was gat-toothed now. He'd come home for lunch to find them all over the place and he rushed hobbling at them, shouting and beating their rumps with his stick. It had taken him more than an hour to get them all out; his hat had fallen off and one of them had trodden on it. He wasn't even any good at handling cows anymore. He remembered what he'd screamed at them—*"Sacré Coeur, Sacré Coeur!"* over and over again.

He laughed suddenly and shut the window. He felt better. He felt thirsty.

That Easter vacation there had been a series of short, blustery spring storms and bouts of sharp, glistening sunshine, sometimes both at the same time so that a great rainbow would arch across the valley. At that time of year there was not much to be done in the garden except to mow the lawn, which Paul did the first week. Yet all the same he was surprised not to have seen the Lombard, whose visits over the years had gradually become more frequent until it was a rare week when he did not come at least once, usually on a Wednesday or a Sunday or a holiday, whenever there was no school. They would share a bottle, white in summer, red in winter, in the garden or, in wet weather, standing under the glass shelter on the terrace; they never sat down. They had developed a kind of comfortable, though speechless, companionship, which Paul had missed now for almost two weeks.

One day toward the end of the vacation—it was a morning of lapidary beauty, flat clouds of mauve and violet and pink with silver edges in a sky washed with the palest green—Paul decided to investigate. It was possible, after all, that the man had fallen ill at last.

He parked his elderly green car in the square and, as he got out, a group of children stopped playing and stared at him. He greeted them and, suddenly recollecting their manners, they all called out their good-mornings.

There was no reply when he knocked on the door of the cottage. He peered in the window, but there was no light within and the panes were too dirty to see anything. He saw only the reflection of the children who had recommenced their play but had now stopped again and were watching him. He turned and waved at them. "Be off with you!" They retreated reluctantly to the other end of the square, where they stood under the trees giggling softly. Paul put his shoulder to the door and pushed—it opened with a creak of hinges and he stepped inside. It was a tiny, dim room, made even smaller by a litter of sacks and boxes and old cartons stacked high against every wall. The smell was appalling and Paul realized that all the containers were filled with the mouldering rubbish of half a lifetime. He pushed his stick against a sack and a buzzing swarm of flies rose protesting.

"Bonjour?" he said, but it came out as a whisper. He cleared his throat and tried again, "Bonjour!" No answer. Gingerly he crossed the floor and pushed open the door in the far wall—the stink was if anything worse and the room beyond was almost totally dark. He fumbled along the wall for a light switch, without success—no electricity, probably. He took matches from his pocket and struck one. It burned dully in the foetid air —of choking rot and decay. A range, a table, a bed in the darkened corner, newspapers stuck to the window, ghostly cobwebs floating from the ceiling, and bottles, bottles everywhere. Just before the match went out he spotted a candle stuck in a bottle on the table; as he took a step toward it, there was a soft crunching under his foot. Cockroaches. He took a shallow breath through his mouth and with two more crunching steps reached the table and lit the candle.

The Lombard lay prone on the bed, his hands folded on his chest, the black hat shading his face. Paul cast his mind back —"Martellini," he said gently, although he knew the man was dead. He moved around the table and raised the candle, then,

170

leaning down, he pushed the hat away from the face. The deep-socketed eyes were wide open and gleamed blackly in the candlelight. There was a band of startlingly white flesh where the hat had covered the forehead and then the hair, thick and dark as ever. Paul put his hand on the white brow—it was icy cold. Without his hat, the man seemed naked and stripped, and the deep eyes liquid and vulnerable, like those of a doe at gaze.

Paul carried the candle into the front room, blew it out and set it down on the windowsill. He stepped out into the fresh air and pulled the door to behind him. The children had advanced again—some of the more daring had probably even peeped in the open door.

"Go home," he said. "Go home to lunch. It's time. There's nothing of interest here."

As if to suit action to his words, at that moment a brief shower swept across the square, scattering the children and hurrying a curious housewife into the bakery. Leaning heavily on his stick, Paul watched the rain bouncing off the roadway, pockmarking the gravel, rattling against the glass sides of the incongruous new public phone booth—a mistake, he thought idly: no one wanted to be exposed in the act of phoning, hardly more, in this place, than in the act of love.

In his slow, hobbled manner he went across to the presbytery and rang the bell.

"Monsieur Molphey!" Marie Nocent simpered—he was not an entirely unknown visitor these days. "Why, you're soaked, come in, come in."

"I wanted to use your phone."

"Of course. Father—Father? It's schoolmaster Molphey." She trotted before him to the dining room.

"Ah, Molphey."

"Fley." They shook hands. "How goes it?"

"Not bad." Fley had not long ago come back from a three-month cure. He was a good deal thinner, but he looked drawn and grey, the loss of flesh sharpening the harsh lines of his face. "You want to use the phone? It's in the hall."

171

Dr. Mullet was having one of his offensive spells when Paul got through to him—he was about to sit down to lunch, couldn't possibly come now, etc. "After lunch then," said Paul, "*he*'s not going to mind." He hung up and went back to Fley.

"What's up?"

"The Lombard's dead."

"You've been to his house?"

"Yes."

"What's it like?"

"Horrible."

"That doesn't surprise me. Sit down. Here, Marie!"

"Yes, Father?"

"A litre of white."

"Oh but, Father, you have been so good. You know what they said. Surely—"

"Don't argue, woman. Get it. The Lombard's dead." He gave Paul a crooked smile. "Nobody's going to do the honours, if we don't. I don't think he had a friend in the world."

"He had a brother once."

"Did he? Before my time. Is Mullet coming?"

"After lunch."

"Typical. Marie!" he shouted as she came back in the room with the bottle—Paul couldn't decide whether she was going deaf or whether Fley simply chose to work off his frustrations by yelling. "Marie, he'll stay to lunch—all right?"

"Oh yes, Father, that's perfectly all right." She smiled. Perhaps, on the other hand, she *liked* being shouted at.

"If Mullet can have his lunch, we can have ours." He poured the wine and they lifted their glasses. "*Santé.*"

"*Santé.*"

Ever since Thibault's suicide, Fley had taken to dropping in on Paul once or twice a month, usually at night. Paul would hear the battered little car grinding up the hill—the priest was a notoriously bad driver and, although he hadn't been hurt yet, his car bore witness to numerous small accidents—and there'd

be a rattle at the door and then they would sit and drink together half through the dead winter's long night.

"You remember that smash-up at Dandin last summer—two
carloads of tourists ran head-on into each other?"

"I think vaguely—wasn't someone killed?"

"Three of them, others injured pretty badly. Blood all over
the place. They ran to get Mullet—his house is only a hundred
metres up the road. He wouldn't go—having his dinner.
They'd have to wait till he'd finished, he said."

"I didn't know *that*. I'm surprised he's still in practice."

"No one reported him. They would have if local people had
been involved—but both parties were from Lyons. They went
to Chemilly instead, and he came right away."

"The new chap? I hear he's a good doctor."

"Good? Pah! He's popular because he gives all the women
their contraceptives, without putting them to the trouble of
going to Croze."

"And Mullet wouldn't do that?" Paul smiled.

"Mullet's a man of principle." Fley gave his harsh, barking
laugh and refilled their glasses. After a moment, he said, "He
knew, you know."

"Knew what? Who?"

"Our friend the Lombard—knew he was going to die. How
long's he been dead, would you say?"

"I don't know."

"Decomposing?"

"No—though everything else in that place is."

"Humm. Then that must be it. Ten days."

"Why do you say he knew?"

"Curious thing happened—ten days ago. He came up to me
one evening just as I got back here—almost ran him down in
fact. He gave me a parcel—a bundle of old newspaper, I
thought it was at first. Then he leaned over and tore away a
corner, and I saw it was money. I asked him what he expected
me to do with it. He stared at me in that way of his, then he

173

jerked his thumb at the church and turned on his heel and went back into his house. I shouted to him that I'd keep it—that he could come and get it any time."

"Well, he won't be coming now."

"No."

"How much was it?"

"Seven million two hundred and eighty-six thousand."

Seventy-two thousand eight hundred and sixty—though he drummed it into his children, Paul was the only person in the commune, sometimes, he thought, in the whole of France, who thought in new francs. Still, it was a lot. "A lifetime's wages."

"Maybe."

"What are you going to do with it?"

"Keep it—what else?"

"Keep it?"

"Not for long—it'll be gone in a year in this parish."

"Oh." Paul blushed at the stupidity of his suspicion—did he think that Fley was going to start dressing himself in Cardin suits?

"Still want your taxi for the old women, Molphey?"

"My taxi—yes, yes of course. Do you mean it?"

"Why not? We'll get Postman taught how to drive and he can run it—he needs something to do."

At that moment Marie brought in the smoked ham. Then there was grilled trout, roast guinea fowl, salad, goat cheese and a lemon tart. They were finishing the third bottle when Mullet arrived and they all trooped across to the house. Paul lit the candle and led them into the back room. As they entered there was a kind of throttled cry from Mullet.

"What's the matter?"

"A rat ran across my foot," Mullet said in a wavering voice.

"What did you expect," said Fley, "white mice? Well, what's the verdict?"

"Give me a moment, in the name of God." The doctor's hands trembled as he undid the shirt and put the stethoscope to the chest. "He's dead."

"You don't say?" Fley ripped the newspaper from the window to give a little more light, then he kicked open the door that gave onto the minute garden. Garden was a misnomer—it was choked with rusty cans and broken bottles and tangled with bramble, and from the stink must have been used as an outhouse. "What of?"

"Heart, I should think. Does it matter? Let's get out of here."

In the square the sun was shining, but Mullet was greyish green and sweating heavily. "I've been in some places, but . . ."

"You lead a sheltered life, Doctor," Fley said. "Well, you'd better get hold of your friend Després for this."

"Després?" Mullet was busily wiping his face with his handkerchief. "Després wouldn't come within half a kilometre of this. I'll tell you, Father, there isn't an undertaker in the department whose men would go into that place."

They were silent. There were small groups of people in the square now, but they kept at a decent distance from the three men—doctor, priest and schoolmaster. The Holy Trinity of the community.

"I think you're right," Fley said. "In that case, it's up to us."

"Not I," Mullet said, hurriedly looking at his watch. "My surgery begins at—"

"Molphey?"

"Yes," said Paul slowly, "obviously we shall have to do it ourselves."

"Excellent." Mullet gave a feverish little grin. He began to edge toward his gleaming black Citroën.

"Mullet."

"Yes, Father."

"Tell Després he can come tomorrow."

"Tomorrow. Yes. Tomorrow." He opened the door of the car.

Fley was raising his voice now. "The coffin."

"Ah—a coffin, yes, quite, of course, naturally." He ducked his head into the car.

"Oak."

"What?" The head bobbed up again.

"The best oak Després has," said Fley in stentorian tones.

"Oak? But who's going to pay for—"

"Doctor—you mind your business, and I'll mind mine."

"Oak." Mullet glanced round nervously. "Very well." He put his leg into the car.

"Mullet!" The name rang across the square.

"Eh? Yes? Yes, Father—what is it?"

"Brass handles," Fley roared. "Best brass handles—six of them!"

Mullet's lips moved and he nodded, then he darted into the car, slammed the door and started the motor almost in one motion. The DS rose on its flatulent cushion of air, turned across the middle of the square, forcing the spectators to jump for their lives, then went rocketing blindly into the main road and disappeared from sight.

Fley glared round, daring anyone to laugh. No one did. He slapped Paul on the back. "Come on—to work, my dear schoolmaster."

Three hours later the back room at least had a breathable atmosphere. They had cleaned the ancient, grease-encrusted range, lit it, and put buckets of water on to boil. The junk was thrown in the garden, the floor washed, the ceiling swept clean of cobwebs. Together they lifted the Lombard onto the freshly scrubbed table. Then they threw out the bed. Fley gave Paul a cigarette and, as they stripped the body, they smoked—it was a wise precaution. When that was done, they each took a bucket of boiling water and, Fley at the head, Paul at the feet, they began to wash the corpse. Yet *corpse* was too impersonal a word, for, although he had to take a hard scrubbing brush to the ingrained dirt, Paul felt an odd tenderness for the incredibly white flesh that emerged as he worked on the crumpled foot.

"You're cheerful," Fley said suddenly. He'd washed the head and now he was shaving the beard.

"What?" Then he realized that he had been humming. He

said, "He was a fine figure of a man." What was it? The Beethoven septet.

"Not bad. How old was he?"

"Seventy-two." Paul had already examined the identity card
in the wallet. As Fley deftly wielded the razor and the man's
true face was slowly revealed, it seemed incredible that he
could have been that age. The features were strong but delicate
—high cheekbones, deep eyes, a slightly aquiline nose, a firm
chin, full lips, strongly marked eyebrows, and, now that Fley
had cut the hair back, a fine brow, high and wide. There were
two deep lines from the base of the nose to the corners of the
mouth, but otherwise the face was unmarked.

"Pretty, eh?"

No, not pretty, thought Paul—beautiful. He said, "He has
a look of dignity."

"They often do in death, my friend. Life is another matter.
Here." Fley handed Paul the bottle.

Paul shook his head and turned back to the legs, and after a
while he heard himself humming again.

He had perhaps five seconds' warning.

He had risen early and opened the windows onto a crisp
autumn morning. The rains of the All Saints holiday had gone
and an anticyclone had moved in from the east with lofty,
bright skies and a sparkling clarity in the air. And there in the
far distance just after daybreak—*grand matin*—he had seen
Mont Blanc—a white, glittering crown floating above the horizon. He had stared at it for a long time almost without breathing. Later, as he made the coffee, he had thought of Augustin's
last letter: *I feel now that I would have been better served by spending
my retirement in the Alps. Here, although the Mediterranean air is
salubrious, so they say, I seem to catch the scent of decay. I long for my
dear Sallanches and the imperturbable mountains. But I am too old to
move, and besides, regret is always foolish.*

As he had set off for school, Mme. Thibault was washing

something in a bowl on her terrace in the warm morning sun. "Bonjour, Madame!" he had called cheerfully and raised his hat. She had looked up with a smile, then such a look of horror passed over her face that he stopped dead.

"What—"

"Run, Paul, run! The wall is falling!"

As he stood transfixed for a second, there was a loud crack. He looked up, and the wall was bulging and shifting like a living thing. He launched himself forward with a desperate, limping stride—five, six, seven—then there was a fearful roar, something struck him on the leg, he stumbled and threw himself into the ditch as a cloud of blinding white dust enveloped him.

"Paul, Paul, are you all right? You're not hurt?" Mme. Thibault pulled him choking to his feet.

"Only my leg—something hit my leg." He coughed. He could see nothing.

"I thought you were gone for sure," she said, leading him into the house. She helped him off with his overcoat, then took him to the kitchen sink. He washed his face, washed out his eyes, rinsed the dust from his mouth, put his head under the tap and let the water pour over it.

As he sat at the table, toweling himself briskly, she handed him a glass of clear liquid. His hand was shaking when he took it, so he drank it quickly and put the glass down. *Marc*—he felt the welcome fierceness in his throat and stomach, but it didn't stop the shaking. He gripped his knees with his hands and tried to concentrate on Mme. Thibault as she brushed his coat and his hat.

"Now, let's look at that leg." She knelt and rolled up his trouser leg. It was no more than a graze, a patch of torn skin flecked with tiny spots of blood. "You'll have a nice bruise there tomorrow," she said, dabbing at the place gently with a strip of linen soaked in *marc*.

She looked up at him and he gave her a smile.

178

"A narrow escape." He knew she'd not failed to notice his trembling.

She rolled down the trouser leg. "You ought to stay home today, Paul."

He shook his head and stood up. With one accord they turned and silently looked out of the window. The billows of dust had cleared. It was not just the wall that had fallen; the whole building—wall, roof, beams and chimney—had slid into the lane, smashed down Mme. Thibault's wall and now lay settling at the foot of her terrace. If he'd been buried in that, it would have taken them hours to get him out. It would have been a death as stupid and senseless as Fley's. And if it hadn't been for Mme. Thibault . . .

"Thank you," he said.

"Don't thank me. You should thank God who sent the weather that brought me out to catch the morning sun."

"Thank God, then." He smiled.

"If only you would, Paul. Ah, but you men . . ." She patted his arm, then helped him on with his coat. As she handed him his hat and stick, he realized it was the first time he'd been in the house since Thibault's suicide. She had never even invited him in for an aperitif. But perhaps things would change now —and he had the sudden feeling that they would.

And it was the first time in all his twenty-seven years of teaching that he had been late for school. It might have been better if he'd stayed away, because he was unable to concentrate all day. He felt too shaken to go home for lunch, so he ate in the canteen, which he hated to do. He knew he wouldn't be able to climb over the rubble in the lane, so at the end of the day he was forced to take the long way around, by the upper road, over the hill, and down the field to the house. When he got in he was exhausted. He lay down on the bed and listened to his heart thumping rapidly. It struck him as odd that he'd not had a day's illness that he could recall, apart from colds and a mild bout of flu—nothing to keep him away from school.

179

What would he do if he fell really ill? Well, call in Thérèse or Mme. Thibault, or Marie Nocent or Mme. Bouquin or Béatrice —there were armies of women to look after him, after all. And the men would send up hare and rabbit and pheasant—they did even now, had done so for years. Ever since the death of the Lombard which had seen the cementing of his friendship with Fley, the dogs of gossip had been called off. And when Fley himself had died, some of the respect in which he was held had rubbed off on Paul—though hardly the affection. Still, the generations of schoolchildren he had taught looked upon him with amiable amusement, partly, he thought, because—with his limping gait, his stiff schoolmasterly mannerisms, his wide-brimmed hat—he was easy to imitate.

He got up and made himself a grog. Why was he thinking in this childish fashion? Why seek to persuade himself that they would have grieved had he been crushed this morning? It was foolish to try to disguise the unluckiness of his escape. The others had gone—Fley dead, Mullet carted off to some asylum —why not him?

"No, not you, Molphey, not you. Not yet," he said aloud. He held out his hand and it trembled.

He made another grog. But he couldn't settle down. He wasn't hungry. He couldn't read, and he couldn't face dragging himself up to the attic tonight. There was still dust in his nostrils, ashes in his mouth.

At length, in desperation he turned on the TV. It was a literary interview program—a round table of six authors. As each one was introduced the camera focussed on them—how young they all looked—and then on their books. He felt a spurt of anger at such blatant commercialism and almost turned off the set. But he didn't, instead he prepared a grog.

". . . much pleasure in inviting back Jean-Pierre Montbarbon, who was our guest earlier this year, but who, it was announced this afternoon, has just been awarded the Prix Goncourt for his remarkably moving first novel, *Passages to Tomorrow*. . . ."

A handsome young man, curly hair, intelligent face, flashing smile.

". . . and now, Jean-Pierre, as you are obviously the celebrity this evening, I would like to start with you. One of the remarkable things—the many remarkable things—about your book is that it is set toward the end of the Second World War. To those of us who were alive and, ha ha, adult then, it is an extraordinary evocation of the period. I think I am right in saying that you were hardly yet born?"

"I was born in 1950."

"Then what I would like to ask is why you chose to set it in that period and, having done so, how you were able to give such a remarkable feeling of actually having lived it yourself?"

"Well, as the old adage goes, it is not necessary to have experienced something in order to write about it. In fact, I would go further and say that in some ways it is an advantage not to have experienced it. Although, as far as the evocation of place goes, I do want to emphasize that I have lived most of my life in Varay-le-Grand and therefore know the . . ."

Varay-le-Grand. Paul remembered it—a small town twenty kilometres or so the other side of Croze, notable for a row of almost intact medieval houses and an admirable two-star restaurant he'd sometimes taken the girls to. He wondered if it was still there.

He yawned and drank his grog. The cover of the book was on the screen now and he saw with wry amusement that it was published by P.P. or P.P.M. as it was now—Pascal, Pierre, Molphey. Edouard had prospered—and would prosper more with *Passages to Tomorrow*.

Stirring more rum and hot water into his drink, Paul felt a pang of nostalgia . . . put back the clock a quarter of a century, and he might have been sitting in that chair the young man graced. Montbarbon, curious name—a brand of lemonade. Although of course there was no TV in those days—and he could never have matched that flashing smile. He was drinking too much—the besetting sin of priests, and schoolmasters. He laughed—he'd be better off on lemonade. Lemonade—filthy stuff. What was this—was he jealous?

Yes, he thought, knowing he was already half-drunk, he was jealous—why else had he not read a novel in twenty years? A whole generation of writers had passed him by. My God, it was shameful. "Molphey, you ought to be ashamed of yourself." Now and again Edouard had sent him a P.P.M. novel, but he'd never opened them. He'd hardly moved out of the nineteenth century, consoling himself with George Sand, dozing with Daudet . . .

He held out his hand—it was steadier now. Recovering. Well, all right, he decided suddenly, he would read Mr. Lemonade's book. He would have to start somewhere. He yawned again. He was tired at last. And drunk. He went to bed, but he didn't sleep for a long time.

He was woken by the sound of machinery. He sat on the edge of the bed and rubbed his face. He felt foggy and sluggish. He didn't have the head for alcohol he'd once had. After long evenings with Fley—and they'd often drink five or six litres between them—he would get up as fresh as the rising lark. Fley. He looked at his hands—still shaky. He took hold of the bedpost and heaved himself to his feet.

Opening the window and looking out, he was startled for a moment at the absence of the barn.

"Morning, schoolteacher!"

He looked down at the blacksmith sitting proudly on his mechanical shovel, and his son-in-law with his yellow truck.

"Good-morning."

"Had a lucky escape yesterday, eh?"

"Yes. How long is it going to take you to clear that away?"

"Oh, all day today, easily. Sunday morning, too, I reckon." He was cheerful—he loved his machinery as a child loves a toy.

Paul shrugged and turned away. This morning, again, he'd have to take the long way round to school and back. And it was more of an effort than he'd thought. By the time he got to the top of the hill he was already exhausted. And then there were several houses along the upper road and every inhabitant was out and ready with comment on the accident. Narrow escape, lucky escape, near miss. He nodded and smiled—it was meant kindly—but in the schoolroom that Saturday morning he had difficulty controlling his temper.

When he got home at noon he was ravenous, and angry with himself for not having eaten the night before. What a waste of an evening—drinking grog and watching those literary antics on the screen. But as he ate lunch—a thick Charolais steak, mashed potatoes, braised leeks, goat cheese and stewed apples —he reflected that at least it had given him an objective for the afternoon. He would go to Croze and buy Lemonade's book and perhaps, a break with seasonal habit, he would buy a new hat too.

As the lane was blocked to the right by the fall of the ruined barn, he was obliged to take the hill to the left. It was the more direct route to Croze, but one that he usually managed to avoid. At the bottom of the hill where the lane ran across the main road there was now a Stop sign and, also, a large stone cross, on the plinth of which was inscribed:

In Memory of
FRANÇOIS FLEY
parish priest

who died on this spot
April 1, 1969

Erected by
his grateful parishioners

God protect
France and
Ste Colombe-sur-Saye

183

Fley's two-horse Citroën had emerged blind onto the main road, then jerked to a halt at the sight of a huge truck loaded with logs. The driver had braked, swerved and passed the crossing—but the jolt of the brakes had loosened the lashings and the entire load of logs slipped with a roar onto the road, so completely burying the tiny vehicle that the driver, on getting down, had said, "Thank God at least it missed the car."

There had been nothing but pulp to put in the coffin.

Paul shook his head. He drove to Croze with more than his usual caution until he reached the top of the hill above the town. Suddenly he remembered the day Augustin had driven him in to buy a gun, when the old man, abruptly abandoning his usual sedate style, had swept down the wide hill with smiling recklessness. Paul looked up at the high, white scudding clouds, a signal of change—the good weather would hardly last till evening—but for the moment the sun shone, and he put his foot down on the accelerator. As the speed mounted and the car began to rock and the air whistled at the window, he smiled, and then began to laugh.

He started to brake on the outskirts of town just as he sped past the place where the Flagys' house had been—now the site of a bicycle factory—and by the time he entered the main street he was driving with all his old caution. But as he went into the bookshop and bought *Passages* he felt a lingering undercurrent of excitement. It was the last copy.

"I could sell forty more if I had them," said the bookseller. "I've nineteen standing orders alone for the Goncourt—and I sold fifty-two of last year's winner."

"Very encouraging."

"Oh I shall do better this year—with Montbarbon being a local man. Not that everybody who buys it reads it. But it's a matter of prestige, if you know what I mean?"

"Have you read it yourself?"

"Not yet—that's a pleasure I look forward to having in the

slack weeks after Christmas. I expect you saw the television show last night?"

"Yes. Yes, I did."

"A brilliant young man. Brilliant. We're all very proud of him—he could hardly be more popular around here if he'd won the tour de France." He gave a deferential little laugh.

"Or committed a mass murder," Paul said, smiling.

"Er. Well. Yes." The bookseller looked at him strangely. "That will be thirty-five francs."

It was a relief to get into the hat shop—a long, tall room, with glass cases from floor to ceiling, a huge oak counter, hat stands, mirrors, a glossy parquet floor, it had probably not changed for a hundred years. A quiet sanctuary of the nineteenth century. The gentle old widow who ran it knew as well as Paul did which hat he would choose—it never varied. But they managed to pass fully three-quarters of an hour together, softly debating various styles, chatting about the changes in Croze, mourning the loss of the railway and the hatless generation of tourists.

Afterward he went into the ironmonger's and bought a rat trap. He was fairly certain there were rats in the old hayloft, for sometimes he'd heard their scurrying above his head as he sat in the parlour at night. Though what they found there to interest them he couldn't imagine, and why he should kill them he didn't know. Perhaps he was unconsciously afraid they would penetrate to the attic and start eating his *pensées*— perhaps.

It was half-past four. He couldn't think what to do next. He didn't want to go home. He decided to take the tour of the ruined abbey, which was, after all, what attracted the hordes of summer tourists—on false pretenses, he thought, as, with three others, he followed the guide. There was only one small tower and the remnants of the refectory left, and the local inhabitants knew better than to waste their money on seeing them. He thought of escaping as he had with Arlette at Fontainebleau, but he felt vaguely sorry for the guide dutifully cracking stale jokes and forcing a pedestrian imagination to recreate what was no longer there. The monks seemed to have been a cross between saintly benefactors and inveterate and power-hungry pederasts. Could one be both at the same time? Without experience of any of those activities, it was hard to judge. He stood in the square, pondering the question. He needed a drink. But not yet.

He got in the car and drove slowly to Varay-le-Grand. He would see for himself if the restaurant was still there. The wind had risen and little flurries of leaves blew across the road. The clouds were thickening and, when he arrived at Varay—putting his car in the restaurant's enlarged parking lot—the crispness had gone out of the air, to be replaced by a more bitter chill. The light was fading as he inspected the row of medieval houses—they had been heavily restored since he'd last been there and looked curiously new and toylike—and by the time he entered the restaurant it was dark, though too early yet for dinner. He went into the bar and ordered a glass of sherry—a request that caused a mild flurry until a bottle of Tio Pepe was discovered in a cupboard. So it was still a goodish place, though the decor had taken a serious turn for the worse. In the old days it had been all dark oak, fat, fruity sideboards, red velvet curtains. Now—perhaps in some desperate attempt to belie its name, Le Moderne—it had been done over in mock medieval. A stone wall with a portcullis-like grill hid the entrance, a stone floor substituted for the worn old oak boards, an immense fireplace of raw stone had been shoved at one end with a cauldron hanging by a chain over great logs that had obviously never been lit. This effect was somewhat invalidated by gilt mirrors and a profusion of inferior watercolors on the walls. What an immense expense must have been gone to in order to destroy a true and unpretentious style. It had destroyed memory too— this was not the place to which he had brought Agnès and Hélène. Which was perhaps something to be grateful for.

But the food was as good as ever. He had parsleyed ham and

trout with half a bottle of Chablis, and a bottle of Marcilly—
a wine he'd never found anywhere else—with the duck à
l'orange, and Floating Islands with half a bottle of Sauterne. It
was a very long time since he'd been in a restaurant and he had
to restrain his tendency to gobble ungraciously—in this he was
helped by the proprietress, who remembered him. They agreed
that their families were well, and then he congratulated her on
the decor. He gave her some gossip about the commune, but it
was too far away to really interest her. She became animated
only on the matter of service, which to Paul seemed excellent
but which to her was an agonizing problem—girls now wanted
to be hairdressers (they always have, thought Paul) or be check-
out clerks in the supermarket, few cared to be waitresses or
would consent to the rigours of training. Paul listened and at
the end of the meal was rewarded with a liqueur—he chose a
Benedictine with some faint idea of honouring the monks,
then wished he had taken Poire Williams.

He had drunk just enough to give his driving that edge of
confidence it so sadly lacked. He needed it, for the wind tugged
and pushed at the little car with malign force. He was glad to
get home and soon had the curtains drawn and the stove lit.
But as he sat down at the table with a glass of *marc*, it seemed
to him that something was missing. And then he realized he'd
left the book in the car—and the rat trap too. He thought of
leaving them there until morning—but that was what his out-
ing had been all about, hadn't it? With a groan, he got up. The
wind buffeted him as he went down the stone steps and, coming back up, he had to put his head down and struggle against
it. Northeast and bitter; he hardly remembered it so strong.

He rubbed his hands briskly and drank half the *marc*. Then
he opened the book to see what it was all about. *Passages to
Tomorrow*, by Jean-Pierre Montbarbon. He turned to page one
and read:

Today in my village the bells rang out for peace over a
dreamless people. But dreams there are . . .

187

S ometime in the night the wind had died, for when at about two o'clock Paul came to the end of the last page and raised his head, the house was entirely silent. He sat without moving in the bitter chill of the parlour, waiting for a sound, a sign—rats' feet in the attic—but there was nothing.

He turned back to the beginning and started again, although he hardly had need to read. He knew it by heart. It had come back at last. *Signals of a New World*. Word for word, only the names altered.

When he finished for the second time, it was beginning to get light. His cheeks were wet with tears and he realized he'd been weeping for a long time, perhaps for hours. Weeping for the beauty of it—and it was more beautiful than he could have possibly remembered. But he had stopped now. He carefully dried his eyes, his face.

He staggered to his feet and went through into the living room and opened the windows. With the feeble coming of the dawn, it had started to snow—soft, desultory flakes. He watched the hidden landscape gradually lighten, whiten. The harsh cold of the morning didn't touch him—only the words, round and round in his head, the words falling like snowflakes in the inner part. His words.

He turned to the living room—his daughters' bedroom, with their chests of drawers and their narrow beds ridiculously awaiting their return. He looked down and saw that he was holding the book. Suddenly he was blazing hot. He raised his hand and hurled the book at the wall; it hit the Sacred Heart and they fell together onto Agnès's pillow. He swiveled back to the window and, gripping the sill, leaned far out.

"Cowards! Thieves! Whores!" he shouted. "It's my book. It's mine. Mine!"

The words fell without echo on the flat stillness of the countryside.

"Hello?"

"Hello—I would like to speak to Jean-Pierre Montbarbon, please."

"He's not here. Who's this?"

"My name's not important. Could you tell me when he'll be back?"

"He won't be back. He doesn't live here anymore."

"Then I wonder if you could tell me where he does live, Madame?"

"Who *is* this—are you a friend of his?"

"My name's Molphey. Not exactly a friend, but—"

"Well, you ought to know."

"What?"

"Paris—he lives in Paris! Why can't you people leave us alone?"

"Where . . ." But the connection was broken.

It took Paul another hour to find out that there was no listing for Montbarbon, J.-P., in the Paris directory. But there was a Molphey, E.T.—Paul didn't know Edouard's private address or indeed anything about his home life, except that he was a bachelor.

"Edouard—Paul here. I'm sorry to rouse you so—"

"Paul—my dear cousin. Delighted to hear your voice. How are you? What can I do for you?"

"Edouard, I'm coming up to Paris this afternoon, I wondered if you'd be free for a drink or dinner?"

"You? To Paris? What a miracle! Of course I'm free or, if not, will make myself so. Why don't you come around to the office about seven—still in the same place, as you know."

"The office?"

"Ah—perhaps you haven't heard the news? We've won the Goncourt."

189

"Yes—yes, I had heard. Congratulations."

"Thank you, thank you. We're all very pleased. I think this time it's deserved, which it isn't always. But it means a lot of work—publicity, interviews, all that sort of thing. I shall be in the office all day. Just ring the bell."

"Very well. At seven then."

"Seven—I'm looking forward to it."

Paul made the coffee, took a bath, shaved. All these things were difficult because his hands shook almost uncontrollably. He cut himself quite badly on one cheek with the razor, and there was an unshaved patch under his chin, but he could do no more.

Standing naked in the kitchen, he drank a second cup of heavily sweetened coffee. He turned his back on the garden and stared fixedly at the wall of the kitchen. It was essential to keep his mind clear, detached—as blank as the wall—on the other side of which was the old wartime scar of bullets. No. No, that wouldn't do.

He dressed slowly in his best—white shirt, black shoes, the dark blue suit he'd bought for Fley's funeral, and Bernard's mauve silk cravat. He had trouble tying it, but it was done at last. Below the knot he stuck Arlette's pearl-headed gold pin.

Then he went upstairs and fetched the case from the hayloft and carried it across to the attic and put it on the table, thrusting aside the papers to make room for it. The thick pile of his labourious jottings slid to the floor, the top sheet floating, then settling. He glanced down—let the rats eat them.

He opened the drawer and took out the gun and the box of ammunition. He held the gun for a moment, then went over to the window and opened it. *You won't have much time . . . Don't hesitate, don't think—just do it.* He brought his hand up quickly and clicked the trigger at the white land.

The action seemed to calm him and his hand was steadier as he loaded the revolver. He put it in the case between the bottles of calvados, then he bent down and gathered some of the scattered pages and scrunched them up and wedged them into the case to prevent the bottles from rattling. He shut the case. He shut the window. He glanced around. Nothing forgotten. He was not trembling at all now.

First he was going to find Jean-Pierre Montbarbon, then he was going to kill him.

The train sped unimpeded by the snow, creating its own small storm of flakes, darting toward Paris like a diesel snake striking at prey. When it drew into the second stop, the artificial storm was lulled; but one could not see far—even the patterned roofs of the fairy town were discreetly concealed. When the train moved, the cutlery jingled like sleigh bells, and soon one was in the blind country again. Paul picked at his lunch, drank water, thought of nothing, felt only a mild surprise at his lack of regret for his vanishing beloved homeland. The case lay on the chair beside him—he was armed against nostalgia. As the train approached Paris it seemed to lose impetus, the snake its venom; it slowed, dawdled as the day faded and Paul, drinking cup after cup of coffee, began to feel an unreasonable impatience.

"What's the delay?" he asked the waiter.

"Work on the line, sir."

"Work on the line?" Paul laughed.

"Yes, sir?" said the waiter.

"Nothing," Paul said.

"Very good, sir."

Work on the line on a Sunday night in a snowstorm? He didn't believe a word of it. They were all liars. Hypocrites. Prostituted, thieving bastards. Damned smiling villains grinning and shaking their curly locks, they . . .

"Waiter!"

"Sir?"

"A glass of water—with ice."

"Immediately, sir."

The train was exactly twenty minutes late. He had well over

an hour to kill. He stood in the Gare de Lyon and looked about him. He hardly recognized it—big blue and white signs, glassed-in booths, moving staircases. It was clean and empty and had no smell. He moved toward the sign that said TAXIS, but he was not looking for a cab. He went down the broad steps to the street. After the heat of the train, the icy cold was bracing. The snow had ceased. It would take him an hour to walk, but there was no weakness in his leg as he moved off toward the bridge, the heart of the city aglow with lights.

"Do I look as different as all that?" Edouard smiled quizzically.

"I'm sorry—I was staring." In fact, he had been wondering how to extract Montbarbon's address in an offhand, unsuspicious manner. He focussed more closely on his cousin—slightly plump now, the dark hair silvering and cut fuller, but still small, dapper, smooth in the same light grey suit. The only substantial change was the absence of the thick glasses which had given him a gentle, unfathomable look. "What happened to your glasses?"

"Good heavens, I'd forgotten I ever wore them. I've had contact lenses for years." He laughed and stripped away the foil from the bottle and twisted the wire.

"And I—how am I different?"

"You?" He eased out the cork, but held it close to the opening to allow the bubbles to escape without overflow—just as Augustin had always done. "You resemble your father more and more. You look rather—rather distinguished."

"A distinguished country schoolmaster?" In his ill-fitting blue suit and a shirt too tight around the neck? Paul laughed dryly.

"Why not?" He removed the cork and poured champagne smoothly into tulip-shaped glasses and handed one to Paul. "You know, my dear cousin, in town one tries hard to marry one's sense of literary fair-mindedness to the inescapable demands of commercial survival, but the unremitting effort required to find merit in the inferior does, I'm afraid, result in a certain shoddiness of style." He raised his glass. "To rural refreshment."

Paul paused. "To urban renewal," he said, doing his best to match that style. They were sitting in dark blue leather armchairs with a low table between them. It was a much larger office than before—with a bar and a television set in one corner; the bookcases were glass fronted and many of the books leather bound. "But surely there are compensations for success?"

"I would put it another way—success is the compensation for all the rest."

"Such as *Passages to Tomorrow?*"

"Exactly. A perfect, if rare, example. Have you read it?"

"Yes, I've read it."

"Well?"

"It is—excellent."

"More than excellent—remarkable! I tell you, Paul, when that typescript arrived on my desk, I read it straight through —and then I started again at the beginning and read it a second time. I could hardly believe it. I couldn't sleep for two nights. Remarkable." He waved his hand at his lavish quarters. "It's that sort of thing that makes this all worthwhile, you see." He stared down at his glass and sighed. "It's the sort of book . . ."

"Yes?"

Edouard glanced up. "I was going to say it was the sort of book I wished you might have written. . . ."

For one poignant instant Paul was tempted to tell him—but he caught himself. He could envisage all too well disbelief hardening into commiseration—and the last thing on the face of the earth he wanted was commiseration. He wanted revenge. He wanted a death. He said, "It was a long time ago."

"Yes—a long time. I'm sorry. I don't suppose you ever . . . ?"

"No."

"No." Edouard drained his glass and refilled it. "Well, I thought I'd take you to a small place round the corner—the food is not notable, but the wines are quite superb. You can tell me about life in the country and what brings you to Paris."

"Yes." Paul quickly drank his wine and held out his glass for more. "What did you mean when you said you could hardly believe it?"

"What? Oh—*Passages.*" He frowned. "I was transposing. Actually of course I did believe it—that masterly simplicity of unaffected style, the total authenticity and originality of that voice. Well, what else could one do but believe it absolutely? All I had to see was the typescript with the title and the author's name and address. I phoned him and asked him to come to see me at once. It was then that I was amazed—he's only twenty-four now, you see. I am not so impressed as others seem to be by the exactitude of detail of time and place—after all, he did live in that little village Varay-le-Grand, not so very far away from you, by the way—"

"I thought I recognized some of the descriptions. Though Varay is something more than a village."

"Well, yes. But that sort of thing is not very important—he knows the country and would have talked to people older than himself. No—it is the *feeling* which one wouldn't believe he was capable of evoking so perfectly: that extraordinary mixture of triumph and shame, of high hope and wracking pessimism, of relief and dread, of exaltation even but also of vindictiveness, of confidence but profound doubt—and the whole of this seen and transformed by his particular kind of unshakable vision."

"He must be a—remarkable young man."

"Yes of course he is—quite remarkable." Then suddenly Edouard laughed and his small brown eyes gleamed. "Why am I talking to you like this? No—in fact, he isn't remarkable at all. Apparently. Not that that means anything, of course— some of the best writers are quite the opposite of impressive face to face, tongue-tied and inarticulate, very far from glittering. And personally I would much prefer to deal with a Pinget rather than a Robbe-Grillet. Of course I'm not saying that Montbarbon is like that—he's certainly not inarticulate, and he's intelligent, he was about to begin an academic career, in fact, when I bought the book, but . . ."

"But?"

"Well, I suppose one might say that he's refreshingly unintellectual—oh, he knows the lingo all right, and is most charming. But he simply isn't interested in all that sort of thing, although he laps up the praise—you saw the reviews, I suppose? Marvellous! Look, I must be boring you with all this?"

"Not at all—I have the feeling you want to get it off your chest. What you're saying is that he is not a serious man?"

"Precisely. Thank you." Edouard took a cigarette from a silver box on the table—Paul took one too. "Yes, you see—one of the things that so excited me was not just the book. It is a very good book, in its way a small masterpiece, but, if we are to keep things in perspective—and I mean in the perspective of literature rather than of publishing—it isn't a *great* book. But —and this is what really excited me—here, I thought, are the *makings* of a great writer, or at least a very considerable one. And how many of those do we have. One or two a generation?" Edouard blew a long plume of smoke and half-closed his eyes. It was very quiet in the spacious room, very calm. Paul waited.

"I knew at once the book would do well—very well. It's excellent in its own right, but also the time is right for just this sort of novel. I guessed it would make a great deal of money— and it has, and it will make more, far more now. But I didn't expatiate on this aspect of the matter to Jean-Pierre, although morally I could not refuse him a substantial advance. I told him to go back to his village—his small town, as you tell me it is. And write. Unfortunately, he wouldn't hear of it—had to be in Paris. So I found him a charming little apartment, sublet by one of my authors, on a quiet street just off Cherche-Midi in the *sixième*. It has trees and greenery and calm, altogether a perfect place to write."

Paul drew on his cigarette—drawing patience from it to listen to this rigmarole. But he was getting close. "Where is this patch of paradise?"

"Eh? Oh—rue Jean Ferrandi, you wouldn't know it. But that's not the point—or perhaps it is. He promises me he's writing—half-finished, he says, with a new novel. But he's never there. The only place I can be reasonably sure of getting him these days is Freddy Two's!"

"What's that?"

"A nightclub, my God! It's one of these Left Bank celebrity places—singers and models and bloody actors and advertising men and Brazilian diplomats. But not *writers!* Not, at any rate, serious writers."

"What's wrong with that—perhaps after all those years of rural deprivation, he wants to live?" He had what he wanted —all he needed now was an excuse to leave.

"Live? That's not living, Paul, and you know it. Success is a desperately treacherous thing. You have to be beware of it. You shouldn't give your heart to success any more than you would to a whore. I told him to go home, he would not go. I found him a place to write, he will not write. Paul, I am frightened for that young man."

"So I see." Paul felt suffused with a queer gladness. The man was more worthless than even Edouard could imagine. And Edouard's worry would be ended too tonight. "My dear cousin, perhaps you should go into the real estate business and forget literature."

"What?" Edouard looked at him in astonishment.

"Well, you do seem to be very good at finding people places to live."

"What do you mean?" As he reached for the bottle, he knocked over his glass.

"I was thinking of Hélène."

"Oh—Hélène!" He righted the glass and filled it.

Paul suddenly felt his mind floating, as though it were part of the faintly undulating layer of smoke above their heads. "And," he said softly, "and Arlette."

"Arlette?" Edouard's face greyed—or was it always grey,

grey as the hair, the suit? "I didn't know you knew that she . . ."

"When did she come to you?"

"Paul—I didn't tell you because she insisted I shouldn't. Believe me. She didn't want to go back, so why . . . ? It wasn't money or anything like that. But they were just getting set up, and they needed an accountant, advice—that sort of thing."

"They?"

"This fellow Vernaie—for the restaurant, you know. I could hardly refuse help, could I?"

"But you slept with her."

"No, Paul, no, I swear, not—"

"Not then."

"No." Edouard sipped his champagne.

"But before—on our honeymoon."

"Paul. Once. I did, yes. It was only once when you, you—"

"When I was out walking the streets."

"Yes, that's it. You were half out of your mind then, but what you didn't see—how could you?—was that she was too. She didn't begin to understand what it was all about. She needed—she needed—"

"Comfort."

"You make me ashamed. But that is the truth. That's all the truth."

"And Hélène."

"Hélène?" Edouard stared. "I am not a cradle snatcher. My God, Paul, what can you be thinking?"

For a sudden intrusive moment of clarity, Paul was thinking of Hélène—it was as if he heard her cry, heard her Béatrice-taught scream of danger in the city. It cut him to the bone—and in his bones at that instant he was certain Edouard knew where she was. He opened his lips to ask and then—then . . . He hadn't the heart for it. It wasn't the point.

He waved his hand as Edouard started to speak; he rose

197

abruptly. "You must forgive me. I am tired. I must go to my hotel and sleep. As for the dinner—another time perhaps."

As Edouard helped him on with his coat in the hall and handed him his hat and the case, Paul was wondering whether he'd be able to get a taxi easily and whether the driver would know where to find Freddy Two's and whether the place would be open on a Sunday night.

Waiting for the elevator to arrive, he looked down on his cousin—silent as the Lombard now—and put his hand on the dove-grey shoulder. "Edouard, it doesn't matter. It is of no importance."

They shook hands. Edouard said nothing. No tear. But as the little cage of the elevator descended—third floor, second, first, the ground—there came a sudden dwindling cry from above: "Paul . . . Paul!" And fleetingly it crossed his mind that Edouard knew very well who was the true author of *Passages to Tomorrow*.

Outside, the snow had begun again, fragmentary and soft.

"Do you have," he said, "any English cigarettes?"

"Of course, Monsieur. Rothman, Dunhill, Benson and Hedges." The cigarette girl was dressed in a traditional maid's uniform, black with a little white cap and apron; she smiled respectfully.

These cigarettes seemed quite different from the brightly coloured packages he remembered seeing behind the bar in the Sussex pubs. "Don't you have—Goldflake?"

"Goldflake, Monsieur?" She lifted an eyebrow. "No, just these—they are the best."

"Then I will take that one." He pointed to a dark red package.

As she left, he glanced quickly across the room again. Montbarbon was still there. He was sitting on the other side of the dance floor with the same girl in the blue dress beside him. They had danced twice, but otherwise they had not moved for over three hours. With an effort, Paul looked away; he did not wish to stare, he only wanted to be sure the boy did not leave unexpectedly—although even if he did, he would have to pass Paul on his way out.

He did not *need* to stare. Already he knew everything there was to know about him—from the curly brown hair to the frank blue eyes, from the lobeless ears to the dimple on the chin, the little tuft of hair that grew out of each nostril, the slightly crooked smile and the habit he had of rubbing the corner of his mouth with one finger—as if to straighten that smile. He talked—how he talked. He must have said more in three hours than Paul himself had said in the last three years (except in the classroom, of course). And the girl listened—or at least she watched his face and the rapid gestures of his hands.

At first, when the impostor had entered, Paul had been nonplussed—he'd expected him to be alone. There were not many people in the nightclub, and he'd envisaged it being done quickly—strolling over casually between dances to the other at his solitary table, taking the revolver from the case and firing at once without hesitation straight into that immaculate white shirtfront. But he couldn't do it in front of the woman—one didn't take a woman hunting. He'd thought she would be bound to go to the toilet eventually, but she had made no move, although she was drinking her fourth whisky. It was as though she was afraid to leave him. She was right.

Paul held up his hand and immediately a waiter was at his side. "A whisky, Monsieur?"

Paul nodded. His sixth. The case was on the chair beside him, the revolver nestling in its bed of crushed paper. What if, after all these years of disuse, it misfired? Then, Paul decided, he would simply beat the boy's head in with the knob of his stick—his arms were still strong, it was only his legs that failed him.

"Thank you." He lifted the fresh scotch and took a sip. What was the boy doing now? Ah, striking a match to light her cigarette. Paul relaxed—she would not be moving for a little while. But she would, she would. And then . . . It was only a little after one, and he was quite prepared to wait all night, to follow him outside if necessary and kill him in the street or even back at his "charming little apartment." But he would prefer it were done here—a public execution would be fitting. It would be a great scandal. Edouard would be pleased—he would be able to sell more books. It would be even better than the Goncourt. He would not ask for any royalties, his sole demand would be the reinstatement of the proper title, *Signals of a New World*. He would have the right to demand that, for it was clear by killing Montbarbon, J.-P., he would establish his own authorship without question. Molphey's crime would prove Montbarbon's imposture. Justice would be done.

And would be seen to be done. Jean-Pierre's mother, up from Varay, would relate—in that unmistakable Norman accent he'd heard on the phone this morning, yesterday morning now—the old family joke of grandfather Emil bringing a present of apples and cheeses and calvados and it turning out to be *marc* and a pile of handwritten pages, which they put in an old tin trunk up in the attic. "Yes, Monsieur le Juge, we drank the *marc*."

Paul smiled. He checked a restless movement. His patience was infinite, but he wanted to piss badly. Well, that too would have to wait. Not long now, not long. And then Edouard would not have to worry anymore about the "great writer's" next novel. It would not then be a matter of laziness or a temporary block, but of permanent silence. And, after all, these days wasn't silence the only true course for a writer? Death would make honest men of them both.

The band began to play again and Paul frowned. He didn't like the intervening bodies, although there were fewer of them now. And the music was raucous, with a kind of artificial feverishness—but perhaps that was necessary to give these half-dead-looking creatures some semblance of life. Not that

200

Jean-Pierre looked dead, admittedly—he was gesticulating away, oh God, he was ordering more drinks. No, a man had stopped at his table, they were shaking hands—the fourth time this had happened. Two couples, a woman and now this man. He would introduce them to the woman—if a wave of the hand was an introduction—and they would smile, chat for a few moments, and then retire. There was something respectful in their attitude. Was this the normal deference owing to success —or did the discretion have another cause?

Perhaps Jean-Pierre and the woman had just become engaged —perhaps they were on their honeymoon. No, not that—a moneyed writer would not take his bride to a Paris nightclub in November. They would be in Rome or Athens—or New York. Like Hélène . . . Paul felt the blood rush to his face and he half rose, then sat down again. Calm yourself, he muttered under his breath. Yet the girl did look a little like Hélène—or Agnès, of course. No, Agnès was safe in her nunnery. Anyway, the eyes were blue.

Paul raised his glass, but it was empty. He ordered another. He had an urge to open the case and remove the revolver—he could take it to the toilet and practise there. Or wait there, lurking. Shot in the lavatory. Blood on the white tiles, easier to clean up. Considerate old Molphey, always kind to the elderly —a life of charity, battling to get a taxi for the ancient widows.

Perhaps it would be kinder if he killed the girl as well—save *her* from widowhood.

Charles would do it: "If any wife of mine ran off with another man, I would kill her. I would kill him too."

Paul laughed just as the waiter placed the glass on the table.

"Monsieur wants something?"

"Er? Yes. Ice—lots of ice."

"Immediately, Monsieur."

What an admirable fellow the waiter was—he would like to have sat him down and explained the joke. The punch line. "You see," he would say, "what I said was: 'One would have to be demented to kill for such a reason!' "

And he was right—what woman was worth killing for? Arlette? Absurd. Fat and happy running the tobacco counter in the little restaurant she'd bought with Guy—Guy would beat her all right if she got out of hand. Or, more likely, she would beat Guy. What had she done to deserve killing? A little infidelity here and there—but all in the family. All in the family, ha ha.

"Monsieur said?"

"Nothing. I was just—remembering."

"Your ice, Monsieur."

"Thank you, thank you."

The waiter had the faintest of smiles on his lips. Paul's old-fashioned provincial shabbiness deserved no more than that—an elderly bumpkin up from the country to gawk at the celebrated and the rich.

"I was here twenty-eight years ago on my honeymoon."

"Really, Monsieur?"

"Or some place very like it. My wife danced with a black member of the band."

"In December we are featuring a black band from New York—the Ebony Six."

"The following year she ran off."

"With the black man?"

"No, a white fellow. A distant cousin. All in the family, you see."

"Will that be all, Monsieur?"

"Yes, that's all." It had fallen rather flat.

The music stopped, the half dozen dancers left the dance floor. There were noticeably fewer people now, more empty tables than full.

He looked across at Jean-Pierre and for an instant caught his eye. The girl was still there—perhaps if there had been a black man in the band she would have danced with him. And then the deed could have been done rapidly, expeditiously—to the sound of an antic dirge. Not that it was what he called music.

202

He began to hum—"*à nous, à nous, la liberté!*"—but he couldn't find the tune.

He reached into his waistcoat pocket and brought out his watch. Ten minutes past three. He turned it over and saw the initials A.G.M. on the back—Augustin Molphey. He'd taken to carrying it years ago after the face of Bernard's shockproof watch had begun to cloud over. He must really get a new glass fitted—this one was beautiful but impractical. It was . . . He looked up quickly. Still there, but something was happening. *She* was talking now—rapidly and earnestly.

The band was packing up and nearly everybody else had left. Paul leaned forward a little; he could almost hear what she was saying, although she was speaking softly. But no, all he caught was the words—*not serious.*

Ah, my dear, he thought sadly—what do you want a serious man for? A serious man will do you serious harm. Better your pretty smiling butterfly—here one day, gone the next. Although Jean-Pierre was not smiling now—he was pouting, beautifully pouting. "Too beautiful to live," as Mme. Bouquin so eloquently put it. Plagiarist, thief, impostor, take him as he is, my dear—you have only a few minutes of him anyway. She was flushed. If it was a serious man she wanted, perhaps he should invite her over—"I am, by an odd coincidence, Madame, a writer too." And I know better now, you see. I would take you dancing in paradise with me, and in the morning say *adieu.*

She was standing up, picking up her purse, pausing. Then one clear word, "Never." Jean-Pierre was not looking at her; she turned—and was gone.

Now.

Paul felt a deathly chill that came like a wind lifting the fumes of whisky from his brain. His heart fell, dropped away, leaving him—heartless. Stone cold. He rose, took hold of his stick, picked up the case. He walked slowly, but without limping, across the ice-smooth dance floor. He stood before the boy.

Jean-Pierre lifted his head. "Oh—it's you. You've been staring at me all night—what is it?"

Paul placed the case on the table and undid the catches.

"I suppose you want me to autograph my book—all right, but I haven't a pen."

He met the boy's eyes—the clear blue, cloudless eyes of imposture, as though nothing had happened, no crime had been perpetrated.

"Well come on, I haven't got all night," but smiling his crooked smile.

A little theft in the attic of the night—an old man's youth. Paul said, "I have something for you." He opened the case—the lid obscuring the contents from the other's view—and looked down at the steely glint of the gun barrel wedged between the bottles.

"For me? A gift?"

"You might say so." He reached in and put his hand on the butt. *Don't hesitate, don't think.*

"Well, so long as it's not a manuscript."

"What?" He raised his head.

"Just don't tell me you're yet another would-be writer." A sigh of elaborate weariness.

The cross-hatching of the metal grip bit harshly into the flesh of Paul's palm. Staring at the young man, he suddenly saw, behind that bloom of cheek, that gloss of hair, a real fatigue, an ageless sterility. *Jamais*, the girl had said. Never!

"Come on then—what is it?" The smile as thin as brittle ice on a spring puddle.

"Something," Paul said slowly, "something that belongs to you." He let go of the gun, withdrew his hand. "Something I do not need." The lid dropped.

"That's extremely kind of you. How intriguing. What—"

Paul latched the case. It lay like a wager on the table between them. He said, "Bonsoir, Monsieur." Then he nodded and turned.

As he limped slowly to the vestibule and was helped on with

his coat, he heard the young man call out, "Freddy—come here. Some old fellow's given me a present. What do you think it is—a bomb?"

Outside on the boulevard it had stopped snowing; underfoot it had frozen hard.

The clouds were low—a pinkish orange reflected from the city's lights. But beneath the still clouds, even at that dead hour of the morning, the silence was not absolute. There was always the muted metropolitan murmuration—to be cut by the shriek of a siren, or the cry of a lost woman.

Moving carefully on the icy crust, Paul turned towards the Gare de Lyon—it was not far, a kilometre or two, and he knew that he would manage it easily. Somehow he felt lighter, stronger, perhaps because he no longer bore the unbalancing weight of the old case.

His hands were free.

He was unarmed now.

In the attic the candle's flame shone sharp and bright with the cold. No heat—but no need of heat up here. He poured the champagne gently, without spill or tremour.

He lifted the glass. The wine was cold too—fresh and immaculate as the last brief snow this night. Perhaps in Paris at the same instant a young man was drinking also, or reading the fragments of Paul's laborious reflections, or toying with a revolver. "Santé," he murmured and put away the thought, as one puts away all childish things.

He refilled his glass. He would finish the bottle slowly—a duty, a ceremony as obligatory as baptism, marriage, extreme unction, to those who might understand them.

He caught a noise. The wind—a rat in the loft—a soft footfall on the stone stair? He crossed to the window and opened it.

He thought he heard his name—"Paul—Paul!"

He leaned out. What ghost was this? Morine crying of his

crime? Edouard uncertain in remorse? Mme. Thibault for her dead man swinging from the rafter? Fley boisterous at the door? Augustin shouting defiance at the hostile dark? Or a daughter's scream or prayer flying up to heaven?

No. Nothing but the wind whispering across the snow, where the sharp stars pricked the night and the great three-quarter moon cast silver light, black shadows over the listening countryside. *In order to survive one must keep some secret part untouched and still and listening—not listening for death in the dark, but for good news in the daylight.* Out there, the stream still ran beneath the brittle ice and somewhere in the tangled undergrowth of the forest the wild boar snorted in a winter sleep. Even the graveyard was alive with vermin life among the old bones.

Slowly he shut the window, stretching the spider webs back into place. A place for everything, and everything in its place. The pages of his daily work still lay scattered across the floor from yesterday morning. He bent down and gathered them together and carefully put them beside the old stacks of manuscript yellowed with years under the eaves where the bats slept in the daytime.

And as he sat on, drinking, he heard his father's voice, as if in answer to a question: *It will never be all over.* Here was a place of good news—where *Signals* was born, where the first thin cries of his daughters had mounted from below on the winter night, where bells had rung out for peace—the noises of joy together. And a place of loss—too many losses—for which he might weep a little, but they were not tears of any great grief; for it seemed to him that everything he remembered, he possessed. All things would come back to him.

Towards dawn, the bottle long since finished, the candle guttered and died. And as the sun rose golden in the limpid sky and daylight flowed across the wide white valley, the bell down in the village began to peal in short, quick strokes.

Paris; Burgundy
January—April, 1980

206

About the Author

Julian Gloag was born and largely brought up in London. After graduating from Cambridge University, he spent several years in New York publishing; then, in 1963, on the publication of *Our Mother's House*, he devoted his full time to writing. Since 1973 he has lived in Paris, but spends much of the year in London and in an old farmhouse in rural Burgundy. He has two children.